KARL KLING

# Takin' Care of Business

*A Brody James Mystery*

First published by Three Dorks Publishing 2024

First edition

ISBN (paperback): 979-8-9876565-4-9
ISBN (hardcover): 979-8-9876565-5-6

This book was professionally typeset on Reedsy.
Find out more at reedsy.com

# Contents

# 1

# You Were an Upside Down Pumpkin

"Okay. Here it goes...," Bullock said as I unlocked the patrol car and opened the back door. I placed the certificate and a small medal on the back seat.

I shut the door and looked across the roof of the car and Bullock was staring at me from the other side.

"Are you going to tell me this embarrassing moment story or not?" I asked.

"I was waiting until I had your undivided attention," he said as he opened his door.

I opened my door and got behind the wheel.

Bullock got in and reached across with his left hand and placed it atop my right hand that was trying to buckle my seat belt.

"You let me know when you're ready to fully commit yourself to this conversation," he said as he patted the top of my hand before moving it back to his side of the car.

"Don't ever touch me again," I said.

"Oh, you liked it, so just settle down," Bullock said as he lowered the visor and flipped open the mirror and began to check his teeth.

"Why do you always do that?" I asked.

"Do what?" he innocently asked back.

"Do disgusting things in my car."

"Disgusting? I don't do anything disgusting."

"Are you kidding?" I asked in amazement. "You're always spitting, and checking your teeth, and you just do other disgusting things."

"So looking to see if I have food in my teeth is now disgusting? You're a piece of work."

"Me? How am I a piece of work? I'm not the one who does weird things in your car."

"First off," Bullock said as he turned toward me.

There was genuine sadness in his eyes. I honestly thought he wasn't happy with me. What a sissy.

"There is so much wrong with your attitude today," he said. "You're upset you got recognized for solving a crime? That in itself is weird. I didn't even get an award and did as much as you did. You don't see me pouting."

I began to pull out of the parking space at the Stonington City Hall.

"Secondly, and quite frankly, more importantly, you're being mean-spirited and cranky," he continued in a huff.

"Fine," I said in a tone that said I was annoyed with this conversation but that he had approval to proceed. "Go ahead."

"Oh, thank you for allowing me to address my dental issues," he snapped back.

"Not that," I said. "I mean go ahead and tell me your story about an embarrassing moment."

"It seems like a year ago when I first brought the subject up, to be honest."

"You're such a baby," I said. "It's literally been only a few minutes."

"Well, it seems much longer than that," he said as he rolled down his window.

"Don't you dare!" I snapped at him.

"What?" he asked as innocently as he could before swallowing.

We stopped at an intersection and waited for a couple cars to pass in front of us who had the right of way.

"Well, I'm not sure if it was something I ate or if I was just sick that day," Bullock began.

"If this is a story about you throwing up in your mom's Tupperware bowl, I already heard that one," I said.

"No, it is not," he said with agitation.

When the cars finished passing, we turned right and continued on our way.

"I've never really been able to figure out what was the cause, but suffice it to say, I wasn't feeling well," he continued.

"Will this be a long story?" I asked knowing the answer already.

To Bullock, there is not a short story. His stories are rarely linear. They're like an audio presentation of that kid's path from school to home in *Family Circus* comic strip.

"Why?" he asked.

"Well, if it's going to be a long drawn out story, we'll drive around for a few," I said. "But if it's quick, and I doubt it will be, we'll head straight to the station and you can finish before we get there, I'll park and then we'll go inside."

"What if it takes longer than all of that?"

"I'm not sure," I said as I scanned the area making sure nothing nefarious was afoot. "I guess it depends."

"I mean, I'll feel bad if I don't finish and we have to sit in the

3

car."

"Will you?" I asked.

"Not really."

"I can't imagine it'll be the first time you finished and then just sat in a car."

He just startled to chuckle. I said it as a joke. A put down. A little verbal jab. It backfired. Based on his reaction, he was not picturing it as negatively as I had initially hoped he would have.

"Well we're going to be at the station in a few minutes, why don't we just roll the dice," I said trying to move on from the uncomfortable nature of the moment.

"I'll make it short," he gladly said.

I was already 0-for-1 on the day. No sense going hitless. I let his comment go unanswered. But, boy, did I have a doozy.

"I'm sitting in class back in third grade," he continues. "Mrs. White. Really old. Like I think they built the school around her kind of old."

I took a deep breath. Probably more like a huff. I knew this wasn't going to be a short story.

Bullock continued, "Mrs. White was the type of teacher who had rules for everything."

"We kind of work in a profession based on rules," I said.

"Laws, Brody, ours are laws," he condescendingly said. "These were stupid rules."

"Such as?" I asked.

"Well, the important one for this story is only one person could use the restroom at a time," he indignantly said. "So I had to go to the bathroom. And Melissa was already using the bathroom."

"Wow, that really sucks," I jokingly said. "And you lived to tell about it?"

"Well, guess what?" he defiantly asked. "Turns out I had to go really bad. Like diarrhea bad."

It was at that moment that I didn't like where this was heading. I knew deep in my heart that I shouldn't let him finish this story. I wondered if having to explain to Captain Alex Leonard as to why I catapulted myself from a moving patrol car was the better of the two options against listening to the rest of Bullock's story.

There was a long drawn out pause. I don't think either one of us wanted him to continue the story at this point. At least I knew I didn't.

We pulled onto Walnut Street and I could see the station. I could see a parking spot that would release me from this hell. With any luck, the silence will remain until I could park and escape.

"So I crapped my pants," he shockingly said. "Yep, all over my chair and the floor."

I was rendered speechless. I wanted to laugh. I wanted to cry. I wanted to run.

"What...did...you do?" I slowly asked as I pulled into a space, put the car in park and turned the ignition off.

"Well the point was made," he said. "She realized the error of her ways and then allowed me to go to the bathroom to clean myself."

"That is embarrassing," I admittedly said as I had so many emotions swirling about in my head.

I wanted to laugh at him. I wanted to empathize with him. Mostly, I wanted to laugh at him. I didn't.

"That's not the worst of it," he added.

Oh dear Lord. There's more. I'm not going to be able to contain this much desire to laugh.

"I had to wear my baby sitter's son's clothes the rest of the day," he said as if I would be in agreement that only added to the horror of the story.

The internal laughter subsided and gave way to confusion.

"I'm sorry?" I asked. "How is that worse than pooping yourself in your third grade class?"

"That dude was a dork and the clothes didn't even match," he incredulously said. "I don't even think what they made me wear was ever fashionable. Not even in the 80s when they bought them."

That reminded me of one of my first little league photos. I was so pleased to wear my uniform, but since it was a little cold that day, my mom – a baseball novice – forced me to wear a long-sleeve shirt under my jersey. A dazzling white dress shirt with collars the size of plane wings. I felt stupid at the time. But I have the picture on a wall in my apartment. And whenever I look at it, it reminds me that even though it was slightly misplaced my mother really loved me and wanted what was best for me. In her way.

"I had to wear an orange He-man shirt with green corduroy pants," he said, bringing me back into his horror story.

I burst into laughter. I couldn't take it anymore.

"You were an upside down pumpkin," I chortled.

Bullock threw his hands in the air and said, "And now you know."

"Wait a second?" I asked. "How did you end up getting these clothes? Did he have extras or something?"

"Nah, my babysitter was kind enough to drive up to the school with them. They were still ugly even if the gesture was nice."

"Well you survived, and that's what's important," I said.

Bullock sat there. Waiting. He knew something was coming. I applauded his patience.

"Now let's go inside and do some police work," I said. "Okay, punkin'?"

"You're an ass," Bullock said.

# 2

# You Become Winter

The month of March is probably the ugliest month in the state of Michigan. With the constant temperature fluctuations, as well as the occasional snowfall, the prevailing colors are a combination of gray, black and a disgusting brown.

There's so many beautiful colors in the spring and summer and the fall is dazzling with its bright reds, yellows and oranges. The winter, with its fresh apron of snow, is beautiful and if you happen to be able to step outside deep into the night with the air crisp and the moon dancing off the snow, it's a breathtaking experience.

But March? Talk about bleak. Slush. Dirty slush abounds. It's wet and dreary and depressing.

"Are you okay?" Bullock asked, snapping me out of my doldrums.

"Yeah, I just hate slush," I dejectedly replied.

"I don't mind it," he said as he raised his head to peer out the window as we splashed through the muck spraying it onto the sidewalk. "It's like winter's holding onto dear life and spring is pushing it's way through. It's kind of like college baseball."

"How's that?"

"When you get recruited, the coaches tell you how much of an impact you'll have and when you get to campus there's some senior who thinks he has a deed to the position and he definitely resents you being there," he said. "The seniors are winter, the freshmen are spring. Until one day, you become winter."

We both sat silently pondering the magnitude of what he said. I myself realized that without knowing it, he gave an indictment of us.

I am spring. Captain Leonard is winter.

And yet. I am winter. And Bullock is spring.

* * *

Cold is relative to the average Michigander. For example, if the temperature says it's 50 degrees outside and it's September, then it's darn near freezing. However, if it's March and you've just spent three months inside with temperatures outside hovering in the teens, well then the same 50 degrees is pretty much viewed as balmy.

On this particular Saturday, the residents of Stonington and the surrounding area, fresh off their hibernation, were enjoying what they considered warm weather and had flocked to the downtown area to get their blood flowing again.

Bullock and I were strolling the streets, giving us a chance to reconnect with many of the shop owners in town, several of whom were propping their doors slightly ajar to allow a cool breeze to send fresh air into their establishments.

The practice allowed us to peer inside, say a quick hello and continue on our way.

"I'm going to get some coffee, you want anything?" I asked Bullock as I grabbed the door to Deb's Donuts.

"You buying?" he asked.

"Nope," I said as I let the door close behind me forcing Bullock to lunge to grab the handle before it shut completely.

"That was rude," he mumbled.

"You'll be okay," I said without any semblance of sympathy.

Like a little dog, Bullock followed me up to the front counter as we both sat on the circular chairs they had. Only one of us decided to spin around in our seat. I preferred to sit like an adult.

"You're like a child," I said.

"You're old and crusty," Bullock said in return. "You're kind of cranky today. We're you unable to secure some affection from Chloe last night?"

"Yep, that's it."

"Really?"

"No, not really," I said.

"Then why did you say it was?" Bullock asked.

"I thought a childish remark deserved a childish response," I answered.

Deb, the owner of the shop, made her way to the counter.

"Officers, what can I get you?" she asked.

"You can get him a better personality," Bullock said, gesturing to me.

"And you can get him a pacifier," I said in return.

Deb looked at me, then Bullock, then back to me.

"One pacifier and one personality, got it," she said. "Anything else? Maybe I can get the two of you booster seats to make you both more comfortable."

I like her. She has spunk. Normally, I don't like spunk.

10

"Large chocolate milk," Bullock said like a child responds when they've been verbally disciplined by their parent.

Deb glanced back in my direction.

"I'll just have coffee."

* * *

If given an option, I like to sit and enjoy my coffee in silence.

"Did I ever tell you the first time I ever thought about being a cop?" Bullock said, as he made it clear I wasn't going to be given the option.

"Don't think you did," I said recognizing that my answer was irrelevant to whether or not he told the story.

Bullock took a sip of his chocolate milk and swung his chair in my direction.

"It was at a donut shop like this when I was a kid," he said. "It was after church. Or maybe before. I'm not really sure. But we were dressed up. I had a tie on. Or a sweater."

"You're kind of hazy on the details regarding this pivotal moment in your life," I said.

"All I know is we we're dressed up and church was involved," he said. "But that's not the point."

"And what is the point?"

"We were sitting at a corner table and I was in the gunfighter's seat," he said pointing to a table off to our side in the corner of the shop.

"I'm sorry, the what?" I asked as I looked at the table trying to figure out which one he was referring to.

"The gunfighter's seat," he said. "Gunfighter's always had their back to the wall so no one could sneak up from behind and shoot them. They could see everything happening in front of them."

"Are you sure about that?" I asked. "I don't know much about the Old West, but I've heard a lot of them got shot in the back playing cards."

"Like who?"

"Wild Bill Hickok," I said.

"And who else?"

"I don't know anybody else, I just know him, I guess," I said.

"And how do you know he got shot in the back?" Bullock asked.

"Saw it in a movie with Jeff Bridges a few years back."

"Have I seen him in anything?" he asked.

I was stunned. I could not believe he hadn't heard of Jeff Bridges.

"King Kong?" I incredulously asked.

"He played the monkey?" Bullock asked, clearly pulling my leg.

"No, you idiot," I said. "He was like the main guy. What about Tron?"

"Never saw it."

"The Big Lebowski? He was the dude."

"Is that supposed to mean something?" he asked.

I was in disbelief. I was almost crushed to be honest. I had nothing left to give.

"Well, other than Hickok," he continued, apparently oblivious to the pain he caused. "Who probably should've used the gunfighter's seat I might add, most gunmen in the Wild West liked to have their back to the wall."

I wasn't over the Jeff Bridges thing. But we weren't going to go back in time and rectify any of this. I pressed forward.

"Did you fancy yourself as a gunfighter back in the day and that's why you wanted to be a cop?" I asked.

"No, I was simply telling you where I was positioned," he said. "I thought I was using a commonly known phrase to describe it. You really make telling stories difficult."

"So I've heard," I said as if his telling of stories was a pleasure cruise.

Deb approached the two of us with a pot of coffee in her hand. Never breaking stride, she refilled my cup and went on her way.

"Did you want more coffee?" Bullock asked.

"I guess so," I said as I stared at my now almost full cup.

"Anyway, my mom and my sister we're facing me," he continued.

"What's their seats called?"

"You're a jackass," he said. "Drink your coffee, shut up and let me continue."

He stared at me for a few seconds. In our relationship, there's always a fair assumption that a smart ass comment is forthcoming. I knew he was expecting one from me. I felt it was even funnier to not say one and just let him sit there staring at me.

"Alright," he continued. "So there we were."

He reached for the sugar bottle and put it up against his glass of milk. He then grabbed the salt and pepper and put them a few inches away from the sugar.

"Why do always do that?" I asked.

He rolled his eyes in exasperation.

"Do what?" he asked.

"Why do you always use items on the table when you're telling a story?"

"First off, I don't always do that," he said. "But I want to give you a visual. Maybe your mind isn't as imaginative as you think it is and this way you get a good idea of what I'm talking about."

"Okey dokey," I said as I shook my head in amazement.

"Anyway, these two sketchy guys walk in and sit at the counter," he said.

"Use the mixed fruit jelly as the guys," I said.

"What's your fascination with mixed fruit jelly?" he asked rhetorically. He grabbed two mixed jelly packets and put them at the edge of the counter.

"Moving on," he said. "The waitress comes up to them and asks them what they want. They tell her two waters and two dozen donuts."

He looked at me with raised eyebrows.

"What?" I asked.

"You'll see," he said. "Oh, you'll see. So the waitress is filling the boxes with various donuts based on what they tell her. She sets two dozen donuts next to the two guys."

"So far this is riveting," I said.

"Well, guess what they do?"

"They bolt for the door."

"Nope," he said with a chuckle. "That's what everyone thinks they did. They didn't do that. They ordered coffee."

"That's it?"

"No, that's not it," he said. "What kind of story would that be?"

"They type of story you always tell."

We tease each other a lot. At that moment, however, I could tell with the look in his eye that he actually wanted to slug me in the face.

Instead, he decided to squeeze the last part of the story out.

"When she turned to get the coffee, they bolted for the door," he said.

"What does that have to do with you being a cop?" I asked.

"Oh, yeah, I forgot about that part," he said. "You see when they came in and sat down I told my mom that I thought those two were going to rob the place. I had an intuition. That got me thinking maybe I'd be a good cop."

"Jury's still out on that," I said as I got up from my seat, took a last sip of coffee and headed for the register.

I wanted to leave him with a positive thought.

"But you're a better cop than you are a story teller," I said.

Maybe not entirely positive.

* * *

As we exited Deb's, I stretched my arms out and took a deep inhale of the late winter air. I scanned the area to get a glimpse at the action downtown. Something caught my eye as I looked about.

Sitting across the street, all bundled up, with her arms crossed, staring off into the distance was my next-door neighbor Betsy. She didn't seem to be doing anything other than staring straight ahead.

She had on a full winter jacket, and the hood was atop her head with a scarf tied around her neck while covering her face. She had on mittens and winter boots. Her posture gave the impression she was miserable. But yet she just sat there.

"What are you looking at?" Bullock asked.

"That's my neighbor, Betsy," I said gesturing in her direction.

Bullock took a look at her.

15

"Why is she just sitting there?"

"I don't know," I said. "She hasn't moved. She's just sitting there, all bundled up, looking miserable."

"Well, why don't you go over there and talk to her?"

"That's not really our thing," I said as I turned to walk in a different direction.

"Your thing?' Bullock asked. "You too have a thing?"

We took a few more steps, but I sensed Bullock stopped walking. I turned back toward him.

"Do we have a thing?" he asked.

If ever a question could be described as sad, puppy-like, this was it.

"And there it is," I said.

"What?," he asked. "I was just wondering."

"Somehow, someway, you always make things about you."

"It's called conversing," he said. "It's how regular people conduct themselves."

"Can we continue conversing as we walk?" I asked.

He begrudgingly started walking allowing us to return to checking out a few more stores. Whenever given the chance, I tried to catch a glimpse to where Betsy was sitting to see if she had moved. Each time I looked, there she sat, staring at seemingly nothing.

# 3

# Damn, He Was Just a Kid

Having some down time while I waited for my girlfriend Chloe to close Brown's Root Beer, the restaurant she owns in town after taking it over from her father a few years ago, I decided to take a stroll through the park and stumbled across a youth baseball game being played under the lights.

I'm not what sure why it was, but playing games in late spring like these boys were, when you're still in school, made the games more competitive. No matter the result, you knew the next day walking the halls and sitting at your desks you were either ribbing last night's opponent or you were the recipient of the ribbing.

I sat atop the bleachers and watched the boys in action.

It took me back to the 1983 Stonington Little League World Series. After pitching the first few innings, I was put out in right field, which for young baseball players is almost worst than sitting on the bench. Which is ironic, because the outfielders with the best arms in high school, college and the pros all play right field.

Nonetheless, my coach decided that was where I was to play.

My Expos team was barely holding onto the lead against the hated Dodgers. Hated as much as you could hate a local team that had some of your friends on it.

Late in the game, a bloop pop fly was going to drop between me and the first baseman. Our first baseman wasn't considered to be a good player, even though he played one of the most important positions on the ball field. He did, however, have one thing going for him. He shared the same last name and address as the head coach. And in youth sports, that's often the deciding factor.

All that being said, I knew he wasn't going to catch the ball. He couldn't catch the ones thrown directly at him, so my assumption was a safe bet.

I ran as fast as I could. Mind you, that wasn't very fast, but it was the best I could do. What I did have in my favor, was a very long frame allowing me to take big strides and when laid out, I could cover a good distance.

Just before the ball dropped, I left my feet and was able to haul it in and prevent the Dodgers from taking the lead.

We would end up winning the game. And the championship. And our first baseman was named team MVP despite being near the bottom of nearly every stat.

Winning the championship was fun and memorable, but I think if we were still in school instead of being the middle of summer, it would've added to that moment.

A crack of the bat and cheering from one side of the bleachers brought me back to present day. A young man crushed the ball and sent it flying over the left field fence for a home run.

My phone began to buzz and I flipped it open to see that it was Stonington police chief Alex Leonard, calling.

"Hello, sir?" I said as I answered the call.

"Brody, I hate to do this on your family time," he said. "But we got a call about a disturbance on Kimble I was wondering if you could check out. We're a little short-staffed tonight."

"No problem, sir," I said. "I'm just waiting for Chloe to be done with work."

"According to a witness, there's a couple people possibly casing some houses," he said. "If you could swing by and check it out, I'd appreciate it."

"On my way, sir."

"Thanks, Brody. I do appreciate it."

\* \* \*

When I arrived on the scene, I didn't notice anything out of the ordinary. There weren't any mysterious vehicles parked on the street. There wasn't anyone milling about. There weren't any dogs barking.

I got out of the car and made my way up to the house of the homeowner who made the initial call.

I knocked on the door and saw the curtain from the front window move slightly with an elderly woman peering out at me.

I leaned closer and pulled out my badge for her to see.

"Ma'am, I'm Officer James from SPD," I said.

"You don't look like a police officer," she said as she let the curtain fall back into place.

I waited there for a moment, and when no one answered, I knocked on the door again.

"Mrs. Rayner?" I called out.

I knocked on the door again.

"Mrs. Rayner, you called about a disturbance," I said hoping she was still within earshot.

I waited momentarily.

"Mrs. Rayner?" I asked for what was going to be the final attempt.

"How come you don't have a uniform?" she said from behind the door. "And how come you aren't driving a police car?"

"Those are good questions, ma'am," I said. "Tonight was my off day and we're a little short-handed so they called me and asked me to come to check things out for you."

Again, a moment of pause.

"How come the police are short-handed?" she asked.

"That's another good question," I said as I realized how strange all of this would be for a senior citizen who just called about people she doesn't know lurking in the area.

"You can call the department and ask if anyone was dispatched and what the name of the officer is," I said.

The front door opened slightly, but the chain kept it from being opened further.

She again peered out at me.

"Show me your badge again," she said.

I held it up for her to see.

"I'm Officer James," I said.

"One moment."

The door shut and I had no idea if she was coming back. I began to look about the property from her porch to see if anything caught my eye.

I decided she wasn't coming back and started to leave the porch, when the front door opened, again, stopped by the chain.

"What's your first name?" she asked.

"Brody," I answered.

The door shut again, but I could hear the chain moving and knew she would be opening the door. Once the door was fully ajar, I showed her my badge again just to be sure.

"Officer James, ma'am," I said. "You reported a disturbance. What seems to be the issue?"

"All I know, is there seems to be two people sneaking about the neighborhood," she said. "They have flashlights, and I think one of them is named Roger."

"Roger?" I asked.

"I'm pretty sure it's Roger," she said. "I was looking out my back bedroom window and while I didn't see the lights, I could hear one of them whispering. He said 'Roger' a couple of times."

"Alright," I said. "I'll take a look around. You should probably lock your doors and stay inside. Once everything is clear, I'll come by and knock on the door. Until then, just sit tight."

I went back to my car and opened the trunk. I pulled out my gun from the safe and grabbed a flashlight as well. I headed back up Mrs. Rayner's driveway and made my way back toward her garage.

I navigated my way through the back yard using my flashlight to check any potentially broken windows or doors. I also used the light of the moon to get a lay of the land so I wouldn't hit anything that could obstruct my path.

I didn't see anything that had been disturbed.

As I made my way through Mrs. Rayner's backyard, I was fortunate that the more recent housing developments were built with regulations not allowing fencing. I began moving toward the next home by crouching down and maneuvering underneath some pine tree branches. But at least I didn't have to hop a fence.

Coming out the other side, I surveyed the property and saw

a flash of light coming from the other side of the neighboring house to Mrs. Rayner. I traversed through assorted lawn chairs, a barbecue pit and numerous plastic toys until I was positioned at the back side of the home.

The light went out.

I took a couple steps closer and drew my gun, when the light came back on, causing me to pause. Before I could take another step, the light went out. The light returned but was dimmer and then was frantically moving back and forth.

It was obvious to me that a flashlight wasn't working properly.

I was just about to spring into action when I heard the person around the corner of the house smack the flashlight a couple of times and say, "dammit."

The voice was female. More importantly, it was familiar.

"Evans?" I asked at a level just above a whisper.

Libby Evans has been on the force for four years. She's a dynamic officer, doesn't pull punches and doesn't ask for, or want, special treatment. I've heard her say on several occasions, "I'm a police officer who's female, I'm not a female police officer."

"Brody?" she answered back.

I lowered and holstered my weapon.

Peering around the corner, I asked, "what the hell are you doing?"

"Says the guy wearing cargo shorts," she said as she continued to fidget with her flashlight.

"I was finishing up a DUI and Captain Leonard said I should help you out with your disturbance call as soon as I could," she continued. "What do you have so far?"

"Not much," I said. "Other than you and your defective flashlight."

"Very funny," she said as she finally got the flashlight to work. She pointed it in my direction, stopping at my torso.

"We're you fishing or something?" she asked.

"I was watching a baseball game," I said.

"I bet everyone there thought you were one of the dads."

I might need Chloe to help me with a wardrobe upgrade.

"Our resident said one of the people we're looking for, might be named Roger," I said returning our focus to the reason we were standing between two suburban homes in the middle of the night.

The two of us headed out to see what we could unearth. Evans and I weaved our way through several homes as we crossed each other moving from front to back of each house.

We had one home remaining when a glimmer of light caught my attention coming from the pocket park across the street. I gestured to Evans to work the flank to the far right.

You don't want to take any chances, but the thought entered my mind as I was crossing the street that any real threat wouldn't find rest in the local park a few houses down from where they committed a crime. Teenagers might do such a thing, because planning and executing criminal activity in detail isn't their strong suit.

As I began to approach the park, I heard someone call out, "Roger!"

It wasn't a yell. It wasn't a whisper. It wasn't even a normal talking voice. It was said in a way that was to get the attention of a specific, potential listener which was loud enough for them to hear, but not loud enough for others to hear. Even though others could hear it. Whatever that speaking style is called, that's how they said it.

Nonetheless, however it was said, the identity of one of the culprits was definitely Roger.

I took a position behind a Juniper bush and peered around to see if I could see anyone or anything.

"Roger?" was call outed again, this time more as a question than a statement.

But, further, more with a strong tinge of exasperation. I started to laugh. I realized what was going on. Roger wasn't a who. It was a what.

I heard footsteps closing in on my location. I stepped out behind the bush and was looking square in the eye of a middle-aged man in a t-shirt, shorts and slippers. And a flashlight. One that works.

"Lost pet?" I asked.

The man, who was startled by me appearing from behind a bush, stared at me and then started to backtrack from me. Probably because I was still in civilian clothes and now I came across as the weirdo in this interaction.

I pulled out my badge while thinking I'll never go on another call in street clothes again. Henceforth, I'm going to put some sort of uniform in my car for situations such as this.

"I'm Officer James," I said before returning my badge to my cargo shorts. "We were called out here for suspicious behavior."

"You don't look like a cop," he said.

"Yeah, so I've been told. And you are?"

"I'm Hal," the man said. "Hal Coulter."

Coming from behind the bushes was Evans, holding a cat.

"I believe I have found our elusive Roger," she said. "I love his fur. What kind of a cat is he?"

"It looks like a hippie," I said.

"He's a Norwegian Forest cat," Hal defensively said as he reached for his pet. "He loves being outside. Too much sometimes."

"Well, you'll probably want to keep a better eye on him," I said. "You wouldn't want him, or you, being harmed by any predatory animals in the area or by a resident who might mistake you for a burglar."

Hal was not amused snuggling Roger tightly.

"Maybe you should look more like a police officer," he said in a huff.

"Well, as long as everyone is safe now," Evans said. "You sir, and your friend, are free to go."

Hal turned and brushed the top of Roger's head, saying, "we're not friends, we're family, aren't we Roger?"

"I'm not talking about the cat," Evans said. "I'm talking about him."

Evans pointed to a man sitting at a picnic table off to our right. His hands were clasped in his lap and his head was slouched over.

"Isn't he with you?" she asked as the three of us, and Roger, looked over at the slumped over figure.

"I don't know who that is," Hal replied. "In fact, I didn't even see him sitting there, to be honest."

I immediately knew this wasn't good. I needed to clear the area, and while I knew Hal Coulter probably had nothing to do with the man on the bench, I let him know we would be in contact. He gave his address and phone number to Evans, who actually had a pad of paper and pen with her. I had neither in my shorts.

After we received the necessary information, I told Hal, "have a good night."

Evans approached the figure at the table.

"You alright over there?" she asked.

No response.

I decided to move slightly to the left as she proceeded cautiously to the right of the man.

She clicked on her flashlight and pointed it at him, revealing a young man in a jean jacket.

"Sir?" she asked. "Are you okay?"

As she kept her light on the young man, I moved quickly and approached him head on.

"Hey buddy, you okay?" I asked as I approached him.

I moved closer as Evans kept the light on the body.

Putting my hand on his shoulder, I began to shake him lightly to get him to wake up.

"Hey, my man, you okay?" I asked again.

I shook a little harder and the body slumped away from me, falling toward the ground while his legs were still intertwined in the legs of the chair.

I grabbed the body underneath both arms and slid him away from the table and turned him on his back.

He couldn't have been more than 15 or 16 years old.

Evans called it in. I gave a quick glance over the body and there was no blood on the table, nor the ground where he was sitting, and none was evident where we laid him down.

A quick search of his body produced drug paraphernalia, a Velcro wallet, a lighter, a small amount of crumbled up cash and a few tokens from The Funhouse, a local arcade in town.

In his wallet we found his Stonington High School ID, a library card and a Funhouse premium member card.

The young man was Tom Downing.

"Damn," Evans said. "He was just a kid."

# 4

# I Hope He Turned Out Okay

There is very little that is more painful to experience as a police officer than the next of kin notification after someone has died. I had to do this twice prior when I was working in Norfolk, Virginia. Both were automobile accidents.

What I learned on this day, was that such notifications are magnified when the deceased is a minor and you're informing their parents. No parent should bury their child.

Nothing about Tom Downing was alarming. In fact, he was as average as average can be. That's where the tragedy hits hardest. There were no red flags. No problems with authorities, no history of being in trouble. Average grades, average life, average kid.

Neither mom nor dad or his sister Jenna had anything negative to say about Tom. There wasn't a girlfriend, no issues at school and a handful of friends who were a small pack of dedicated, like-minded young men.

Until that moment in the park, Tom Downing was an everyday teenager walking the halls of every high school in America. A kid that few remember years down the road. Now, after years of walking among his classmates like a shadow passing through unnoticed, he will become the most talked about person for weeks. Rumors will fly and the nobody kid will be center stage in the most salacious tales that will be concocted, truth be damned. For this brief moment in time, he will be the most famous person at Stonington High School.

Our job will be to find out how he got there.

* * *

"I don't want to sound naive," Captain Leonard said as he stood behind the podium in the conference room.

"I know Stonington is not immune to the scourge that are drugs on our kids," he continued. "We've been very fortunate to not have a young person die from an overdose during my time here. I want to know everything we can find out about this and do everything we can to stop it from happening again."

Bullock leaned over toward me and whispered, "should we start at New Horizons?"

New Horizons is a drug rehabilitation center in town that is somewhat controversial in that neighbors of the facility are not too keen about addicts wandering their streets. Every issue that could otherwise be found in every other neighborhood is conveniently placed at the feet of these men and women. Sure, some are destined to return and would do things unfathomable to the fine folks of that area, but many are just like the taxpayers. Only they are cursed with something they cannot shake free of.

It also was a facility that Bullock and I became more familiar with during our investigation of the Gary Hutchins and Rebekah

Wertheimer deaths a few months ago.

"Either there or the high school," I answered Bullock.

"Maybe we just hit both while we're at it," he said back. "Are you in the mood for chicken? I could go for some chicken, right about now."

I didn't respond.

"We could get chicken after, I guess," he said.

\* \* \*

As the room cleared, Bullock and I approached Captain Leonard.

"We're thinking we'd go to the high school and then maybe to New Horizons," I said.

"We'll also get some chicken after," Bullock interjected. "Would you like us to bring you some back?"

Based on Leonard's look, I assumed he was not in the mood for chicken.

"Maybe we can get an idea of who's dealing," I said. "We'll see if New Horizons has heard of anyone dealing product that is causing adverse reactions. Other than the norm."

"Well, proceed with caution," Leonard said. "We ruffled the feathers of the folks at New Horizons last time, and they're good people and we're not accusing anyone of anything because, quite simply, we don't know anything."

"Will do, Captain," I said.

\* \* \*

"So how was it?" Bullock asked as we drove toward Stonington High School.

"How was what?" I asked.

"Working with Evans," he said.

"We've worked with Evans before," I said. "She's a good cop. She's smart. I like her."

"I know *we've* worked with her before," he said. "But neither of us have worked with her before."

"Is this some sort of riddle?"

"No, I mean, the two of us worked with her before but neither of us have worked with her before....alone."

"Well, if we worked with her, we wouldn't be alone."

"You know what I mean," he said. "You're just being difficult."

"What's the point of this?"

"What do you mean?"

"I mean, what's the point of this?" I asked. "Why are you asking such a stupid question? Evans is a good cop. She's good people. And you better not be asking what I think you're asking."

Bullock paused. I could see the Rolodex of ideas spinning in his head. He let out a childish giggle.

"Oh...no...not that," he said. "I wasn't asking about that sort of thing. I never thought of it that way."

"Well, you better not."

"I was just wondering, you know, if you liked her as a cop," he said.

Now I paused. It was my turn to laugh. He laughed like a little kid who saw boobs for the first time. I laughed at him. This guy is a piece of work.

"What's so funny?" he asked.

"You," I said. "You're funny."

"Why am I funny?"

"You're not interested in what I think of Evans," I said. "You want to know if I thought Evans was a better officer than you."

"Okay, first off, that's not true," he barked back. "And secondly, well, that's not true."

"Which part isn't true?" I asked.

"Both parts," he said. "Both parts are not true. Number one: I just wanted to know how she did in the field, in case I am ever in the same situation."

"And number two?" I asked.

"And number two," he said before pausing. "Well, quite simply, I don't believe anyone is a better cop than me."

"So if, by chance, I did think she did a great job in the field," I said. "And if, by chance, I thought to myself, 'she's better at this than Bullock,' you wouldn't be offended because you know in your heart that's not true?"

He didn't say anything, but I knew he was boiling inside. It was giving me great joy.

Finally, he couldn't contain it any more.

"Do you think that?" he asked.

Fortunately, we reached the high school. He was going to have to ponder this exchange on his own.

* * *

We approached the front entrance of the school. As with many schools, they unfortunately felt the need to protect their students by having a security system to restrict free entrance. Too bad they didn't have such a device for narcotics that easily pass through these doors.

I pushed the button to notify them of our arrival, while Bullock put his face uncomfortably close to the camera.

"Back up," I said. "They won't know who we are."

"I'm sure everybody knows the great and powerful Brody James," he said as he backed up anyway. After the main office buzzed us in to enter the school, we drew the usual stares from the kids in the lobby area.

Some had the look of excitement as if they were going to be privy to a titillating moment involving some unsuspecting student. Some had the look that they feared *they* were the unsuspecting student. Others gave off the usual teenager vibe of being unbelievably annoyed.

"Do you realize that one of these dorks could be working with you in 15 years?" Bullock asked.

"Me?" I asked. "What about you?"

"Oh, I'll be long gone by then," he said.

"Is that right? And where might you be?"

"I don't know," he said. "Maybe I'll be a college baseball coach."

I grabbed the doorknob to the front office. But before turning and entering, I looked at Bullock.

"Kind of a weird career change, don't you think?" I asked.

"I don't know," Bullock said. "There's some things I want to do, ya know?"

I stepped back as a very motivated and agitated young lady wanted to go into the office. I held the door open, she just passed by us as if we were part of the scenery.

"You're welcome," I said, which didn't elicit a response from her.

Turning back to Bullock, "such as?"

"I don't know," he said. "I always wanted to coach. But I also want to own like a super cool bar. Or maybe write a book. Or be in a band."

"What instrument do you play?" I asked.

"I don't know how to play an instrument."

"You sing?"

"Not really, I just know that if I was in a band, I'd be a great lead singer because of my energy."

"I don't think that's how that works."

"Look at Mick Jagger," he said. "He's not that good of a singer, he just jumps around a lot in concert."

"Well maybe that's how he is now, but back when they started, he was a really good singer."

"Well, whatever, I just know that there's a lot of things I could do. I just don't want to be an everyday kind of person. I think I've always pictured myself as 'the something' rather than 'a something'."

"You could be the captain here," I said.

"I don't think so," he said as he walked through the doorway.

"Anyway, I'm pretty sure you'll be the next captain," he added.

For a brief moment, I pondered what he said. I never really thought of it before to be honest. Captain Brody James. Holy crap. In a flash, I saw me old and gray and Chloe was holding a grandchild while another clung to me leg. stepped. That was all too real for me.

"Doesn't really matter anyway as Captain Leonard has a few more good years in him," I said as a way to hold back the scary idea of aging and growing and maturing.

\* \* \*

By the time I had reached the front desk, Bullock was already fully engaged in a conversation with the woman behind the desk.

Upon my arrival, Bullock stopped mid-sentence, "and this is my partner Brody James, who you probably already know."

The woman offered no reaction. Not only did her silence say she didn't recognize me, it also confirmed what I had suspected. She never heard of me.

"Well," he continued. "He's pretty much a Stonington High School legend. You probably have a wing dedicated to him somewhere, I imagine."

Turning toward me, Bullock continued.

"Brody, this is Mrs. Samuel," he said. "Mrs. Samuel was explaining to me that the principal, Mr. Yarbrough, was in a meeting and if we'd like to wait for him, we could have a seat."

"I guess we can wait a few minutes," I said as I started to scan the various fliers of school activities that were on display.

"Kids must be getting excited about summer starting soon," I said aloud while not diverting my attention from the plethora of information. Chess club, band, a poetry club to name a few.

I don't remember having this many choices to me as a student here. Maybe they were available and my indifference to them was more telling of who I was as a teenager than how schools have change.

"We all are," Mrs. Samuel said in a tone of exasperation.

She apparently was looking forward to summer more than the students.

"Do you enjoy what you do?" Bullock asked.

"I love it," she said. "It's not a 9-to-5 job working with kids."

"Because of all the after-school activities?" I asked holding up a piece of paper announcing a bash fishing club held throughout the summer months.

"That, but more so, you get to know so many and you feel for them as people and their struggles," she said. "So you take a lot home with you. It can be exhausting by the time you get the end of the school year."

"I bet," Bullock said.

The door to Mr. Yarbrough's office opened and out stepped the young lady I encountered earlier.

She moved with even more determination, but this time with a scowl on her face.

"I'll talk to your teacher, Meredith," Mr. Yarbrough said toward her. She did not respond. Again.

"Meredith," Bullock said. "Means great ruler."

"How the heck do you know?" I asked.

"Alicia has some baby books lying around the apartment and I like to look through them."

"Do you now?" I asked. "And do you memorize the meanings of all the names. That would be quite impressive, my friend."

"Nope," he said. "For some reason, hearing her name triggered the memory. Weird, isn't it?"

Mr. Yarbrough turned his attention to me and Bullock and said, "how can I help you, officers?"

He turned back into his office and Bullock and I followed.

"This isn't a real formal visit," I said. "Obviously, the overdose of Tom Downing probably shook the school a bit."

"You can say that," he said as he sat in his chair behind his desk.

He placed his hand on his desk and asked, "Should I call for the district's legal counsel?"

"Not at all," I said as I sat in one of the chairs in front of the desk. Bullock leaned against the open door behind me.

"We want to know how we can help you," I said. "Is there anything that you've noticed that we may want to keep an eye out for? Any trends you've noticed?"

"Nothing out of the ordinary," he said. "I'm not naive. I know we have marijuana being used by our students, and we assume that there's other drugs being sold as well, but we haven't been privy to any student using the sort of narcotics that could kill them. Hell, I've been here so long, I remember in the early 80s when the kids had their own smoking lounge. I don't think that'd fly today."

"Is there anyone who you think might be the point man on any drug activity on campus?" I asked.

"Officers, if I thought one of the kids here was responsible, I'd be conflicted in wanting to help you guys solve this case..."

"And protect the lives of other students," I interjected.

"True," he said. "But as I was saying, I'd be conflicted. I'd want to prevent other kids from meeting such a fate, but I also know I have a duty to protect the kids in my charge and their rights."

"We basically want to the same thing, Mr. Yarbrough," Bullock said as he moved closer.

I wasn't a confrontational maneuver. It was more of a physical embodiment that we were all on the same team. That we needed to be closer as a unit rather than adversarial.

"Well, the good news, gentlemen," Yarbrough said. "Is that I think I can sleep comfortably at night knowing that what I'm about to tell you protects my student's interests in both regards."

"Go on," I said as I adjusted in my seat to get closer to him as if he was going to whisper his next few words.

"There's a young man," he said. "He's no longer a student here. Thankfully. His name is Lucas Winters. He was, I'll say, a rumored, dealer of drugs when he was a student here. He graduated last year. I don't envision him taking a different path in life and he still knows a lot of the kids enrolled here. You might want to check him out."

I got up from my seat and extended my right hand.

"We will definitely check him out," I said as Yarbrough arose and shook my hand and then offered the same to Bullock, who scooted past me to bid the principal goodbye.

"Mrs. Samuel will be able to let you know his home address," he said.

Bullock turned to walk out the door and bee-lined for Mrs. Samuel's desk.

I started to walk out as Yarbrough came out behind his desk and placed his right hand atop my shoulder.

"I still have hope that Lucas will change his ways," he said. "Most kids are just good kids who are sometimes a little misguided."

"That's not always the case," I said as I reached his office doorway.

"Not always," he said. "But sometimes. Sometimes you get a good kid who does the occasional dumb thing. I recall a young man who always had a reason as to why he never did his homework back when I had him as a student in my science class. He also thought it was funny to put plastic wrap on toilets, and to my recollection, bet other kids he could throw snowballs through open school windows. I wonder what ever happened to that kid? I hope he turned out okay."

I turned to Yarbrough, gave a wry smile, and said, "he turned out okay."

"That's good to hear, Brody."

\* \* \*

As soon as I got back to the office, I hopped onto my computer to see what I could find out about this Winters kid.

"You got plans for the weekend?" Bullock asked.

"Not really," I said while not diverting my eyes from the computer monitor. "You?"

"I'll probably start getting the baby's room ready."

"Isn't she due in like two months?" I asked.

"Yeah, but we want to be prepared in case something happens sooner."

"Well, I hope not."

"Why?"

"I heard that premature babies all come out weird."

"Bullshit," he said. "Nobody has ever told you that."

"Okay," I said as if my information was accurate and his willingness to dispense with it was at his own peril.

I found some information on Winters and used my finger to scan the monitor screen line by line.

"A lot of petty stuff, nothing too major," I said.

"Like what?" Bullock asked.

"A couple shoplifting incidents," I said. "Looks like he broke into a shed once."

"No, I mean, what kind of weird?"

I hadn't really ever talked about babies of any sort to anyone. What I said just sounded like it'd be true to me. Now was my chance to make it true. Very true.

"I wouldn't worry about it," I said. "I'm sure it'll be fine."

"It?" he said.

"He, she, whatever," I said. "You'll have a healthy baby. Alicia is good stock. I'm sure she'll be strong enough to overcome anything out of the ordinary."

"Such as?"

"No extra limbs or anything like that," I said. "I read a recent study that said that the vast majority of premature births result in some sort of extra limb. Or was it one fewer limb? One of the two."

"That's bullshit," Bullock said. "Your attempt at humor has failed my friend."

"I laughed," I said.

"Well, you're the only one," he said. "Like every other joke you tell."

"Statistically speaking, 50 percent is actually pretty good," I said. "Since there's only two of us here, and one was laughing, the percentages are in my favor."

I looked up from my computer. Bullock was sitting with his arms crossed with a less than enthusiastic look on his face.

I got up from my chair and slapped him on the shoulder.

"Come on buckaroo," I said. "Let's head over to New Horizons and see if they can help us out with whatever is hitting the streets and maybe even a little bit of info on this Winters kid. And if you behave, we can get you you're chicken nuggets."

\* \* \*

39

As we entered the main lobby area of New Horizons, the receptionist called back to Sebastian Bannister, the Executive Director of the facility.

"Officers, he'll be right with you," she said as she hung up the phone.

Bullock leaned against the counter and grabbed one of the suckers they had on display in a little red metal bucket.

"You like working here?" he asked as he unwrapped the sucker and plopped it into his mouth.

"Beats working at Browns," she said.

Bullock turned to me and reiterated what she said, "Beats working at Browns."

"You worked at Browns?" he asked.

"Nope," she said. "Just never thought working fast food was my kind of gig. It's the first thing that popped into my head. My dad eats there all time. I want to work somewhere where I like to feel I'm helping people. I'm majoring in psychology at State. It's why I intern here."

"Good for you," he said as he pulled out the sucker and then proceeded to return it to his mouth, only to bite down on it and eat it.

"It's called a sucker," I said. "Not chew this shit out of it...er."

Sebastian appeared from the hallway.

"Well if it isn't my two favorite police officers," he said.

"Oh, you're making me blush," Bullock said. "How are you Sebastian?"

"Splendid," he said. "Did you two know that our facility has been able to help rehabilitate over a dozen people in the first quarter alone? While it appears that some people only see our residents as criminals, there are others who know many are on a path of redemption."

"Many, not all," I said popping his sanctimonious bubble.

Sebastian gave no response. Bullock slid toward Sebastian and rested on the front counter.

"Listen, I get it," Bullock said. "We're on the same front lines, though, my friend. You have one way to deal with the problem, we have another. But remember this. You would rather change someone outside of the prison life rather than locking them up. But we…"

Bullock leaned in toward Sebastian and placed his hand on the counselor's shoulder.

"We'd prefer," he continued. "To lock them up rather then send them to the morgue. And now we have a dead young man and we just want to get out in front of this before we find another. You have to agree that stopping this is much better than cleaning it up."

I figured the pump was primed.

"We got a name of someone," I said. "I'm wondering if you have any info on him that could be helpful. His name is Lucas Winters."

Sebastian shook his head in the negative.

"Doesn't ring a bell," he said. "He has never been with us."

"Maybe not," I said. "But has anyone ever mentioned him? Even in passing?"

"Nope," Sebastian answered. "Believe me, I hear a lot of names that I probably shouldn't hear, and that name is a new one to these ears."

"Hear anything about bad product?" Bullock asked.

"Haven't heard anything in that regards as well," he said. "But as I tell my residents, all product is bad product. At the moment, it doesn't appear that the individual is part of our merry-go-round, yet."

"The merry-go-round?" I asked. "Interesting analogy."

"The dependence merry-go-round," he said. "Listen, the merry-go-round continues to turn. Right now, the three of us are part of the ride. We'll eventually find our way off, and others will come and go in the meantime, but the ride isn't going to stop. There's no end to the ride, it just keeps turning every single day. Our job is to make sure we get as many off the ride as safely as possible. Including ourselves."

"You make it sound bleak," Bullock said.

"I make it what it is," Sebastian said. "We're not preventing anything on the macro level, we're just trying to salvage as much as we can on the micro level. It's the cross we bear. You hope to get to them before the EMS has to. I also hope to get them in one piece after you're through with them."

"And we hope not to get them back from you," I said.

"Exactly."

\* \* \*

Bullock and I headed to the car after our dead end at New Horizons.

"I used to like merry-go-rounds," Bullock said. "Now I don't think I'll ever be able to enjoy one again."

"Is it because you're a grown man?" I asked.

"No," he said. "It's because of how Sebastian compared it to what we do."

"Oh, gotcha," I said. "I thought it was because you're a grown man and it's a kids ride."

"Well, that too."

42

We decided to head over to the address we were given for Lucas Winters and see if that would produce anything that would help us on our case.

"I hope we find something out, otherwise it'll be bupkis," Bullock said.

"We'll have bupkis, not it'll be bupkis," I said.

"Whatever."

"You sure have fallen in love with that phrase, though," I said.

\* \* \*

"Is this it?" Bullock asked. "It's a warehouse."

"I can see that," I said.

"Did you go to the right address?" Bullock asked.

"I know how to drive."

"I didn't say you didn't know how to drive," he said. "I'm wondering if you're not good at directions, that's different. What's the address?"

"I'm at the right address!" I said. "760 McWilliams Park."

"It's a warehouse," he said. "I know it's a warehouse," I said. "We have sufficiently established that this building is a warehouse."

"You think he actually lives here?"

"I doubt it," I said as I opened the car door. "But let's check it out anyway."

\* \* \*

Bullock cupped his eyes and placed his face close to the window to peer inside.

"Looks abandoned," he said. "I'm not sure anyone would live in a warehouse, but maybe that's me."

I looked over the exterior of the building and checked a couple doors, which were locked.

Bullock walked past a couple of windows that didn't look promising, then approached another and looked inside.

"Looks like someone is storing stuff inside, but not really using it for business," he said.

Checking another door, I asked, "like what?"

"There's one of those scissor lifts, you know the kind where you stand on it and it goes up and down," he said.

"I know what a scissor lift is," I said. "Is that it?"

"There's some workout stuff, a camper, a grill," he said. "Who grills inside a building? That's just weird. And unsafe, if you ask me."

"There's a camper inside the building?"

"You think our Mr. Winters is living in a camper inside the building?"

"Possibly."

"And also possibly on the brink of burning the whole place down while he roasts some wienies."

"Possibly," I said. "Let's head over to the city and see who owns this building. It's a stretch, but maybe he's picking up some cash by renting it to Lucas Winters."

"Or the guy broke in and the owner doesn't even know he's there."

"There's that too."

# 5

# Sorry I Look Horrible Today

Bullock and I stood at the counter of the Assessing & Property Department for the city of Stonington. We were waiting to find out who the owner is of the property on McWilliams Park.

Bullock pulled out a couple of quarters from his pocket and dropped them into the cardboard display case that offered candy as a fundraiser for the local Lions Club.

"I don't really like chocolate mint candy," he said as he unwrapped one and plopped it into his mouth.

"Then why did you buy it?" I asked.

"Well, for one, it helps out this organization," he said pointing to the logo on the box. "And secondly, I'm hungry. I didn't get my chicken."

"Are you a member of the Lions Club?" I asked.

"Nope," he said. "I'm not even sure what they do to be honest. But I'm sure it's a good organization. All those animal clubs are. Lions, Elk..."

"Water Buffalo?" I asked.

"I'm not familiar with them."

"It's from the Flintstones," I said to him, hoping for a reaction that I never received.

He had no idea what I was talking about.

"You never watched the Flintstones?" I asked in absolute astonishment.

"Not enough to remember Water Buffaloes, I guess."

"I don't think you watched very many episodes of the Flintstones, if you don't remember anything about the Water Buffaloes."

He's never watched the Flintstones. He hasn't lived a full life.

Andrea, the employee who was helping us with our request, returned to the counter with an opened manila folder.

"So it says here that the building was finished about fifteen years ago," she said. "Looks like they had a business in there, some sort of sports thing, but they moved out a couple years ago and it's been vacant ever since."

"Who owns the building?" I asked.

"The construction company who built it," she said. "Barton Construction."

"Do you happen to know anything about Barton Construction?" Bullock asked. "Such as who owns that, is it local, that sort of thing?"

"According to this, it's owned by Don Barton," she said. "And he lives here in town."

"Can you give us his address and phone number, please?" I asked.

"Sure thing," she said as she took out a small piece of paper and wrote the pertinent information down.

With paper in hand, we thanked Andrea for her help and headed back to the station.

\* \* \*

"Are you on hold?" Bullock asked.

"Yeah, I'm on hold," I said. "What else do you think I'd be doing? You think I'd just hold the phone next to m ear for no reason?"

"Maybe," he said.

"Why don't you just eat your beef jerky and leave me alone while I make this call."

Bullock sat down in his chair and placed his feet atop his desk. He removed the jerky from its plastic wrapper and tossed the whole stick in his mouth while placing the plastic in his trash can.

"Okay," I said into the phone. "I see. Well, we're not sure how it involves Mr. Barton. We're just trying to get some questions answered."

Bullock stood up and approached me at a distance that I wasn't comfortable with.

"What is she saying?" he asked.

He was close enough to whisper it into my ear. I waved at him to back up. He took a step back. I glared at him and gestured for him to back up even further. With an overly dramatic huff, he took a few more steps back.

"Is this far enough, your highness?" he said.

"Thank you," I said into the phone as I tried to ignore Bullock. "Please have him call me as soon as he can. Thank you."

"Well?" Bullock asked before I even hung the phone up.

"His assistant said he's a very busy man," I said.

"Sure he is."

"The company builds and manages many different properties,

47

so she assured me that there is no way that he specifically would know what happens on a daily basis at each and every site."

"All we want to know is who the hell is using the building?"

"I know, seems simple," I said. "We'll see."

"By the way, do you have plans for this weekend?" Bullock asked.

"Didn't you already ask me that?"

"Yes, but that was just small talk," he said. "This is actually a specific question. Alicia wants to have people over for a get-together of some sort and she told me to ask people here if they'd want to come over."

"Did she call when I was on the phone?"

"No," he said. "Why?"

"When did she tell you to ask me?"

"Sometime over the weekend, I think."

"We've spent pretty much the last two days together and now you ask me?"

"I actually already asked you, remember," he said. "Anyway, what difference does it make? She told me to ask and now I'm asking. Anyway, I was eating the beef jerky and it made me think how thirsty I am and how I could go for a beer and then I thought that I needed to get beer for this weekend and that made me realize I didn't know how much beer because I don't know how many people are coming over. So are you coming over?"

"I have to talk with Chloe first," I said. "What's the occasion?"

"I'll only tell you if you promise not to make fun of Alicia."

"Why the heck would I make fun of her?" I said. "I like her. It's you I don't really care for."

"Ha ha," Bullock said before his face turned serious.

He leaned towards me and whispered, "she's afraid that after the baby is born that we'll never have nights out with adults

48

again."

"That's probably true."

"So more importantly than you not making fun of her, definitely don't say it's true. So let me know as soon as you can."

"Are you saying don't take two or three days?"

The phone on my desk rang.

"Officer James," I said as I answered.

"Yeah, Officer James, this is Don Barton, my secretary said you wanted to know something about one of my buildings," the voice on the other end said.

"I really appreciate you calling me back," I said as I sat down in my chair and grabbed a pad of paper and a pen. "I was wondering if you could let me know the status of the building at 760 McWilliams Park. Specifically, if someone is living in the building?"

That last sentence drew the attention of Bullock who came toward my desk and was looking over my shoulder.

"Not that I'm aware of?" Barton said. "Is that it?"

"Well, we're looking for a Lucas Winters and he listed that address as his last residence," I said. "Not telling you anything you don't know, but that property isn't residential. Do you know Lucas Winters?"

"I see," he said.

A strange response. More of how it was said than what was said.

"So you know Lucas Winters?" I continued.

"He's my stepson."

I wrote down "Lucas Winters = Barton stepson" on the sheet of paper.

Bullock tapped the paper with his index finger and then walked around in a circle.

"Does Lucas live at the property in question?" I asked as I watched Bullock stop his pacing and walk toward me excitedly. Bullock nodded approvingly and pointed at me feverishly as if I asked the greatest question ever.

There was a moment where neither me or Barton said anything.

"Mr. Barton?" I asked hoping to elicit a response.

A few seconds later, he responded, "not that I'm aware of."

"Okay," I said. "If you're not sure if Lucas is living there, would you know where he is currently living?"

"I would not," he said. "Listen, I don't mean to be short with you, but Lucas and I aren't exactly close. I'm sure you are aware he's had some minor issues with the law. I'd love to help you out. I really would. But right now isn't a good time. Is there any chance we can meet in my office tomorrow? I'd love to go into more details, but right now I have some things I need to address with my business."

We agreed on a time and he gave me the address to his office. I hung up the phone and leaned back into my chair.

"He wants to meet with us?" Bullock asked. "That's weird."

"Why do you think that's weird?" I asked.

"You don't think it's weird?"

"I do," I said. "I was just wondering why you think it's weird."

"Just tell us if your stepson is living there dude," he said. "How hard is that?"

"He said he's not."

"I mean there's nothing illegal about him allowing his kid to live there," he said. "At least, not enough to involve us, right? Do you think he's lying?"

"That's why I think it's weird," I said. "It was like he didn't want to tell me anything, but yet, wants to tell me something.

Not sure if the kid is living there and he's trying to hide it or if the kid isn't living there and for some reason he wants to shed some light on the situation, but not over the phone."

I nervously tapped the pen on the notepad. It's a default mechanism when I'm trying to sort through things in my head.

"What do you want to tell me, Don?" I asked aloud.

Bullock clicked off his desk lamp.

"Maybe we'll find out tomorrow at 11 am," he said. "Maybe he's in the mob and thinks his phone is bugged."

Bullock started on his way home, but not before stopping and turning back toward me, "Don't forget to ask Chloe if you're coming on Saturday. It really will mean a lot to Alicia."

* * *

I opened my apartment door and headed up the stairs.

Steam was coming from the kitchen area and Chloe was standing at the stove lifting a lid over a boiling pot.

"I'm making spaghetti, if that's okay," she said.

Chloe stood there in jeans, a t-shirt covered by an apron, with her hair in a bun. She was the most beautiful woman I have ever seen.

"Sorry I look horrible today, just haven't had much time between getting some work done," she said totally oblivious to how I saw her.

I honestly believe that women, on the whole, view themselves much more negatively than others see them. Particularly those that love them.

She poured the spaghetti and water into a colander sitting in the sink. Steam engulfed the entire kitchen area.

I reached into the colander and grabbed a few pieces of spaghetti. As I was putting them into my mouth, she said, "careful, those are hot."

She was right. There were indeed hot. Pretty much burned my mouth. I tried to cool it off by doing that open mouth panting thing that never works. It was as ineffective as ever. To the faucet I went to scoop a handful of cool water into my mouth.

"It's hot," I said as well as I could with a burnt mouth full of spaghetti.

"It's probably because of that cooking thing," she said. "Why do you always do that?"

"I don't know."

I honestly didn't know. It's like a primitive animal instinct. I see freshly cooked food and I want to eat it. I also believe there's a little bit of being a rebel or something. As if I'm some sort of bad boy by taking spaghetti out of the pot when told not to. Nothing I'd brag about on the streets, as I don't think that would get me much cred, but nonetheless, there's a sense of stepping outside the rules that is exhilarating.

Chloe poured the spaghetti into a serving bowl and walked around to the dining area and placed it onto the table.

"Hey, by the way," I said. "Bullock asked if we wanted to come over Saturday night for a party that Alicia is planning."

"Did you tell him we were helping my parent's with their move?"

"Yeah, I told him that."

"Did you?"

"Well, I told him that I wasn't sure what you had planned and that I'd ask you and I'd get back to him."

Chloe placed two glasses and silverware onto the table.

"Can you grab the broccoli?" she asked. "It's on the stove

still."

I stood looking at the small pot.

"You have to strain the water out first," she said without the ability to actually see me.

How does she do that?

"A bowl is in the cupboard behind you," she continued utilizing her sixth sense.

"I know," I said.

She knew I didn't know. I knew she knew I didn't know. I didn't want her to know that I knew she knew. But she knew that too.

"So you forgot that we are moving my parents into their condo this weekend," she said.

Carrying a bowl of broccoli to the table, I said, "I didn't forget. I didn't exactly remember that it was specifically this weekend, but if given a multiple choice option, I would've nailed it. I think."

Chloe clasped her hands and that was my sign that she was prepared to say the dinner prayer she learned when she was a child.

After grace, she said, "I'm willing to bet you don't have the answer to my next two questions, but I will ask anyway. Am I supposed to bring a dish and are we celebrating something specific where I should also bring a gift?"

"None of that sounds familiar," I said. "However, Bullock said Alicia is worried that once the baby arrives, that they won't have much of a social life. But we're not supposed to say anything about it."

"I bet she's experiencing a lot of emotions right now. I will find a nice housewarming gift."

"Well she's in a relationship with Bullock, so it doesn't have to be anything special."

"Be nice," she said. "And you shouldn't talk behind people's backs."

"Good point," I said. "I'll have to try to remember what I said and tell him tomorrow. Getting his reaction makes it much better anyway."

"That's not what I meant."

"No, but still."

# 6

## I'm Like The Jefferson

Bullock and I were driving through downtown on our way to meet with Don Barton.

"What do you think his story will be?" Bullock asked as I was trying to find a parking spot.

"I honestly don't have any idea," I said. "I've been trying to figure out his angle all night."

After parking, we made our way toward the two-story building on Main Street where Barton had his office. I glanced to my left as we approached the door and noticed that sitting across the street was Betsy.

Same bench. Relatively same pose. Not as bundled up with the warmer temperatures since the last time I saw her sitting there, but nonetheless, everything else was relatively the same. Except this time she had a notepad and was writing something down. When she lifted her head, we made eye-contact.

At that point, Betsy picked up the bag that was next to her, placed the notepad inside of the bag and got up from the park bench and walked in the opposite direction.

Bullock noticed I paused.

"You okay?" he asked.

"I just saw Betsy."

"Again?"

"Yeah," I said. "It's weird."

"Why is it weird that you saw her in the downtown area?" he asked. "It's a small town. We all bump into friends all the time down here."

"I know," I said. "But she was sitting in the same spot."

"What do you mean, 'the same spot'?"

"She's sitting in the same exact spot," I said. "Remember the last time I saw her down here? She's there again. Same spot."

Bullock looked around the downtown area.

"There's only like four benches on this block," he said. "It's not like she had a lot of choices. Come on. Let's see what Mr. Barton has to say for himself."

We opened the door and checked the directory to the right. The downstairs of the building is a medical supply store. The top floor had several offices for various service industry businesses: an attorney, a CPA and a financial planner. Barton owned the building and his office was at the end of the hallway.

"Have you ever seen anybody in that medical store?" Bullock asked.

"Can't say either way," I said. "Never really thought about it."

"Too focused on where you're weird neighbor is sitting?"

At the top of the stairs, we turned right, passing three other doors before we reached the end of the hall.

"First off, she's not weird," I said. "She might be eccentric, but she's not weird."

Bullock reached for the doorknob to open Barton's office.

"And secondly?" he asked.

56

"She's not weird, that's all I'm saying."

* * *

Don Barton was a large man in height and width. He had a raspy voice, a rough exterior and a firm handshake.

"Don't mind the clutter," he said after shaking our hands. "I sit here and I hate every second of it. Rather be out on the job, swinging a hammer. You know what I mean?"

"Absolutely," I said as I recalled the time I had great difficulty hanging a picture in my living room.

I'm not what I would call a toolsy guy.

Barton plopped down in his chair almost as if he collapsed into it. The sound the chair made was as if he forced every bit of air out of the cushion. Bullock shot me a look that screamed, "did you hear that?"

I tried very hard not to laugh and act as if I hadn't heard it at all.

"How can I help you officers?" he asked.

"To be honest, we're not exactly sure," I admitted. "As you may recall, we had a young man overdose..."

"Shit, let's get to the chase," Barton abruptly said. "Some kid overdosed and someone told you that Lucas has to be involved. Probably a fair assumption. That clown was always involved in something."

"Was?" Bullock asked.

"Listen," Barton said. "I ain't all chummy with Lucas. We're not...who was that dude who did those paintings?"

Bullock and I looked at each other hoping that the other had a beat on which painter Barton was trying to describe. Not trying to judge, but solely based off our brief history with him, I assumed he was referring to the guy who painted dogs playing poker. At least, that's what I pictured in my head.

"The guy who did, like, family paintings of Americans?" he continued. "Rockefeller maybe?"

"Norman Rockwell?" I asked.

Barton slammed his hands down on his desk in celebration making Bullock jump a little.

"Yes!" he said. "Rockwell. Well, no matter, the point is we ain't in one of those paintings. All happy and shit. Me and his mom aren't exactly doing so well either."

"Mr. Barton," Bullock said. "You said Lucas 'was always involved in something.' What did you mean by that?"

"He was," he said. "Past tense. Was. I don't think he's doing any of that stupid shit anymore."

"Why's that?" I asked.

"It was part of our deal."

"Your deal?" Bullock asked.

"I gave the kid some money, you know, to get him back on his feet," he said. "His mother doesn't know about it, and she'd be pissed if she found out. She'd be pissed no matter what we did. That's just her nature. Basically, she's a bitch."

Other than his rough exterior, Don Barton seemed like a real sweetheart.

"And what do you get out of it?" I asked.

"Out of what?"

"The deal," I said. "You said you made a deal. What's he giving to you in exchange?"

"I set him up with a bullshit job, that's all," he defensively said.

"And what exactly does he do?" Bullock asked.

"He's manning one of our properties," he said.

"So what I'm hearing is you set him up with some money, and in exchange you also gave him a job," I said. "That's quite the deal for him."

"It's a good deal for me, trust me," he said. "Dealing with his shit for the last several years, I'm glad to get him on his feet so I don't have to spend anymore mental energy. That's a lot more off my plate. Money I can make back. My time, and my energy, I can't."

"So where is this job?" I asked.

"Why?"

"We'd still like to talk to him."

"Why?" he said with disdain. "I told you, he's not around here doing that stuff he used to do. Why do you need to bother him?"

"Maybe he knows something that could move us in the right direction," I said.

"Maybe he doesn't," he said turning this conversation more confrontational by the second.

"True," I said. "Maybe he doesn't. But we won't know that until we ask him."

Barton gave out a heavy sigh and scratched his forehead like he was pondering his options.

"He's down in Monroe," he finally said. "We have an empty industrial building down there. He's supposed to watch it. Take care of the property. Make sure no weeds are growing. Just make it ready if we get a potential tenant."

"Could you provide the address?" I asked.

Barton grabbed a pen and a small piece of paper and wrote the address down. He handed the paper to me and then tossed the pen onto his desk as if that act would fully convey his annoyance with this whole situation.

"We thank you for your willingness to help us," Bullock said.

"Thanks for the help," I said as I tapped Bullock's shoulder signifying he can lead us out of the office.

\* \* \*

Chloe was working late so I heated up some leftovers from last night's dinner. With the sun still a few minutes away from setting, I decided to enjoy my meal in the quiet of my balcony.

I balanced the plate on my glass of milk, opened the balcony door very carefully as not to spill my entire dinner, and set everything on the patio table that Chloe recently upgraded us to from the set I picked up many moons ago at a garage sale. Or was the set given to me? Nonetheless, I wouldn't be gifting my initial set to any of my future children when I die. Chloe made sure to get rid of that as soon as she got the new set.

"Ever since you got yourself a lady friend," the voice of Betsy said from the next balcony. "You no longer have to eat TV dinners, I see."

"I'm like the Jefferson," I said. "I'm moving on up."

"Classic TV right there," she said. "Back when comedy was funny. Not today. Comedy is just stupid today."

"You sound like Archie Bunker," I said.

"Are you just going to roll through the entire lineup of 70s hit shows?"

I took a sip of milk and stabbed at a few green beans with my fork.

"Nope," I said as I shoved the food into my mouth.

60

I'M LIKE THE JEFFERSON

After taking the bite, I decided it was a perfect time to inquire about her affinity for a certain park bench in downtown.

"Hey," I said. "I saw you downtown today."

Nothing but silence from Betsy. Apparently, other than busting my chops over my meal, she wasn't in a mood to talk.

"My partner Bullock and I were down there to talk with someone, and I spotted you sitting on a park bench."

"Is that so?"

"I was pretty sure you saw me as well," I said. "I thought it was weird."

"You thought me sitting on a park bench in downtown on a sunny day was weird?" she asked. "Or you thought me potentially seeing you downtown was weird? Which, otherwise normal activity, did you find weird?"

"Not specifically seeing you downtown, was weird," I said. "But because I saw you a few months ago and you were sitting on the same park bench."

"Is this the shit they're teaching at the academy, now?"

I must've struck a nerve. She had never been so brash with me before.

"I just thought it was weird, that's all," I said almost apologetically.

I turned my attention back to my meal, cut a piece of pork chop and started chewing. We both sat in silence for the next minute or so. With most of my mind on the peculiarities of my exchange with Betsy, I probably chewed much longer than is required for pork.

My curiosity was overwhelming me. I just couldn't let it go.

"Are you working on something?" I asked.

"Aren't you just the eager beaver tonight," she said. "No, I'm not working on anything. I'm enjoying my retirement. I thought I could do that downtown. I didn't realize you had it under surveillance."

"I just saw you writing some stuff down."

"Are you watching me, James?"

Betsy had never had such a forceful tone before. She also never used my last name before. It had less a familial feel to it. It was cold. It was confrontational.

"Nope," I said. "I just saw you downtown and you were writing something and I wondered what you were doing. I didn't mean to offend."

When I played back what I just said in my mind, I realized how misconstrued it could be from her perspective. I went back to eating. She pulled out a cigarette and lighter and vigorously puffed away.

"So what did you do?" I asked.

"You're just not going to give it a rest, are you?" she asked in exasperation. "I was downtown. I wasn't doing anything, but thinking I was enjoying my day."

"No, I'm not talking about today," I said. "You mentioned you're retired. It got me thinking that I don't know what you did for a living."

"It doesn't matter," she said. "I retired. I wanted to be left alone, if you want to know."

"Were you in construction?"

"What? Why the hell would you think I was in construction? No. I wasn't in construction."

"Lawyer?"

I got her to laugh.

"Are you just going to ramble off every job you can think of?"

"Pretty much."

"I was a writer."

"Like books?"

Betsy took a long puff of the cigarette. Blew out the smoke. Coughed a little.

"Nothing like that," she said. "I did some freelance stuff."

"Anything I would've read?"

"I honestly wasn't sure you knew how to read," she said followed by a small chuckle.

I even had to laugh to myself, and then took a sip of milk. Our relationship, albeit temporarily strained, was back to our usual banter.

"By the way," she said. "Milk with pork is disgusting."

"I like it," I said. "What do you think I should be drinking?"

"I don't know," she said. "Anything but milk."

"But I like milk."

"You said that," she said as she got up from her seat.

Betsy went into her apartment and I sat there with some questions.

Why was Betsy so defensive regarding me seeing her down-town? Why was Betsy so coy about her career? And why is she so against milk?

# 7

## I Bet You Do

Chloe came out of the bathroom with a green floral sundress, a white sleeveless long duster cardigan vest and sandals. She was stunning.

As she stood there in all her splendor, her expression turned sour.

"Are you going to get ready?" she asked.

"I am ready," I said.

I looked down at what I had on and realized that my thinking that my Cure t-shirt, cargo shorts, socks and tennis shoes was perceived differently in her mind. And now looking at the two of us, together, she may had a point. But maybe she'd realize that I looked acceptable.

"Are we going to Wrestlemania?" she asked.

I was mistaken.

"First off, I wouldn't wear a Cure shirt to Wrestlemania," I said. "And secondly, I've only been to Wrestlemania once, and that was when I helped my friend Bill work a concession stand for Wrestlemania III at the Pontiac Silverdome. And it was really fun."

"I'm sure it was," she said. "But we're going to Alicia's for the first time and I'm sure she's pretty nervous. I want it to be nice for her."

"Well, *I'm* going to Bullock's and I don't care how nice it is for him," I said.

Chloe approached me, ran her hand down my right shoulder and arm.

"I just find you so attractive when you're dressed nicely."

"How attractive?"

"You'll never know unless you change."

"When will I know?" I asked. "Will I know I right now?"

"No, not right now," she said. "I just did my hair."

"Tonight?" I asked. "Will I know tonight?"

"Just go find something nice to wear and we'll worry about when later."

I started down the hallway to my bedroom.

"I hope it's tonight," I giddily called back to Chloe.

Ever so faintly I could hear her say, "I bet you do."

I hope it's tonight.

\* \* \*

I stood in my closet trying to find the specific shirt that Chloe would find irresistible. I narrowed my choices down to three possible candidates: my Honolulu blue and silver Lions polo shirt, a forest short-sleeve button-up shirt and a white polo shirt with red stripes my mother bought me for Christmas a couple years back.

Since I didn't want to look like *Where's Waldo*, and I was pretty sure Chloe wasn't as keen on the Lions shirt as I was, I went with the green shirt.

I changed into khaki pants, slid on a pair of brown leather loafers and I was all set to hit the town.

\* \* \*

"See, this is why I love you," Chloe said as I approached her as she stood in the living room.

She came close to me and adjusted my collar and then kissed me on my cheek.

"You took careful consideration and matched your outfit with mine," she whispered into my ear, which sent shivers up my spine.

My heart began to race as nothing but glee overwhelmed my senses.

"It's going to be tonight," I thought to myself.

I was so glad I didn't pick the Lions shirt.

\* \* \*

Bullock's party was a mishmash of people from the various aspects of his, and Alicia's, network of friends and co-workers.

Captain Leonard and his wife either were unable to, or didn't want to, attend, which meant that Chloe and I were the oldest people in attendance. That was a weird feeling.

A couple of Bullock's teammates from his college baseball

team made it, and the one thing I learned about former college athletes is they have a lot of stories about their playing days. You literally can't bring up any subject without them being able to turn it back to a story regarding their collegiate years.

I mentioned that I had lived and worked in Virginia for a few years and it was met with "dude, we played Apprentice College on our spring trip. They're from Virginia. Do you know that school?"

It was mentioned that I had spent time in the Navy.

"Bullock, what was that school that wore those Navy jerseys that had that sick catcher?" one of them asked.

Nick, a teammate of Bullock's, asked me what I did for a living and I said Bullock was my partner. He gave me a very confused stare.

I stressed that we were partners on the police force. Once that was cleared up, Nick was excited to tell me he had a friend who played at Adrian College who became a police officer. Which reminded Nick of the time that Saginaw Valley State, where he and Bullock played, had a walk-off win over Adrian. His buddy wasn't playing there at that time, as he and Bullock were freshmen, and his buddy was still in high school.

Whatever the topic, the conversation usually returned back a few years to their glory days. So I decided to make a game of it and tried to come up with the most obscure things I could think of just to see if they could turn the subject back to college baseball.

Sure enough they could.

Even when I mentioned papayas and jazz music.

* * *

Fortunately, after several testosterone-filled conversations, I was able to finally find a few moments to be alone with Chloe. We sat in the corner of the living room enjoying a couple of hors d'oeurves and drinks.

"How's it going?" I asked her hoping she was having more fun talking with the women at the party than I was listening to the men.

"Not too bad," she said. "Alicia really liked the floral arrangement I gave her."

"That's good," I said as I popped shrimp with cocktail sauce into my mouth.

"I haven't seen her in awhile," Chloe said.

"Maybe she's in the bathroom."

"Maybe," she said unconvinced by my suggestion. "But it feels like a long time, longer than a bathroom break would take."

"Well, we can obviously rule out her and Bullock doing it in their bedroom if it was longer than a bathroom break."

"Don't be crass," she said.

Proud of myself, I took a sip of my diet soda.

"I'm going to go find her," she said.

Chloe handed me her plate and walked away. I wasn't too angry about that, as now I had a few more things to eat.

* * *

After awhile, even I began to wonder where Alicia was. I actually was wondering where Chloe was, but I figured wherever Alicia was, Chloe was there as well.

I got up from the chair and looked for a garbage can for the plates I was still holding, as well as seeing if I could see Chloe in the room somewhere.

After depositing the plates into a trash bag that was placed next to the front door, I weaved my way in and out of the mass of younger people searching for my girlfriend.

I finally found myself standing outside the bathroom door. I gave it a little knock as I hoped that whomever was in there was Chloe.

She, in fact, did respond with a soft, "occupied."

"Chloe, it's me, Brody," I said in a tone loud enough I hoped she could hear but not too loud so other people would know I was trying to talk to someone in a bathroom through the door.

A few seconds passed, and she didn't respond.

I gave another soft knock on the door and said, "Chloe? Are you alright?"

No response.

I stood there waiting for what felt like an eternity. I heard the door open slightly and Chloe's head peered around. She had tears running down her face, her cheeks red and eyes puffy.

My heart stopped. I was panicked. What was going on?

Chloe slowly opened the door and gave me a head nod to signify I could enter.

Alicia was crouched down on the floor between the toilet and bathtub. She was a mess. I looked at Chloe in confusion.

"She lost the baby," Chloe said.

I knew I was going to have to be the one who was going to tell Bullock, my best friend, possibly the worst news he may have ever heard.

\* \* \*

I was sitting back in the corner chair. Slumped was more like it. I had my hands folded underneath my chin, with my elbows on the arm rest, and my legs stretched out before me.

The gathering had dwindled to only a small handful of what would be described as the closest of friends to Bullock and Alicia.

Chloe and the other women had circled Alicia, who was now sitting on a love seat across from me in the living room.

Aside from me, there was only three other men remaining, including Bullock. He was standing in the kitchen resting on the stove. His two friends, Nick and Andy, flanked him. They too stood in a similar stance. Andy with his back pressed up to the refrigerator and Nick leaning on the counter to the left of the stove.

None of the three spoke.

In fact, no one was speaking. No one knew what to say that hadn't been already said.

"I'm so sorry," was the prevalent comment.

It never felt enough each time it was said.

But what else could be said?

\* \* \*

The drive home was solemn.

Whenever we took Chloe's Camaro Z28, the one she got from her father, she always liked to drive. I drove this time. Chloe just sat in the passenger seat and stared out the window.

I had never thought about kids in the micro sense. Children had always seemed to be the thing I'd end up with, but never did I think specifics such as names, gender, number or anything else.

Bullock and Alicia had picked out a name. They were going to name their daughter Kendan Harley. Bullock's dad is named Ken and Alicia's dad was Dan. He passed when she was 18-years-old, just before graduation.

I had, however, never got that intimate with the idea of children. I wasn't sure Chloe had either, but based on her state of mind at the moment, I had the feeling if it wasn't at the forefront of her mine before, it was now.

Chloe has an angel's heart as well. I knew she hurt for Alicia, someone she had just met. That was Chloe's nature. She had empathy. But at this moment, I knew her sadness was more than just her compassion for Alicia.

As I drove I began to wonder if in the next few years, maybe even months, if we should consider having children. We should probably start planning for a wedding first, a conversation we never had openly together. We were both in our 30s and the clock was ticking much faster for Chloe than it was for me. It's a door that can't be opened once it's shut.

# 8

# No Comment

Bullock had a few days off to mourn.

In a brief conversation I had with him over the phone he told me it was weird. Alicia was absolutely devastated over the loss. Obviously. Bullock said that while he was sad by the loss, he felt that he didn't have the connection with Kendan that Alicia had already established biologically. His grief was a combination of being sad that he lost a child he never met, but also he was just as sad for his girlfriend. She was hurting deeply. And he was hurting because she was hurting.

"I don't feel like I would be a very good dad," he said. "Shouldn't I be more upset of losing Kendan than I am? I feel like I'm more sad for Alicia, does that make sense?"

I realized that while I am no way an expert on the subject, I was at that moment the big brother he needed. I had no words of wisdom. I kept saying how sorry I was.

And then I added, "I'm not sure why this happened. That's a hard one to explain or even try to. You and Alicia are upset for the same exact reasons: you both lost a child and your partner lost a child. Be sad together. Don't be sad as individuals. God put you with her, maybe for this specific reason, I don't know. But maybe that's why you're there, because you can handle it."

Never before had I said anything spiritual to another person. I'm not sure why I said it. It just came out. I'm not even sure it was good advice. Time will tell.

Nonetheless, I was riding solo for a few days at the office. My desk phone rang. Apparently, I had a visitor I wasn't expecting asking for me at the front desk.

\* \* \*

As I approached the lobby area, I could see a smaller gentlemen with a satchel over his shoulder standing at the bulletin board. He wore a plaid short-sleeved shirt, a combination of browns and greens, with cotton slacks. His tennis shoes were a bit worn. I had no idea who this person was, nor what he wanted.

"Can I help you?" I called out to the man.

He turned around and adjusted his glasses.

"I hope so," he said. "My name is David Bell."

He said it in a way that apparently I was supposed to recognize who he was. When I didn't respond in a way that indicated I was familiar with him, nor his name, he followed with, "from the *Herald*."

*The Stonington Herald* is an institution in town. It's been the local newspaper from pretty much day one when the town was established in 1876. To be honest, I have never been much of a newspaper reader. Whenever I did read the news, it was a much larger paper, and it was usually just the sports section.

"How are you David?" I asked.

"Pretty good," he responded. "Is there somewhere we can chat for a few moments. I have a couple questions, and I'd prefer to not ask them in a public forum."

I looked around the lobby and he and I were the only two there.

"I think you'd prefer I didn't ask out here," he said, as if he knew what I was thinking as I scanned the room.

That was intriguing for sure. Why would I care where I'm asked questions from someone I just met?

"There's an interrogation room we can use," I said. "Is this going to be an interrogation?"

"I'm not sure yet," he said.

Now I was definitely intrigued.

\* \* \*

David and I walked into the interrogation room and I quickly took my usual position, which ironically is totally opposite of the gunfighter's seat. Sitting in the first available chair, facing away from the door, forced him to walk around the table and be on the side where we normally place the people we're trying to extract information from.

Once he settled into his seat, I asked, "how can I help you?"

David began to pull a couple of manila folders out of his satchel, as well as a notepad, a couple of pencils and a small handheld tape recorder.

Ignoring my query, he began to place the various items into a particular alignment before him.

"Do you have a lot of free time on your job?" I asked. "Because I don't."

74

David looked up at me and smirked.

"I assure you, you'll have time for this," he said.

"If you say so," I said.

David opened one of the folders, and after looking over whatever was inside, closed it and looked at me.

"You haven't been with the force very long, have you?" he asked.

I was sure he knew how long specifically I had been with the department. I figured it was a rhetorical question, so I didn't feel a need to answer.

"Is there something you want to ask me?" I asked. "Because if you do, just ask it. Not a fan of beating around the bush."

David adjusted his seat forward so he could rest his arms on the table between us.

"It's just that, in my time with the Herald, which has been almost a decade, I don't recall too many suspicious deaths in town," he said. "And yet, since you've been in town, we've had two such deaths in Stonington specifically."

"Is there a question?"

David grabbed a second folder. Opened it, glanced it over. Shut it.

"I see you got an award for almost, in a roundabout way, of solving one death," he said. "Gary Hutchins. Drove over a cliff. Seems like you were able to only confirm that he died. Is that right?"

David pulls out a couple copies of *The Herald.*

He tosses me one across the table. I had to spin it slightly so I could see whatever he wanted me to specifically see.

"Here's my story on your department solving the crime," he said as he put his index finger at the headline. "I didn't bother to write about you receiving the award. I'm not sure why you received an award for something that wasn't really solved."

"That's your opinion," I said.

I've known this man for a few minutes. I felt comfortable thinking he was a prick. If I had a subscription to his paper, I would've canceled it. Maybe I'll subscribe just to cancel it.

David tosses another edition toward me.

"Actually, that's a lot of people's opinion," he said.

I didn't reach for the newspaper. I didn't like where this appeared to be headed. David reached across the table and opened it up. After thumbing through a few pages, he stopped, and laid the paper fully opened in front of him.

"Let's see here," he said as he guided his finger across the page. "Here's a reader who says, and I quote, 'Officer Brody James is hardly a first class detective with a series of false steps and assumptions'. That's from Eleanor Thompson. Do you know her?"

"David," I said as I stood up. "I'm not sure what's going on here, but I have actual work to do."

David leaned back in his chair and folded his hands behind his head.

"Officer James," he said. "I don't think you're a hero cop. But that's another story. What I found interesting is that we've had two mysterious deaths here in Stonington, and that obviously, was something I found interesting. I thought to myself, when was the last time we've had a death that involved police? Do you know how long it's been? I do."

I stood silent.

"The last time," he said, as he pulled out another manila folder and opened it. This time he didn't peruse it and close it. This time, he spun the folder around and slid it in my direction.

I didn't look at the contents of the folder. I knew what it was going to say. David also knew I knew.

"As I was saying," he said. "The last time was in 1982. Do you know what happened in that situation, Officer James?"

I knew.

"Well, by your silence, I believe you do," he said. "In the summer of 1982, a young man fell off a roof and landed next to a pool. There was only one witness. The homeowners weren't home at the time and didn't know anyone was on their property. Seems that two young boys entered their back yard, climbed on top of the house, and according to the only witness, the young man - a Charlie Plunkett - was trying to jump from the roof into the pool. He missed. Broke his neck and died at the scene. Do you know who that witness was, Officer James?"

I knew.

"It was you," he said. "Don't you find it interesting that a town that goes decades between mysterious deaths has only one connection to all three? That's you. You were there when Charlie fell. Or was pushed. You waltzed into town and a classmate drives off a cliff and another just happens to overdose. And now you discover someone dead in a park? Four deaths. Somehow all connected to you."

I grabbed the door handle.

"David, I don't know what your angle is," I said. "But I'm not going to sit here and be accused of - I don't know what you're accusing me of - but I don't find any humor in this whatsoever."

"Me neither, Officer James," he said. "But I do have one question. On the record. Do you have a comment as to why three deaths - four if I include Rebekkah Wertheimer's overdose - can all be connected to you?"

"No comment," I said as I walked out the door.

# 9

# And All Hell Breaks Loose

Bullock and I could hear Chief Leonard through his closed door. To say he was angry, was an understatement.

I sat there with a copy of the recent *Herald* on my desk.

The headline, above the fold, read: "Cop can't explain connection to area deaths."

David Bell was insinuating in the article that maybe I was honored for solving murders that I may have had a hand in. He suggested that a thorough investigation be had to see if there were any mysterious deaths during my time in Virginia as an officer, or any of my assignments during the military.

Leonard slammed his phone down followed by, "same to you!"

"Damn, Brody," Bullock said. "I'm gone for a few days and all hell breaks loose."

I just sat there silently staring at the headline.

"Brody, get in here!" Leonard called out from his office.

* * *

I sat down in Leonard's office. I had a quick flashback of my days of being called into the principal's office. Several times.

"I've been here in Stonington for a hell of long time to have to deal with this shit," he said. "We should sue them and that little punk editor."

"I don't think we can, sir," I said.

"Well, we should," he said as he paced back and forth behind his desk.

He grabbed his chair, spun it around a few times and then grabbed it to stop its rotation. He dropped down into the chair, spun it so he was facing me and looked at me with steely eyes.

"Son, I know all about the case you worked on and you did a hell of a job," he said. "What do I need to know about this young man and the pool?"

I tried to swallow, but my throat had dried. I pressed on as best I could.

"To be honest, sir, it was the worst day of my life," I said.

\* \* \*

There was a knock on my bedroom door.

"Brody, your friend Charlie is here," my mom said.

"Can he come up to my room?" I said. "I've almost got the high score on Pitfall, and if I do ,I can take a Polaroid of the score and send it in to Activision and they'll send me back a patch."

"You know the policy," she said. "No friends in bedrooms. I'll tell him to wait in the living room. I'll put on the television for him."

"Thanks mom," I said.

\* \* \*

I sprinted down the stairs, jumped off the final three steps and landed with a thud near the front door.

"Charlie," I called out. "You're not going to believe what I just did. It's epic."

"What did you do?" he asked while he tried to extract himself from my dad's Lazy-Boy chair.

"I got 20,000 points in Pitfall!" I said with great pride.

"Bro! You can get a patch," he said. "That's so gnarly."

"I know right."

He slapped me on my back and then we awkwardly stared at each other for a few seconds like the socially awkward preteens we were.

"What do you want to do today?" I asked.

"You want to go pool jumping?"

\* \* \*

Pool jumping was pretty much the way it sounded. The key was to find backyards where the pool wasn't being used, had easy access to, didn't have a dog, and we were pretty sure we could escape without any problems.

For the most part, it was simple.

We weren't committing crimes, at least in our eyes. We would hop a fence, jump into someone's pool and swim as far as we could. You got out as fast as you could and hopped a fence on the other side of the yard and went about your way.

Once in awhile, someone was home. We got yelled at several times, chased a couple times and one time we heard they were going to call the police. We went straight home and hid for the rest of the day, that time.

On this very unfortunate day, no one was home. And the pool was super nice. Which allowed us to stay much longer and be more adventurous.

* * *

"Do you want to go over to that rich neighborhood past Simonds Elementary?" Charlie asked. "We've never been over there to pool jump. I bet they got all sorts of nice pools."

"Sure, doesn't Paul live over there somewhere?" I asked.

"I think so," Charlie said.

He stopped walking, looked at me with a wide grin.

"He has a pool, bro," he said.

The two of us picked up our pace.

* * *

We hopped the fence to Paul Schumann's house.

The family had an above ground pool, which made our task a little more challenging. I got to the top of the ladder and yelled out, "gottay."

When I came out of the water, Charlie was looking at me standing atop the ladder to the pool.

81

"What did you say?" he asked.

"Gottay."

"What the heck does that mean?"

"I don't know," I said. "It was the first thing to come to mind. I wonder if I can get other kids to say it?"

"I doubt it," Charlie said.

He looked around the yard. It looked like the Schumann's were doing a roofing project. There was piles of shingles everywhere, a nail gun and nails were sitting on a picnic table, and a ladder was still leaning against the house.

"Are you thinking what I'm thinking?" Charlie said.

"I don't know," I said. "I was thinking why did they leave all this stuff laying around. I bet they might home soon. Maybe the just went to the hardware store? What are you thinking?"

"Not any of that," he said. "I was thinking we can make the pool from the house."

"You want to jump off the house?"

"We can make it," he said with great confidence.

"Are you out of your mind?" I asked.

Charlie jumped off the pool ladder and sprinted toward the construction ladder. He looked up at the roof and back toward the pool. He was determining whether his assertion was accurate. He convinced himself it was.

Up the ladder he went.

"Come on ya sissy," he said.

I know I'm not the first person to begrudgingly do something because of peer pressure. As I climbed the ladder, it hit me that I was petrified of heights and the reality was starting to sink in.

My steady but slow pace was not fast enough for Charlie.

"Come on, moron," he yelled down to me. "We won't have time to jump."

"And wouldn't that be a shame," I thought to myself.

When I go to the top of the ladder, I thought for sure it was going to tip back and I was going to die.

Charlie held the ladder for me.

"Be careful," I said to him.

It took some time, but I finally was on the roof. I looked down and it was at this moment that I knew I didn't want to jump. I also didn't want to climb back down. And if Charlie jumped, who was going to hold the ladder anyway?

Charlie was looking over the edge, a few feet away.

"I'm not so sure about this Charlie," I said as a last-ditched plea to not continue.

"I'm doing this," he said. "It's going to be epic. Kids are going to remember me for this."

No truer, or tragic, words were ever spoken.

Charlie backed up and started sprinting to the edge. As he was about to jump, his left foot caught the gutter. That was the last moment I, or anyone, saw Charlie alive.

* * *

"I don't remember ever getting off that roof," I said. "Some kids at school said I pushed Charlie, or that we got in a fight, or something like that. I never wanted to be on that roof."

Captain Leonard sat there, just listening.

"What's weird about that whole thing," I said. "Was that I became really interested in scouting and swimming and stuff like that. I never really thought about it. But maybe deep inside, I don't know, maybe in some way I wanted to be able to survive or maybe help someone. It sounds crazy. I guess I don't really know."

Leonard got up from his chair and looked out his office window.

"We all have different reasons for taking the paths we took," he said. "But what I do know is, you're a good man and a good cop."

"Eleanor Thompson doesn't think so."

"Who the hell is Eleanor Thompson?" he asked.

"Nobody," I said. "Not a big deal."

"Well, then don't you worry about Eleanor Thompson or anyone else," he said. "You're good at what you do. Maybe this tragedy with Charlie was the thing that moved you in the right direction."

Leonard moved around his desk, sat on the edge near me and looked me in the eye.

"I'll handle Dave Bell," he said. "You keep doing what you do."

\* \* \*

In the next edition of the *Herald*, there was a guest editorial. It was written by Chief Leonard. He took the newspaper to task and commended me, and all of his officers, for the exceptional work we do for the department and the community.

I give the paper credit for running it. I also felt that in the back of my mind, this wouldn't be the last time I had a conflict with David Bell.

* * *

I was sitting at my desk, when Bullock came out of the break room with a jello cup.

"Did you see what Leonard said about me?" he asked.

"You?"

"Well, he had to include everybody to not show favoritism," he said. "But we all know who he meant when he said 'the quality and passion for the job is evident'."

"By the entire department," I said. "The rest of the quote was 'by the entire department'."

"Whatever," he said as he sat in his chair. "Hey, Brody, do you have any whipped cream?"

"At my desk?" I asked. "No."

"I love whipped cream," he said. "I could eat a whole can. Alicia said you're not supposed to eat a whole can of whipped cream, but I think you can. I just spray it right into my mouth. Damn, it's so good."

"You eat whipped cream in one sitting?"

"If I could, I would," he said. "No, I sneak shots of it when I think she doesn't know."

"And you consider yourself to be a man?"

"A man who produces quality work and has passion for the job," he said.

I spun my chair around. He was licking his spoon. I sat there for a few seconds and my mind returned to the child he lost. It seemed like an odd moment, but it was pressing on my mind, so I forged ahead.

"Hey Bullock," I said to get his attention.

He looked up at me, with the spoon dangling from his mouth.

85

"How are you and Alicia doing?"

Bullock's demeanor totally changed. From a kid licking a spoon that had Jello on it, to a quality police officer and a dedicated boyfriend, in one moment.

"We're doing okay," he said as he hung his head and stared at the spoon.

"Thanks Brody."

I didn't know what else to say. I turned my chair and wiped my eyes.

# 10

## My Allergies Are Acting Up

Not deterred by David Bell, I returned my focus to finding out anything I could about possible drug activity in Stonington.

Bullock and I drove down to Monroe to see if we can find Lucas Winters, and hear directly from him about his whereabouts, as well as any knowledge he may have about the drug scene in Stonington. At least any he'd be willing to share and that wouldn't incriminate himself.

As we pulled into the parking lot of the address provided by Donald Barton, it was evident that he wasn't getting the value he was paying for in regards to his stepson maintaining the property. No matter how much he was paying Lucas. Weeds were growing everywhere and the property looked closer to being abandoned than being ready for future rentals.

There weren't any vehicles visible on the property, and we weren't exactly sure which was the front door. Bullock and I walked the perimeter of the building and would peer into various windows, but it was hard to see clearly as most were covered in dust and cobwebs or were blocked from the interior by boxes or shelves.

Most of the doors were locked as well, and there weren't any sounds coming from inside the building which would give us the impression that anyone was there.

Bullock grabbed another door handle and both of us were shocked when the door actually opened.

No lights were on inside the building, so we both pulled our flashlights out and turned them on. The door we entered through accessed an open section that was used for storing industrial materials. Not much was left, but enough remained that we had to watch our step. The floors were filled with grease stains and debris and the air was filled with dust particles. The interior gave off a vibe that nothing had happened in this building in quite some time. It smelled industrial. At one time, it was the lifeblood for people's careers and livelihoods. Now it sits, long forgotten.

Bullock started down a hallway that led toward offices. I was keeping an eye on our backside, when I nearly ran into Bullock.

"Reefer," he said.

"What?" I asked.

I had an idea what he said, but wasn't sure he actually said it. And if what I thought he said, was what he said, I was confused why he said it.

"Ganja," he said. "The devil's lettuce. Spleef. Mary Jane."

"What about it?"

"You can't smell that?" he asked.

"My allergies are acting up. I can't smell much of anything."

"You're a dork," he said. "Nonetheless, I smell marijuana."

I took as large of a breath I could. I honestly didn't smell anything. Bullock was watching me inhale. I felt compelled to confirm his discovery.

"Yeah," I said. "I smell it now."

I may have convinced myself I had actually smelled something. But I trusted my partner. He felt someone was here, or had been recently. And based on what we had been told, we were pretty confident that Lucas Winters was living there and was there at that moment.

Bullock peered around the corner. He looked back and me and gave me a nod to follow him.

We both turned the corner and Lucas was sitting in an recliner, headphones on, eyes closed with a bong on his lap.

Bullock gave a look over the area to see if any weapons were near Lucas. None could be seen. Bullock tapped Lucas on the shoulder.

"Holy shit!" Lucas yelled out. The bong went flying and it's contents spilled. "What the hell, dude?"

Lucas fell out of the chair and was trying to get his bearings when Bullock leaned down and picked him up and put him back in the chair.

"What the hell?" Lucas said as he processed our presence.

When it clicked, he asked, "You two got a warrant?"

"We don't need a warrant," Bullock said. "You, my friend, are a person of interest and this was the address we were given and we saw you through the window. We knocked on the door and it opened, so here we are."

"That's bullshit," Lucas said as he attempted to look out the dirt-filled window.

"It doesn't matter, Lucas, we're here now," Bullock said as he sat down on a folding chair next to Lucas. "We have some questions. It may not lead to anything other than you giving us some information and we'll overlook the possession charge that is staring at us in the face."

"Who told you I was here?" he asked still peering out the

window.

"No one else is with us, if that's what you're trying to figure out," I said. "For what it's worth, your dad gave us the address."

"Step-dad," Lucas quickly said. "What questions do you have that are so important you had to come all the way down here?"

"Did you know Tom Downing?" Bullock asked.

"Doesn't sound familiar," he said. "Why did you say 'did'?"

"He overdosed back in Stonington," I said.

"Really?" Lucas said.

He appeared to be putting things together in his mind.

"Damn," he continued. "That sucks."

I grabbed another chair, unfolded it and sat down. Bullock and I flanked Lucas.

"Listen, guys," Lucas said. "That's why I got off that shit."

"You stopped doing drugs?" Bullock asked as he looked at all the paraphernalia all over the office.

"I stopped doing those kind of drugs, man," Lucas said. "Weed is a plant. It's natural. If it's natural, it's good for you."

"I don't think that's necessarily accurate," Bullock said.

Lucas began to rub his eyes and fidget in his chair.

I snapped my fingers.

"Lucas, pay attention," I said.

"I'm paying attention, dude," he said. "I just have to piss, you know what I'm saying?"

"We'll let you go to the bathroom in a minute," I said. "Do you have any idea who might be dealing back in Stonington?"

"Nah, dude," he said. "I've been down here for awhile. I don't know nobody back there anymore. I ain't about that town anymore."

"That's why you came down here?" Bullock asked.

"Nah, Donald said I could live down here as long as I didn't interfere with anything," he said.

"What do you mean by that?" I asked.

"His business, you know," Lucas said.

"I'm not following," Bullock said. "You worked for him?"

Lucas closed his eyes, rolled his neck until it cracked a couple of times, and set his head on the chair back.

"My mom wanted me to get a job and kept bugging him to hire me," he said. "Like I'm construction worker material."

He sat back up, rested his elbows on his thighs and clasped his hands together. He dropped his head into his hands, rubbed his face and looked back up at us.

"Donald put me in an office job, putting paper into folders and shit like that," he said. "Boring! You know what I'm saying? Anyway, I'm not like a genius or anything."

"You don't say," Bullock said.

"I get it," Lucas said. "You don't look at me and think I'm smart. But I'm not stupid. I would glance at some of the papers and I noticed that the materials he was charging customers for, was not the materials he was using."

"Really?" I said. "Such as?"

All of a sudden, Lucas sprang to life. It was like he was waiting for someone to ask him an important question like this all his life.

"So they'd be hired to do a roofing job," he said. "But they weren't even using actual roofing materials. They'd just put up, like I don't even know what it is, but it was like patch work and this spongy material. It sure as hell ain't roofing."

"If you don't know anything about construction, why are you so sure they weren't using the right materials?" Bullock asked.

"I don't know dude," he said. "He just said to me one day to make sure not to show what we're using to the customer. It was probably cheaper material. And how would people really know? How often have you been on a roof?"

For a brief moment, I had an image of Charlie and I back on the Schumann's roof.

"It's been awhile," I said.

"Exactly," he said. "So they charge a lot of money to do a job that most people won't even realize ever. It's kind of genius. Anyway, one day I brought it up at dinner and Donald was pissed because my mom was asking a lot of questions. Fortunately, for Donald, I had some issues so he just blamed my condition."

"And that's how you ended up here?" I asked.

"Donald brought me into his office and offered me a lot of money to just go away," he said. "I told him I didn't have anywhere to go, so he gave me a lot more money and this building. I figured it was a good deal for me, so I just left. Been here ever since. There's no phones here, so I pretty much lost contact with my boys back home. Made some good friends in town here and that's that."

"That's that," I said. It wasn't a question.

Wasn't really a statement either.

"So you wouldn't know anything about drugs being dealt to high school kids in Stonington?" I asked. "Is that you're saying?"

"Yeah," he said. "Sorry I can't be more help officers. But I ain't in that life no more."

Lucas Winters didn't get us any closer to the truth.

* * *

"Do you believe him?" Bullock asked on our drive back from Monroe to Stonington.

"I don't know, maybe," I said. "Why make that up?"

"What are we going to do about it?" he asked. "I mean the stuff about his dad scamming customers."

"I guess we'll tell Leonard," I said. "Maybe we have to tell the building department or the county or something. I'm not exactly sure who's jurisdiction it is for overcharging someone for construction work."

"Is it a crime?" he asked. "I mean it should be, but what do we do about it? I don't know anything about roofing materials. I couldn't tell you what should or shouldn't be used."

"Me neither," I said. "We'll get the preliminary information and then we'll probably hand it off. I'd hate to have our focus diverted to this when we're trying to find out who sold deadly chemicals to a high school kid."

\* \* \*

"Well, there hasn't been one formal complaint filed against Don Barton or Barton Construction," I said as I studied my computer screen.

Leonard asked us to get a little bit more information, much to my chagrin.

"Maybe the kid was right," Bullock said. "Maybe no one knows that he charged them for one type of material and then used much cheaper materials. Would you know the difference?"

Not looking up from the computer, I said, "no, I would not."

"So if there's no formal complaint, there's not much we

can do, right?" Bullock asked as he rose from his chair and approached my desk.

I could tell he was as eager to pass this case, if there even is a case, to someone else.

"I mean, we have one guy's word and nothing else," he said.

I turned in my chair to face him.

"Captain Leonard said that for now, we can have it on file, but nothing more until someone comes forward that says they've been wronged," I said. "According to the Better Business Bureau, there hasn't been any complaints."

Bullock rested both arms on my partition wall.

"We got bupkis," he said.

"Why do you keep saying that?" I asked.

"I don't know, it just sort of works, you know?"

"You made fun of me for saying it and now you keep saying it," I said. "That's more annoying then you making fun of me for saying it."

"That's before I knew how useful it is," he said. "It summarizes situations succinctly. There's irony to it, though."

"How's that?"

"If I didn't have that word," he said before pausing. "I'd have bupkis."

"You're an idiot," I said.

Captain Leonard came out of his office and headed straight toward me and Bullock.

"We got the toxicology report on Thomas Downing," he said. "Looks like he ingested methylenedioxymethamphetamine and mixed it with vodka."

"Bet you can't say that twice," Bullock said.

"Ecstasy?" I asked.

"Back in the day, it was also called molly," Leonard said.

94

"Well, both of those would have been a lot easier to say than whatever you started with," Bullock said. "Next time, just say molly."

Leonard wasn't amused.

"No matter what we call it," Leonard sternly said. "The young man died from it. About a decade ago, we had a few kids get caught up in the rave scene and we'd scoop them up as they tried to make their way back home. Nothing life-threatening, but we did have a couple kids mix it with Viagra. Lowered their defense mechanisms. Hard to recover from being sexually assaulted."

He paused. He had the look of a man who had seen some things that he had stored away for quite some time and is once again reliving another person's horror story.

"Gentlemen, I need you two to get to the bottom of this," he said. "Go back to the Downing family, see if this news can jog their memory and give clarity to what might have happened. I'm going to contact Mr. Miller and see if he'll allow us deeper access in the schools."

"Who's Miller?" I asked.

"The Superintendent of the schools," Leonard said.

"Maybe we could do an assembly," Bullock gleefully said.

"That's what I was thinking," Leonard said. "Give me what you got on the building issue and I'll pass it on to someone else."

Thanking God, in my mind, I gathered all the documents, shoved them haphazardly into a folder and handed it him. He sorted the papers in a more presentable way and went on his way back into his office.

"I was kidding about the assembly," Bullock said. "Do you think he was kidding?"

"Well, it doesn't sound like it," I said. "Tell you what, champ, I'll let you have all the speaking parts."

"Thanks a lot," he said as he stood there trying to internally determine whether or not Captain Leonard really wants us to do a school assembly.

I saw no reason to get clarification.

# 11

# Their Pain Was Just Beginning

Bullock and I sat down with Patricia and Edward Downing.

We had to explain what we found in their son Tom's system, and then we had to try to get them to help figure out how he put himself in that position.

The common problem with these exchanges is that parent's will often blame themselves, or make the assumption that we are somehow blaming them. With the questions we have to ask, it's very easy to see how the latter would appear to be the case.

"Have you had any fights with Tom?"

"How are the finances?"

"How is your marriage?

"Did your child start running with the wrong crowd and why do you think he did?"

Legitimate questions that could help us solve his death, and possibly more kids from dying, all say in a roundabout way: Why weren't you better parents?

The reality is, that often times, those questions are asked for a reason. And the reason is, why aren't some people better parents?

* * *

I sat in a chair facing the two parents, who were seated on a couch with their front picture window behind them.

"Last time we spoke, Mrs. Downing," I said. "You couldn't remember if Tom had started a new friendship with someone. Has anything changed in that regard?"

"Why would it be different?" Edward tersely said.

"We're just trying to see if new information comes to light," I said as an attempt to keep emotions in check, and not get this headed in a wrong direction.

Patricia rubbed her hand across Edward's right leg in an effort to calm him down or console him. Or both.

No one wanted this conversation to be confrontational, but it can often become that as both sides want answers and neither wants to have to defend themselves.

"Like I said, Tommy only had a few friends," she said. "They've been buddies since elementary school."

Bullock, standing behind me, was taking down notes of the conversation. We wanted to have written record to see if there were similarities, or potential discrepancies, from our previous conversation with the family.

Every question asked was, upon review later, met with near identical answers as to what was previously said.

Except one.

It wasn't so much a different answer, but it was a slightly different question that elicited a different answer.

Previously, Bullock had asked, "To your knowledge, was Tom involved in drugs in any sort of way?"

This time, he asked basically the same question, but only with a twist, that he himself admitted later was done by happenstance.

"You haven't seen any drug use, to your knowledge, here at the home?"

Edward Downing tensed his jaw. His breathing became more labored, more deliberate. His gaze was undaunted.

Patricia Downing slid closer to her husband. She slid her left arm between his right arm and side and clutched Edward tightly. She rested her head on his shoulder and began to weep.

"Mrs. Downing," I said. "Did Tom have a drug problem?"

In between teardrops, she shook her head in the negative. When asked before if Tom was involved in drugs, they answered that specific question honestly.

The front door of their house opened and in walked their daughter, Jenna, one year older then their son Tom was.

Jenna froze in her steps and stared at the four adults sitting in her living room.

"What's going on?" she asked.

* * *

Jenna sat in a dining room chair and was flanked by her parents.

Bullock sat to the young girl's left, while I was directly across from her. I slid a display of flowers to unblock my view of her.

Jenna sat there crying, with her head hung and her arms crossed as if she was very cold. Patricia's sobbing had subdued. She was now focused on being as emotionally supportive of her remaining child as she could. Edward was more distant. His battle seemed to be more internal. He lost his son. His daughter may have played a role.

I think both parents feared that was the case but was hoping it not to be. We were about to find out.

"Jenna, did you provide Tom the ecstasy?" I asked. "Do you still have some of the same supply that you gave Tom?"

Jenna wiped her nose with the sleeve that was clenched in her hands. She nodded in the affirmative.

Patricia placed a hand on each of her daughter's shoulders and rubbed vigorously but compassionately. Edward turned his head toward the ceiling in dramatic fashion and turned his back on his wife and daughter.

"Why?" he screamed out.

Bullock stood up and placed his hand on the man's side and ushered him into the living room.

"He was going to ask out a girl," she said between spit strands stuck between her upper and lower lips. "He was super nervous. He asked me if I had anything that could calm him down."

Patricia took her right hand and held it to her mouth and began crying while stifling the noise as much as she could.

"How much did you give him?" I asked.

"I dunno," she said. "Four or five, maybe. I told him not to take more than one."

"Then why did you give him so much?" I asked.

"I don't know," she said. "I thought maybe if she said yes maybe he could...I dunno...like have a good time."

"He also drank a lot of vodka," I said. "Did you get that for him too?"

"I don't know," she said. "Maybe, he got it out of dad's cabinet."

This became more a tragedy with each bit of information we discovered.

"I have two more questions and then we'll be done," I said. "Do you know the name of the girl? And, more importantly, where did you get the ecstasy?"

"Gwyneth," she mumbled.

I began writing the first name down, "do you know her last name?"

"Penrose," she said. "Apparently, she's super popular and Tommy thought if he asked her out and she said yes, that he'd be super popular. He said he was tired of being...just being...you know? He wanted to see how the popular kids lived."

I wrote down the girl's last name in my notebook.

"Jenna, I really need you to understand how important it is that I know who provided you with the ecstasy," I said. "I also need whatever is left of the drugs. If you still have them."

I reached over and touched Jenna's arm. She was in an unfortunate situation no matter where she went with her answers. She was filled with guilt, sadness and anger. But she also could default to self-preservation. I hoped that connecting with her humanity, she'd want to prevent this from happening again more then trying to make herself less culpable.

"They've been laced with fentanyl," I said trying to look her eye-to-eye. "We need to not only dispose of what you have, if you still have some, but we also have to find out where it's coming from before anyone else gets hurt."

"Carson McCall," she mumbled.

I wrote his name down.

"Jenna," I said. "If you still have any left, we need to take it. We'll analyze it so we know exactly what we're dealing with. Can you give us what you have? Can you do that for me?"

Patricia released her hands from her daughter's shoulder allowing Jenna to get up from the table. The teenager slowly walked out of the kitchen, through the living room and up the stairs. Bullock followed behind her with Edward Downing in tow.

Patricia sat down in the chair, eyes puffy and red, and reached across the table and moved the flowers back to their original position. She evened out the table cloth that, from my viewpoint, was already even. She did that a couple more times.

The trio returned from upstairs. Bullock handed me a small plastic bag with about a dozen pills inside.

"Are you going to be okay?" I said, looking directly at Edward.

"This family can't have any more pain, officer," he said before slumping into the door frame. He leaned his head back and stared at the ceiling.

Patricia hung her head. Neither of them appeared to be aware of what was about to happen.

Jenna sat on the couch, all balled up, with her left thumb in between her teeth.

I got up from the table and followed Bullock toward Jenna.

"Jenna," Bullock softly said. "Could you stand up for me?"

Confused, Jenna stood up. Bullock gently grabbed her right arm and placed it on her back.

"You have the right to remain silent," Bullock said.

Internally, I disagreed with Edward. Their pain was just beginning.

# 12

# Maybe You Could Be An Astronaut

"Have you ever thought about getting a tattoo?" Bullock asked.

I sat there waiting for the driver of the car in front of us to apparently make the most critical decision they've ever had to make.

"Let's go!" I barked out.

"Did that help?" Bullock asked.

"Well since they haven't moved, I'm assuming it didn't," I said.

"Maybe they have capiophobia?"

Finally the car turned right. I pulled up to the stop sign, looked to the left and then to the right, and proceeded straight through the intersection.

"What's capiophobia?" I asked.

"The fear of being arrested," Bullock said as he looked out the side window back toward the road we just passed. "Weren't we supposed to turn right?"

"Yes," I said. "But I didn't want to be stuck behind that douchebag any longer."

"So, we're going to out of way and making this trip a little longer?" he asked. "And that's because we want to save time?"

"Yes," I said. "Yes, we are."

Bullock rolled down his window and starting tapping the outside of his door with his fingers.

"I might as well make myself as comfortable as possible, then," he said.

"Have you ever thought about getting a tattoo?" he asked after a few minutes of silence.

"I have a tattoo," I said. "It's not that warm to have the window down, you know."

"Do you want me to roll it up?" he asked.

"Yeah, if you don't mind," I said. "Maybe a little."

Bullock pushed the lever to raise the window, ever so slightly.

"Is this good?"

"A little more."

Bullock raised the window, although I couldn't tell the difference.

"Is this good?"

"Are you going to move it up as little as possible and ask me each time if it's good?" I asked.

"Not sure," he said raising the window a little more. "Is this good?"

"Yes, its' fine!" I said.

"I thought so," he said in a tone of victory in his voice. "How much longer?"

"A couple more minutes," I said as I pulled to a section of the road with a yield sign.

I never understood yield signs. Why not just put a stop sign? Are people's lives that adversely affected by coming to a stop for a few more seconds? Most yield signs are on rural roads, which are often obstructed by trees or shrubbery, forcing you to pretty much stop any way. I just don't get it.

"So, what's your tattoo?" Bullock asked.

"I have a couple," he said. "A lot of people who serve do and they get theirs when they serve. But I got one right out of high school."

"Oh yeah, that young?" Bullock asked.

"Well, my dad was against tattoos," I said. "He figured you get a tattoo you're pretty much one step away from prison."

"A lot of guys in the joint say their life of crime started after they got a tattoo."

"I kind of won him over," I said. "I got a tattoo of a lighthouse on my right arm. It's pretty cool. My grandpa liked lighthouses, so I figured it'd be hard for him to complain about something that had to do with his dad. That and I really wanted to honor my grandpa."

"That's sweet," Bullock said. "You're a real softy Brody."

"Do you have any tattoos?" I asked.

"Nope."

"Are you thinking about getting one?" I asked.

"Nope."

"Then why did you bring up tattoos?"

"Oh, I was thinking about that show *Fantasy Island*," he said. "I thought that show was weird. Why would you go on that island? All sorts of spooky shit happened out there and rarely was the person entirely happy at the end. I just can't picture why people would pay to go there. It had the guy who did ads for Corinthian leather and his helper was Tattoo."

"Okay, first off," I said. "I can't picture you watching *Fantasy Island*. Secondly, the guy was Ricardo Montalban. Pretty famous actor other than *Fantasy Island*. He was Khan from *Star Trek*."

"Never saw it."

"You watched *Fantasy Island* but never saw *Star Trek?*" I asked.

I couldn't believe it. One was a popular show, but a lot of popular shows in their time are forgotten. The other was a pretty famous movie. Popular movies outlast popular television shows. At least when thinking of these two.

"Doesn't matter," I continued. "Because he was famous. And classy. That's why he did the Chrysler ads. They were like a classy car company in the 70s."

"I know about Chrysler," he indignantly said. "I'm not an idiot."

"Well, he didn't do commercials for the leather,"I said. "In the Chrysler ad, Montalban would say the cars came with Corinthian leather. I'm not even sure that's a real thing now that I think about it."

"So, he's a liar," Bullock said.

"Well, I'm not sure it's not a thing," I said.

"And if it's not?" he asked.

"Well, then he'd be a liar," I said. "But a classy one."

I slowed the car down to look at the number on the mailbox next to the street.

"This is it," I said.

\* \* \*

I knocked on the front door.

"He ain't here," a gruff, female voice said from the other side of the door.

"Mrs. McCall?" I said. "I'm Officer James from SPD."

"Don't care," she said. "I know who you're looking for, and

he ain't here."

"We're looking for Carson," I said.

"I just said, I knew who you were looking for," she said with great agitation. "The little asshole ain't here. Haven't seen him in awhile. Don't know when I'll see him. Don't care if I see him."

Bullock tapped me on my arm. I turned toward him and he whispered, "lovely woman."

I couldn't help but chuckle.

"Can you let him know we're looking for him if you see him?" I said.

"He knows you're looking for him," she said. "You guys are always looking for him."

That much was true.

Our young Mr. McCall has been charged twice for driving under the influence, once for retail fraud and once for entering a posted farm property.

In that particular case, Carson was asked to leave the property of a girl he was seeing at the time. Since she lived on a family farm, and he was asked to leave and refused, he served 30 days for trespassing on a Fenced or Posted Farm Property. All told, he has spent 304 days in local jails.

"Are you two just going to stand on my porch all day?" the woman yelled out toward us.

\* \* \*

"Do you want to drive?" I asked Bullock on our way back to the car.

"Seriously?" he asked.

"Yeah," I said.

"Are you afraid you'll run into that person at the intersection again?" he asked.

"Careful," I said. "Or I'll rescind the offer."

I tossed Bullock the keys. I don't have children, but I can't imagine any future child of mine being more excited when I finally toss them the keys to have them drive.

"This is awesome," he said.

It was a welcomed change insomuch as it would give me time to figure out where we stood as far as the case. I was starting to already regret the offer. Bullock, before we even got in the car, was adjusting the side mirror.

Once I was comfortable in my seat with the belt secure, I watched Bullock adjust the seat forward. And then back a little. And then forward a smidge. And then...

"For goodness sake, we're not going that far," I finally blurted out.

"I can't get comfortable," he said. "You and your freakishly long legs."

Bullock turned his attention to the rear view mirror.

I rolled my eyes and gave out a huff of disapproval.

"You going to be okay over there?" he asked as he buckled his seat belt.

"It's quite possible that I might be able to solve this entire case before we even leave this driveway."

"You think so?" he asked. "Could you solve it? All by your lonesome? No, you couldn't. So maybe stop with the bloviating and maybe relax, enjoy the ride and let me show you what a good driver looks like."

\* \* \*

All-in-all, Bullock did a good job driving.

"Thank God I survived that ordeal," I said as we pulled into the station.

No sense in letting him know what I actually thought. His ego would balloon and that would be insufferable.

"Do you ever think you could be a race car driver?" he asked.

"Nope," I said. "About a year or two into my stint with the Navy, I figured I was either always going to be in the service or switch to police."

"I think I could be a pretty good race car driver," he confidently said.

"Is there anything you think you can't do?"

The long pause was a signal that he was literally going through his mental Rolodex of potential jobs, and my assumption was that he hadn't yet landed on one he didn't think he could do.

"Maybe you could be an astronaut," I suggested.

I knew he was legitimately pondering the idea.

"Nah," he finally said. "I don't like heights."

"Well, that has to be reassuring to have one off your list."

"I'd be a pretty sweet astronaut if it wasn't for that, though."

\* \* \*

Bullock and I were barely settled back at the office when Captain Leonard summoned me to his office.

"Have a seat, Brody," he said.

Leonard looked solemn. It was unnerving.

"You okay, Captain?" I asked.

I was partly concerned for him, but I was more concerned for myself as I've never been keen on being called into anyone's office, particularly when I wasn't given prior notice, or had knowledge what it was pertaining to.

He pulled his chair toward his desk and sat upright with both arms on his desk and his hands folded together.

"I have an idea," he said.

Seems promising. At least not ominous.

"It's not earth-shattering," he continued. "But it does lead to somewhere that is coming a lot closer than I envisioned it would."

We slid back towards ominous.

He used both hands to brush the dust off the desktop.

"I'm old," he said. "I'm not dying or anything, but my time in this career is coming to an end. Be it two years, five years, ten years; I don't know. When you're focused on the day-to-day, you don't see the end creeping up until one day you realize that you have to start planning for your departure. That time is now."

He scooted his chair out from the desk, stood up and put both hands on the desk, leaned toward me and seemingly stared right into my soul.

"You're my replacement," he said.

To be honest, that seemed to be the prevailing thought. At least with Bullock. Once he put that bug in my ear, if I were to be honest, I periodically lingered on the idea.

"We have to figure out the specifics," he said. "But for now, suffice it say, we need to start the process for you to be the logical heir."

He stepped behind his chair and pushed his chair in. He turned and stared out the window. It seemed rude to break the silence and interrupt whatever thought, or thoughts, he was having. I didn't know what to say, anyway, so I just sat there waiting for him to speak.

"It's why this David Bell is making me so mad," he said. "We can't have unnecessary baggage ruining this transfer from me to you."

In my best old-school mafia voice I could muster, I asked, "You wants me to whack 'em boss?"

Leonard chuckled. Thankfully.

"No," he said. "We just need to position you in positively in this community."

I felt like I was going to be running for the position of Chief without there ever being an election.

"My idea is pretty simple," he said. "Whenever we have the major events, I want you to be on point with these. Such as our Shop with a Cop program, you need to be the face of that. I want our citizens to feel comfortable with you."

"Sounds easy enough."

"The other part of that equation is for everyone here to be comfortable with you as well," he added. "Therefore, I'm going to move you around periodically. I'm going to assign you to work with Evans on her shift for a week or so. I'm not saying I'm going to have you with someone new every week. But just enough so that they all have a feel for your style. Does that make sense?"

To be honest, I understood the idea even if I didn't like the idea of having a constant flux in my schedule. Bullock and I have a routine. Chloe and I have a routine. It would probably get some getting used to, but if the Captain is right, it does make sense for me to get to know the other officers.

"Understood, sir," I said.

"Don't get too excited Brody," he said. "This is the first day of a plan that may take years."

"Yes, sir," I said. "Thank you, sir."

\* \* \*

"What the hell?" Bullock said.

"Captain said it'll be one week," I said.

"So just like that, after all we've been through, I get thrown to the side like some jilted ex-girlfriend."

"Can you not phrase it like that?" I asked. "There's very little in this world that is more disturbing than you comparing yourself to an ex-girlfriend of mine."

"You wish you could be my girlfriend," Bullock said as Mike Garrett, a four-year veteran of the force, walked by.

Garrett raised his eyebrows and shook his head.

"Keep walking, Garrett," Bullock sternly said.

Turning to me, "he probably wants to be my girlfriend."

"You're not going to stop using that analogy are you?" I asked.

Bullock let out a huff and sat there pouting.

"You'll be fine," I reassuringly said. "Maybe you and Garrett can work together. Maybe you'll get, I don't know, Drake. Or Norris. Those are all good guys. You know, you have more experience than Norris, you could be the point man for the week."

"As opposed to what?" he asked. "Are you saying you're the point man? That's what you think? I thought we were partners.

You know? In this together. Butch. Sundance. Turner. Hooch."

"Well, you're definitely Hooch in this relationship," I said.

"I'm Turner, you're Hooch," he said as Garrett walked by again, this time caring a coffee cup.

"You two are very weird," he said not breaking stride.

"Move along, Garrett," Bullock said.

"Well, I'm glad you thought of us as Butch and Sundance, even Turner and Hooch," I said. "The way this conversation was going, I thought for sure you were leaning toward Harry and Sally."

"Who?"

"Harry and Sally," I said. "From *When Harry Met Sally?* The movie."

"Never saw it," he said.

"Have you watched any movie?" I asked. "It's a romantic comedy. Rent it for Alicia. She'll love it."

"She likes *Die Hard* and *Lethal Weapon* movies," he said. "I watch those with her."

"Rent it anyway," I said. "Maybe show a soft side. You'll thank me for it."

# 13

# Remember The Plan

It was a little after six o'clock in the morning. I was exhausted. I hadn't had that kind of shift since my days manning a post on a naval base.

I walked up the stairs to my apartment, tossed my keys toward the bowl that sits on a table at the top of the stairs. I missed. I didn't care.

I went straight to the refrigerator and grabbed a gallon of milk. At that moment, I was very thankful Chloe didn't live with me. Otherwise, I would've had to get a cup of some sort. Not tonight. I took off the cap and drank straight from the jug.

After putting the lid back on, I set the jug back in the fridge, shut the door and stared at the little magnets. I had no idea where any of these magnets came from. Well, except for the two pizza place magnets. Those were obvious. Are magnets given as gifts? Do people buy magnets for themselves?

After a few minutes I realized I had, at least mentally, dozed off. I may have, actually, fallen asleep standing in my kitchen.

I headed for the bedroom, disrobed of my uniform en route, tossing garments here and there, until I finally reached the bed in just my underwear.

Plop. I fell into the bed.

* * *

The ringing of my phone brought me out of my sleep. After I was able to get my senses in order, I realized that the phone was in my pants. I just didn't remember where I left them.

Sitting up in bed, the ringing stopped.

I dropped my head back into my pillow. The ringing returned.

I pulled myself from out of the covers and scanned the floor of my room. Nothing. The ringing continued.

I walked down the hall, when I saw my pants next to the bathroom door. I picked them up and dug my phone out of the pocket.

"Hello?" I slowly asked.

"Morning, honey," Chloe said. "Well, actually, good afternoon."

I turned back to look into my room and the clock on the nightstand. It was a few minutes past noon.

"Good morning," I said. "Or afternoon."

I walked toward the kitchen, opened the fridge, held the phone with my shoulder to my ear and grabbed my trusted gallon of milk out.

"So, how was it?" she asked.

"It was okay, nothing too eventful," I said.

I took a big gulp of milk from the jug, which caused me to drop the phone onto the floor.

I scrambled to get pick up the phone as quickly as I could.

115

"Get along well enough?" she asked.

I was going to roll the dice and assume the first part of that had something to do with me and Evans.

"Yeah, she's a good cop," I said as I sat down at the dining room table.

There was no attempt from Chloe to clarify a misunderstood question.

"She definitely has some ideas about the department," I continued. "There were all good and productive suggestions."

"Did she tell you her ideas because she just is that way or did she tell you her ideas because she thinks you'll be the boss soon?"

"I don't know," I said. "Maybe a little of both."

I really wasn't comfortable with any of this talk about me becoming captain. Even if it wasn't in the very near future. I'm not sure I even want the job. I can see that a more office-oriented, regular hour, less chance of being in danger sort of job would appeal to a significant other. I just wasn't sure I wanted that as a career destination.

"Other than that, not much happened?" she asked.

"Like, what do you mean?"

"Well, I thought since you didn't really ever do a night shift here, I was wondering if it's boring or full of excitement or something in between."

"Pretty boring," I said. "We did have two different car accidents involving teenagers. One decided to cut across traffic and ran into the Mary's Chicken sign. The other was learning to drive and ran into a curb on a bend. Said he didn't see the curb. Not sure why not. There's a big freaking tree right there. You'd think he would've wanted to at least avoid the tree."

"Well, I am certainly thankful that everyone was alright."

"Yeah, but I thought the dad was going to kill the kid who hit the curb," I said. "Apparently, they just bought the car on Monday and the kid totaled it two days later."

"Well, for my sake, I hope all your nights are just as eventful this week," she said.

"Yeah, I don't expect much more than this," I said. "Maybe Friday and Saturday we'll get some of the usual weekend action."

"Well, I pray that you don't."

\* \* \*

The second day was very similar to the first night. Nothing too eventful. Other than me erroneously thinking that Evans had said all she had to say about her ideas for the department.

I started to look at her differently. It dawned on me somewhere in the early stages of our third night riding together that I was looking at her like I'm wondering if Leonard looks at me.

I didn't even have the job, however, but I felt like I was looking at my replacement.

\* \* \*

Our third night started out much like the previous two. We rode around town and didn't experience anything eventful.

As the late spring day sunk into the night I made a suggestion that we stop at Brown's Root Beer for a quick meal. I also made mention that I hadn't seen much of Chloe that week, and it would be nice to find out she didn't run away with someone else.

We walked in, found a table close to the door and looked over the menu.

"Do you know if they have strata here?" she asked.

"You've never been here?" I asked in complete astonishment. "I've only lived here more than a year and I eat here all the time."

"Gee, I wonder why that is?" she said.

"I would eat here even if it wasn't for Chloe," I claimed.

"Yeah," she said. "I bet."

"What's strata, anyway?" I asked.

"It's basically a mix of egg, cheese and bread and some other things," she said.

"I thought that was quiche."

"Quiche is different, especially in France, where they're more of a custard tart," she said. "In America, quiche and strata are similar except I think strata has bread and quiche doesn't. Maybe that's a frittata?"

"A what?" I said before thankfully having my attention diverted by Chloe walking toward the table.

"And what can I do for the best officer in Stonington?" Chloe said. "And while I'm here, what can I get you as well, Officer James?"

"Very funny," I said.

"Girl power!" Evans said as she raised her hand to high five Chloe, to which Chloe gladly participated in.

"You two through?" I asked.

"Someone isn't getting a lot of sleep," Chloe said to Evans. "He's usually not this cranky."

"I thought he was the same exact cranky as usual," Evans said before throwing up another high five. Chloe, again, smacked hands with apparently her new best friend.

"Is that your thing now?" I asked.

"Maybe," Chloe said. "Are you jealous we don't have a high five?"

"We don't have much time, so can we get a rush on our order," I said.

"Yes, sir!" Chloe said. "Please proceed with your order, sir!"

Chloe pulled out her pen and paper and stared at me. I'm probably going to have to answer to this, I thought to myself.

"Go ahead," she impatiently said.

"Two roast beefs and a root beer," I said in embarrassment.

"And for you?" she said in a friendlier tone as she turned to Evans.

"Do you have strata?" she asked.

"Nope," Chloe said.

She leaned toward Evans and whispered, "but I'll have the boys in the back whip you up a frittata. You want it with bacon or without?"

"Without please," Evans said with a wide smile.

"How come I never get anything off the menu?" I asked.

"You never ask," Chloe said.

* * *

After our meal, Evans and I returned to patrol the mean streets of Stonington. For the most part, all was quiet in our little neck of the woods.

"Let's do a sweep of downtown one more time," I said. "If all is good, we can head back to the station for the rest of shift."

We headed south on Carpenter as it switched from a residential

119

neighborhood to the two-story downtown buildings that define the area. A few of the buildings were erected more than a century before, and have maintained much of their original structure with a few nip and tucks, now and then.

As we came up to an alleyway, a young man wearing blue jeans and a red hoodie came sprinting out of the alley and tried to stop his momentum by running smack into a No Parking sign.

As soon as he gathered himself, he looked in our direction. He was a deer in headlights, just standing there frozen. In a instant, he reentered our world and took off in the other direction.

Evans was already accelerating when I said, "well, I wonder what we have here?"

The young man was running at a nice pace.

"Do you think he runs track?" I asked.

At that moment, he ran into a bench and took a horrific spill.

"Well, it sure as hell ain't hurdles," Evans said as she slowed the car down allowing me to hop out.

The young man found his bearings and got back on his feet. He took off just before I could apprehend him. I pursued him while wishing Bullock was there as he is way faster than I am. Then I wished I was at least driving, and Evans was chasing this guy, regardless of how fast she is. Then I wished if he would only stop running that would be super helpful.

The young man turned right onto Main Street and must've been tiring as I was gaining ground. I took a leap and was able to tackle our sprinter to the ground. We rolled and tumbled for a few before coming to a stop in front of the building where we met Don Barton.

I turned him over face down and cuffed him.

"Why are you running from us?" I asked.

"I didn't do it," he said.

"Do what?"

"I didn't kill him."

"Tom Downing?" I asked.

"Who the hell is Tom Downing?"

Are you kidding? Another dead body?

Evans pulled up and when I looked toward her I noticed somebody walking quickly away from us. It was Betsy.

A lot of things were filling my head. Right now, I needed to figure out who this kid is, what was he talking about and if we had another death in Stonington. Then I was going to have to figure out how to approach Betsy, because she was either a witness, or worse.

* * *

Jack Ramirez. 16 years old. Looking to score and found himself in much deeper waters.

Evans put Jack in the back of the patrol car she parked on the street, blocking the alleyway.

As we walked down the darkened pathway, I looked back and I could see Jack's face illuminated by the streetlight. Less than an hour ago, he was making, what he thought, to be an adult decision. Now he's rendered to nothing but a scared child fearing the worst of what was about to happen.

Evans and I slowly walked down the alleyway, with our service weapons drawn. I was angled off her flank and a little behind her.

Beams of our flashlights flickered back and forth helping us assess what, or who, could be waiting for us.

As we reached the backside of Barton's building, we saw a young man at the foot of the stairs leading to the second story offices. His head was leaning against the railing of the staircase and his lower body was spread out at the bottom of the steps on the pavement. A ball cap laid next to his body. His hand clenching a plastic baggie full of pills.

Shot once in his right cheekbone and another into his chest. Due to the available space to maneuver, it must've been close range.

"Damn," Evans said.

I checked the area surrounding the body and was able to find two casings.

"Evans, can you go get the markers out of the car?" I said.

I grabbed an empty beer can and marked one of the shell casings and I slid a rock near the second casing.

Using my flashlight, I looked over the area to make sure there was only two shell casings, and there weren't any errant shots fired. We have enough dead bodies. I didn't want there to be collateral damage from whatever was the root cause of this murder.

I could hear sirens getting increasingly louder and the flicker of red and blue lights lit up the alley.

Trailing Evans was Captain Leonard and our Crime Scene Investigator, Irwin Noble.

"I just needed the crime scene markers, Evans," I said. "I didn't need the whole police force."

"What do we have, Brody?" Leonard said, none too amused by my attempt at humor.

"We discovered our DOA after chasing down a Jack Ramirez," I said. "Right now, we haven't ruled him out as suspect, but we didn't find a weapon on him. We also haven't found one on the scene. He came sprinting out of the alley when Evans and I approached the area."

"Do we have an ID of the victim?" Leonard asked.

"No sir," I said. "I was securing the scene and looking for evidence of additional shots being fired other than the two in our victim. Looks like a 9 millimeter was used."

Evans swapped out the impromptu scene markers with our department issued markers. Noble was clicking away with his camera, getting every possible image of the scene he could.

Leonard gestured for Noble to come closer.

"Film this please," the Captain said.

Noble gave a quick glance of the body, snapped a few pictures, and then began filming. Leonard rolled the young man over to his side and grabbed a wallet from the back pocket and rolled the body back.

"Looks like we found our Carson McCall," he said as he pulled a driver's license from the wallet.

I pulled out my cell phone and dialed Bullock to let him know we found our elusive young friend, although he wasn't going to be much help at this point.

Once my brief conversation with Bullock ended, I returned my attention to the crime scene.

"What are we thinking happened here?" Leonard asked.

"He could've been coming down the stairs and was ambushed when he got to the bottom," Evans said.

"He must've known his killer," I said. "At least enough to have product out for a sale."

Noble placed the small baggie into a larger plastic bag and marked it as evidence.

"Our victim may have been already standing at the base of the stairs and simply fell back after being shot," Leonard offered.

"Well, well, well," a voice said as it approached.

It was none other than our local newspaper editor.

"Why wouldn't there be a dead body and Brody James at the same location at the same time?" he sarcastically asked.

"Evans, get him out of here," Leonard angrily said.

"I got every right to be here, Captain," David Bell said.

Looking in my direction, he added, "and I definitely have a few questions for you Officer James. I'm assuming you were the first on the scene. Was that before or after the victim died?"

Captain Leonard stepped in front of me before I could do anything regrettable.

"Remember the plan," he whispered in my ear.

"Let me know when you'll be available for additional questions of our latest Brody James' murder scene, Captain," David said.

"How did you get here so fast?" I asked David. "We're you lurking in the alleyway?"

"It's called a police scanner," he said. "Trust me, I keep this thing on all the time to keep track of you."

With that, Evans ushered our local scribe down the alley to the sidewalk where a small gathering of residents had amassed.

\* \* \*

According to the data, there were 728 guns sold last year alone in Stonington. Of those, 204 were 9-millimeter handguns.

While there's approximately 10,000 residents in the city alone, Stonington is surrounded by four townships, which give the area another 20,000 or so residents.

Most gun owners pass the weapons onto the next generation and they become family heirlooms that extend even further down the tree. There could be over 2,000 9-millimeter handguns in the area, just from the last decade alone. And those are the ones that were legally purchased.

It's going to take a lot of luck to find this weapon. In the meantime, there was an issue that was at the forefront of my mind. It was gnawing at me, and it was time to get to the bottom of it.

# 14

# Use The Black Marker

I knocked on the door. Knocked was selling it short. I practically pounded on the door.

"Annabeth Garrison!" I called out. "It's the Stonington Police. Open the door!"

I continued knocking frenetically.

"Annabeth!" I said. "It's Officer Brody James of the Stonington Police. I need you to open the door."

The door to her downstairs neighbor opened slightly.

"Brody?" the woman behind the door asked.

"It's okay Bridget," I said. "I'm here to speak with Annabeth."

"Who?" Bridget asked.

Before I could answer, Annabeth's door opened.

"Don't ever call me that again," Betsy said. "I told you that in private. What the hell do you want, Brody?"

I barged past Betsy and headed up her stairs. I barely got to the top before I turned in her direction.

"What the hell have you been doing downtown, Betsy?" I said.

"Do you got a warrant?" she said as she made her way past me and straight into her kitchen.

She grabbed a glass of bourbon that she must've recently poured as the bottle was unopened next to the glass with the cap a few inches away. She took a long sip and then turned to me.

"Well, do you?" she asked.

"I'm not here as the police," I said. "Officially."

"You announced yourself to the whole complex that you're here as the police," she said. "It's almost midnight and you've already publicly embarrassed me. I'll ask one more time. Do you have a warrant?"

"No."

"Then I'm going to have to ask you to leave, Officer James," she said. "And if you ever barge in here like this again, I'll have your badge. Do you understand?"

"Betsy," I said in a less confrontational manner. "What is going on with you?"

She took another sip of bourbon and stared at her kitchen cabinet.

"I saw you flee from the scene where a dead body was discovered," I said. "I got probable cause. As your friend, if there's something I should know, you need to tell me. You need to tell me now."

She took the final sip of the bourbon, set the glass down and poured some more.

"I appreciate what you're trying to do, Brody," she said. "But I've been down this road before. I don't trust the police. I like you. I like you, Brody, the man. But I don't trust you, Brody, the cop."

"If that's the way you want to play this," I said. "So be it. I'll be back tomorrow and by then anything I could do to help you will be long gone."

"Don't forget your warrant."

\* \* \*

I could barely sleep as I knew that despite not having to report to the office until 6:00 pm the next day, I was going to go in early and talk to Captain Leonard about having to arrest my next-door neighbor in front of everyone in our apartment complex. The annual apartment picnic that was a month away was going to be awkward.

\* \* \*

With very little sleep, I headed into the office a little after 9:00 am and went straight to the Captain's office.

I gave his door a little rap.

"Brody, what the heck are you doing here, son?" he said. "You're going to burn yourself out."

"I need to talk to you about additional information in the case that I haven't shared with anyone yet."

"Have a seat," he said.

I proceeded to tell him how I had seen Betsy downtown a couple of times sitting in the exact location, seemingly staking out the building that includes Don Barton's office, as well as a couple other businesses on the top floor, and the medical supply company on the first floor.

That information wasn't exactly moving his needle.

"I saw her again last night, leaving the area right when we apprehended Jack Ramirez," I said.

"Are you saying your neighbor is somehow involved in the

death of Carson McCall?" he asked.

"No," I said. "I mean I don't think so. Maybe. Maybe not. I'm not sure. When I went to her apartment last night..."

"You confronted your neighbor last night about this?" he asked. "Officially? Or as her friend."

"Both," I said.

"There's no such thing as both, Brody."

"I announced myself as a police officer," I said. "But I really meant to go as her friend."

"I'm sure that went over well," he said.

"I just want to know why she was there and why she left the scene so mysteriously," I said. "For the second time, really."

A knock on the door frame of Leonard's office halted our conversation as we both turned toward the door.

Garrett was standing there.

"Sorry to interrupt," he said. "But Brody, you have someone waiting for you in Interrogation Room #3."

* * *

I opened the door to the interrogation room.

"Looks like I can cancel the warrant request," I said.

Betsy was standing across the table dressed as professionally as I had ever seen her.

"I figured you needed my help," she said as she opened her briefcase and tossed the latest edition of the local newspaper on the table.

The headline read: A BRODY JAMES MYSTERY.

Underneath was: "Local cop involved in another death."

Looking down, at my picture and name sprawled across the newspaper, I said, "A Brody James Mystery? Sounds like the name of a series of books. And not very good ones. I'm like the Nancy Drew in town."

Betsy sat down in the chair and gestured for me to do likewise. I thought I was in charge in this situation, but nonetheless, I did as she suggested.

"First off, Nancy Drew books were what got me interested in solving mysteries," she said. "Secondly, you've got a problem, and I'm here to help."

"How's that?" I said as I sat down.

"Let me tell you a little story," she said.

"Will it answer my question about why you've been staking out a specific building in town?" I asked.

"Probably not."

"How about why you fled the scene last night?"

"Probably not," she said. "But in my defense, I didn't know there was a dead man on the other side. But let me tell my story and we'll see where we go from here."

I adjusted how I was sitting in the chair to get comfortable.

"This David Bell," she said. "I know the type. I was David Bell back in my day. Not as frumpy and disheveled, but you get the point."

"You were a reporter?"

"Yes," she said. "And a damn good one. So good that I often got in front of the story. I started out on the police beat for the *Lansing State Journal.* I learned pretty quickly that there isn't really a justice system. It's a collection of people all using a set of circumstances to advance their own situation."

"That's a little jaded," I said.

"Maybe," she said. "But not untrue."

She pulled out some folders from her briefcase, spread them across the table and began opening them. Each one contained various news clippings. I don't think she wanted me to read what she had presented, it was more of a statement to add to her story.

"All of these were things I pursued diligently," she said.

"Until you got your man," I said.

"That's just it," she said. "I didn't care who I got. The more salacious, the better. I was an addict. I just didn't realize it. I also didn't realize that I wasn't stirring the pot as much as I thought I was. Someone else was stirring the pot and I was the ladle. Until it all came crashing down."

"What happened?" I asked.

"We're not going to get into that," she said. "It's irrelevant to what is going on now. I'm here for two reasons. Number one, David Bell is a little yapping dog and you need to neuter him."

"Interesting analogy."

"And number two," she said. "There's something wonky going on in at Good Health."

"Good Health?" I asked.

"The medical supply building downtown."

"I thought Medical Supply Company was it's name."

"That would be a really lame name."

"True," I said. "It's no Brody James Mystery."


* * *


"So, Betsy," Bullock said. "What's it like living next to Brody?"

"Probably less annoying than being his partner," she said.

"You guy's best friends, now?" I asked. "Seems to be contagious in this town."

Captain Leonard walked into the conference room.

"What do we know, people?" he asked.

"Captain, if I may," I said as I walked to the dry-erase board.

I reached down and grabbed a marker from the stand and in the middle of the board wrote the name: Tom Downing.

"Green?" Bullock asked. "Why'd you use the green marker?"

Everyone turned and stared at Bullock for a few seconds. I continued on my way drawing a circle around Tom's name and wrote Carson McCall to the upper right. I circled Carson's name and drew a line connecting the two.

"We know Tom got the ecstasy, albeit indirectly, from Carson McCall," I said. "We do not know where Carson got the drugs nor what role he specifically has in all of this other than being the dealer to Tom's sister Jenna, who then gave them to Tom."

Bullock stood up and approached the board.

"But what we do know," he said as he grabbed a black marker and showed it to all present as if he was declaring victory, "is that Carson was found dead outside of the offices of Don Barton."

Bullock wrote Don's name down, much smaller, and off to the left.

"And Don's stepson, Lucas Winters," he said as he wrote Lucas's name down separated by a slash from Dons, "is known to have been involved in, or still is, the dealing of drugs to high school students."

Bullock drew a line to connect with Tom.

The door to the conference room swung open and Evans came in looking a little frazzled.

"Sorry, I'm late," she said. "Wasn't expecting to be called in early today."

"No worries, Libby," Captain Leonard. "I appreciate you coming in so soon."

"We have a guest?" Evans asked as she walked toward Betsy and stuck out her right hand. "I'm Libby Evans, and you are?"

"She's Betsy," I said as the two women shook hands. "She's my next-door neighbor."

"Should I have brought Agnes today?" Evans asked.

"Who's Agnes?" Bullock asked.

"She's my next-door neighbor," Evans said.

"I asked Ms. Garrison to join us," Captain Leonard said. "She has information that can be helpful to this case."

Leonard got up from his seat, grabbed the markers from both me and Bullock, and gestured for us to sit down.

"Here are my questions," he said as he set the green marker down.

Bullock smacked me on the arm with pride and whispered, "he's using mine."

I rolled my eyes and turned my attention back to the Chief.

"What are we saying regarding where we found McCall?" he asked.

Betsy raised her hand.

"If I may interrupt?" she asked.

"Go ahead," Leonard said as he wrote down "connection" on the board.

"Do I stand?" she asked.

"Not unless you want to right something down on the board," Leonard said.

"Use the black marker, if you do," Bullock added.

"I think there has to be something with Good Health," she said, preferring to remain seated. "I don't have anything specific, but it's a feeling I have. Have any of you ever notice

133

anyone ever being in that building?"

Bullock smacked my arm again, "that's what I said!"

"When?" I asked.

"When we went to meet with Don Barton," he said. "We were walking up the stairs and I asked you if you had ever seen anyone in there."

Leonard turned back to the board and wrote down "Good Health" with a question mark.

"It's always closed," Betsy said. "They've been there a long time, but I did some research on other buildings and the rent in the area is astronomical for a business that would seemingly never be open."

"Evans," Leonard said. "Betsy was an investigate reporter a few years ago."

"Many years ago," Betsy added.

"Nonetheless," he said. "Over a period of time, she noticed that she never saw anyone in the store. Neither employee nor customer. So her intuition kicked in and she began to actively monitor the building and nothing ever changed."

"Does anyone know what they even do?" I asked. "I mean, I see wheelchairs and crutches and things like that in the window. I thought they just sold stuff like that to, I don't know, old people."

Leonard underlined Good Health twice on the board.

"Evans," he said. "Let's see if we can't delve deeper into what this place actually does to pay the bills."

"Yes sir," she said.

"I'd like to help with that," Betsy said. "As Brody said, their customers might be old. And I'm the oldest one here. I can come up with an ailment or two if need be."

"Thank you, Betsy," Leonard said.

"Now, can we connect McCall with Winters?" he asked as he drew an arrow between the two names.

"Bullock," he continued. "See if you can find a connection between these two young men."

Leonard then circled Don Barton several times.

"Brody," he said. "This is your guy. Let's approach it by asking the other tenants first if they know, or heard anything, and then finish with Don. That way it doesn't seem suspicious."

Leonard stared at the board for a few minutes and then turned to the four of us.

"Our little town is changing," he said. "We need to change it back."

# 15

# At A Dead End

"She's an investigative reporter?" Evans asked as we drove through town on our final night working a shift together.

"I didn't really find out myself until yesterday," I confessed. "I guess she got burned out from it or something. She didn't really elaborate on it and if there's one thing I learned about Betsy, never try to pry."

"I bet," Evans said.

"I'll say this, though," I said. "I've learned a lot about some people recently. For example, you're a hell of a cop Evans. It was a lot of fun working with you."

"But you can't wait to get back to Bullock, I bet," she said.

"Oh, I don't know about," I said. "I'd phrase it more that I look forward to returning to the day shift. And seeing Chloe a little more than I have. Bullock is Bullock."

"Do you think Betsy's writing a story about all of this?" she asked.

"I don't think so," I said. "I mean, I don't know for sure. I just thought that maybe her instincts kicked in, and got the juices flowing. You know what I mean? I don't think she's getting back

136

in the quote unquote game. Maybe she is. You'll like working with her I bet."

"Really?" she asked. "What makes you think that. You, obviously, know her more than I do."

"It seems like the thing I should say," I confessed.

"I just don't want to end up in a book or any type of story," she said. "They always make the young, blonde girl stupid."

"You're not stupid," I said.

"I know that," she said. "I just don't want to be portrayed as stupid."

"I don't think she's going to write about it anyway," I said. "So I wouldn't worry about anything."

\* \* \*

After the week of working the night shift with Evans, I was given a two-day break, which helped me gather my senses back.

Staring at myself in the mirror, I realized that I still felt worse than I looked. And I didn't look all that great to begin with. I cupped both hands and filled them with water and splashed my face to remove as much shaving cream as I could.

My immediate task, other than finish getting dressed, was to spend the next day canvassing the tenants in Barton's building and see if any of them could provide helpful information.

Bullock was focused on any connections between Carson McCall and Lucas Winters while Evans teamed up with Betsy regarding Good Health, while simultaneously hoping the latter doesn't put her in a book.

137

\* \* \*

I took a sip of coffee, poured the last bit down the drain and placed the mug in the sink.

I headed down the stairs and opened the door to see Betsy was closing her front door at the same time.

She greeted me with, "Officer James," and a head nod.

I replied to her greeting with, "Stonington Police Consultant Betsy."

I guess neither of us were "good morning" type of people.

"It'll be nice for the other residents to know you're not arresting me," she said.

"I'm not arresting you, yet," I said.

She laughed. That was reassuring.

"Good luck with questioning all the tenants on the second floor today," she said.

"Good luck figuring out what's happening at Good Health."

We went our separate ways for the day.

We often found ourselves at the end of the night, each on our own balcony, recapping the day's events. I think we'll probably skip that until we meet again in two days with Captain Leonard and everyone on the case gives their own update.

\* \* \*

I parked on Main Street, just a few doors down from Barton's office. It gave me the chance to pass the front of the building so I could get a brief look inside Good Health.

Dark. No posted hours. Not even remotely opened. No sign of Evans or Betsy, either.

I went to the door that lead to the second story and checked the directory to get a list of as many names as possible of all the businesses I will be interviewing today. Aside from Barton, there were only three other tenants on the second floor.

The first person on the list was attorney Constance Capel. I started there and work my way down the hallway toward Don Barton's office.

* * *

The lobby of the office was sleek and contemporary. The walls were classic pewter and there were glass blocks creating a half wall in front of the receptionist area. The carpeting was a nylon, multi-level loop featuring a mix a blue and gray.

While it was certainly stylish, it lacked a welcoming feel, and more importantly, chairs for people to sit.

The young lady sitting behind the desk had a cheerful countenance to her.

"How can I help you, Officer?" she cheerfully said.

"I'm Officer James of SPD," I said. "And you are?"

"I'm Sera."

"Sera," I said. "I'm sure you are aware that a young man was killed last week just outside your door."

"I thought he was killed in the alley," she said.

"Yes, he was killed in the alley," I said.

"Oh, you said outside our door and I was thinking that maybe it was in the hallway," she said. "And I thought that I hadn't seen any blood or anything and that I probably would have seen something like that if he was killed in the hallway."

"True," I said. "If he was killed in the hall, you probably would've seen evidence. The reason I'm here is I'd like to talk to any employee that was working that day. It would've been last Thursday."

"There's really only two of us in this office," she said. "It's just me and Ms. Capel."

"Interesting," I said. "Is Ms. Capel here today?"

"No," she said. "But if you have a card, I can tell her you dropped by and have her call you."

I pulled out my card, wrote my cell number on the back and handed it to Sera.

"What time did you leave Thursday, if I may ask?" I asked.

"I left around 4, maybe 4:30," she said.

"Did you hear or see anything that was out of the norm?" I asked.

"I'm sorry, but I didn't."

"I notice you don't have any chairs for people to sit here in the lobby," I said. "What sort of law do you folks do here?"

"We do international trade and customs law," she said. "We have clients in Canada and Mexico, so we have offices all over."

"Really?"

"Yeah, we have an office in Florida, Texas and Ontario," she said. "Ms. Capel started the business when NAFTA was enacted and it allowed her to connect clients from different countries," she said.

"NAFTA?"

"The North American Free Trade Agreement," she said. "It passed about a decade ago."

I honestly didn't know what NAFTA was, but it seemed to be a good thing for these folks.

"Okay, if you could let Ms. Capel know that I stopped by and the reason for my visit, I'd appreciate it. Thanks!"

* * *

Next stop was the accounting firm of Drake & Brahms.

While Constance Capel's office was modern, Drake & Brahms was a few decades behind. The walls had fake wood paneling. The chairs, tables and paintings were probably the decor when they opened the office. Which according to the sign on the door was 1984.

Sera was not waiting behind the desk in this office.

"Welcome, officer," said a portly, middle-aged woman with graying hair, glasses that had a chain around her neck, and a silk-shirt with a vibrant floral design.

"I'm Officer James," I said. "I'm here to talk to any employees who may have been working last week when the young man was killed in the alleyway."

"Oh, goodness," she said. "We heard about that. I can't believe something like that has happened in Stonington."

"We're you here that day?" I asked.

"I was," she said. "But I went home a little after 5 pm."

"And you didn't see or hear anything out of the ordinary?"

"I did not," she said.

"Do you mind giving me your name?" I asked. "It's for my report."

"Not a problem at all, officer," she said. "It's Delilah. Delilah Rendon."

"Thank you Delilah," I said as I wrote her name down. "Are there any other people who were here Thursday, and if so, are they here today?"

"It's just me, Alexander and Jim," she said. "They're the two owners of the firm. They're both here in the back. Do you want me to get them?"

"That'll be nice," I said. "Thanks."

Delilah disappeared down the hall. While I waited, I wrote both names down beneath Delilah's. She returned a few minutes later and gestured for me to follow her.

"The boys will meet you in the conference room," she said.

The meeting was brief and uneventful. Neither man saw or heard anything the day in question. Both had departed well before the shooting occurred.

Delilah followed me back toward the lobby area.

"You guys busy this time of year?" I asked making small talk.

"Our busy season is tax season," she said. "But we have a couple steady clients that keep the doors open the rest of the year."

"Well, thank you for your time," I said. "You have a great day."

\* \* \*

While one office was nouveaux in style and the second was caught trapped in time, the office of Colton Moore was more conventional: standard office furniture you can get pretty much anywhere on the cheap that is supposed to convey wealth. Or at least the possibility of wealth.

Editions of *Forbes*, *Barron's*, *Kiplinger's* and *The Wall Street Journal* were spread out on nearly every table space available.

There was a front desk that met any visitor, but no one was sitting there when I entered. Looking over the desk as I approached, everything was neat and tidy. Either the cleanest person ever sat there or no one actually sat there. Or hadn't in some time.

In the office behind the front desk, I could see a figure moving in the frosted glass window between the office and lobby. The figure moved toward the door.

"Can I help you?" he asked with suspicion as he came out to the lobby. The man had a freshly pressed shirt with cuff links and a high-end designer tie. His navy slacks had pinstripes and his shoes had a shine to them.

"Colton Moore?" I asked.

"Yes, sorry, officer, is there something wrong?"

"I'm Officer James," I said. "As you may be aware, a young man was murdered behind this building late last week. I was wondering if you had seen or heard anything out of the ordinary that day."

"Man, I heard something about that," he said as he looked back toward his window that looked out into the alleyway. "I wish I could help but I was out of town on business all of last week."

"Gotcha," I said. "Work? Pleasure?"

"Oh, um, a little of both, I guess."

"Last time I did that I went up to Mackinac Island. Where did you go?"

"Oh, me, I just went down to the Cayman Islands," he said.

"Wow," I said. "That was my second choice."

"Was it really?"

"No," I said followed by a small laugh. "But maybe someday, right?"

"Yeah, absolutely," he said. "You should definitely go when you get the chance. Water is so blue and the beaches are phenomenal. I highly recommend it."

"Might have to do just that," I said. "Hey, is it possible to speak to any other employees who may have been here while you were gone?"

"Unfortunately, I'm the only one working here," he said. "Don't have any staff right now, but if I can get some of these accounts I'm working on, I will be hiring some help pretty soon."

"Well, Mr. Moore," I said. "I do appreciate your time. Good luck with the business."

"Thanks," he said as he extended his hand out. "Good luck with your case, officer."

We shook hands and I headed to the last stop hoping it was only a dead end in the sense that it was at the end of the hall. Otherwise, the only thing I seemingly accomplished was removing possible witnesses off our list. None of these people, so far, said they were around at the time of the murder.

* * *

When Bullock and I entered Barton's office the last time, Don Barton himself was waiting to greet us. This time an assistant was sitting at the front desk.

A woman in her 30s, who was dressed a little risque for a professional setting.

"Hello," I said as I approached. "I'm Officer James of SPD."

"I thought I recognized you," she said.

"Do we know each other?" I asked.

"Not officially," she said. "You just look like the guy on the front page of the newspaper."

I took a deep breath as I definitely don't want to be recognized in such a fashion.

"I'm assuming you're investigating the murder?" she said.

"Yes, I am," I said. "Can I have your name please? It's for the report."

"It's Lydia," she said. "Lydia Wright. Is that all you need? Do you need a phone number or something?"

She smiled almost seductively. Or maybe seductively. I was never good at recognizing the difference between friendliness and flirting.

"For the report," she added.

"I'd appreciate that."

Lydia wrote down her phone number on a piece of paper and handed it to me while never breaking eye contact.

"Lydia, did you see or hear anything last week on Thursday, the day of the murder?"

"Unfortunately, I did not," she said.

"Is Mr. Barton here? I'd like to ask him a few questions as well."

"He's not here today," she said. "And if it's the same question you asked me, he wasn't here last Thursday either. He was out a few days. But I can let him know you stopped by."

"I appreciate that," I said.

"Anytime, Officer. Anytime."

I walked out of the office, shut the door behind me and stared at the empty and dimly lit hallway before.

I was literally at a dead end.

# 16

# Who The Hell Is Blimpo

"I can't believe how hot it is already and it's only June," I said. "The kids aren't even out of school and it feels like it's 100 degrees."

"I didn't realize that whether or not kids are in or out of school impacted the temperature," Bullock said.

"You're a dick sometimes," I said as I reached for a tissue and wiped my forehead.

"What? You made it sound like it gets hotter because the kids got out of school. You're using a causal argument there. And I, for one, won't have any of it."

"What the hell are you talking about?" I asked.

"I honestly don't know," he said. "I kind of went down a rabbit hole there and just kept digging."

"Whatever, dude," I said. "How did you fare connecting the two hoodlums?"

"Is it Wednesday already? I thought it was Tuesday."

"It is Tuesday," I said. "You can only connect the dots on Wednesdays?"

"Captain said we'd tell each other what we found on Wednesday, and since it's not Wednesday, I don't have to tell you what I was able to discover."

"Did you eat too many donuts this morning?" I asked.

"No such thing."

"You're acting incredibly weird," I said. "And that, for you my friend, is really saying something."

Bullock reached into his desk and pulled out a packet of small store-brand donuts with only two of the original half dozen remaining. He grabbed one, crumbs landing on his chest, and plopped it into his mouth.

"I knew it," I said.

I sat down in my chair and moved the mouse back and forth to start my computer.

"Is your login still 'SlapMe69'?" Bullock asked.

"I think you're confusing me with your mother," I said.

As soon as I said the last syllable of the sentence, an object hit me in the back of my head sending crumbs everywhere. My desk, my chair, the floor.

"You really wasted a donut?" I asked as I started brushing crumbs off my uniform.

"It was worth it," he said. "Don't talk about my mother."

"Sorry," I said, thinking I had actually made him mad.

"She worked hard on those streets."

I guess he wasn't as mad as I thought.

"You can go get a broom and a dustpan and clean this up," I said.

"Why?" he said. "It was your donut. You touched it last."

* * *

147

"Here, hold this," I said as I handed the dustpan to Bullock.

I started sweeping up the crumbs into a small pile waiting for Bullock to put the pan down.

"I'm guessing you actually didn't get anywhere," I said.

"What do you mean?" he asked as he bent down.

"You said you were waiting until tomorrow because Leonard said so," I said. "But I know you, and if you had something juicy, you'd spill it to me as fast as you could."

Pointing under my desk, he said, "there's some more crumbs over there."

I started to gather them into a pile with the broom.

"Also," he said. "I don't want you to say the word juicy to me ever again."

"You can stall all you want," I said as I brushed the last crumbs into the pan. "But I know you didn't get any further on your end."

I took the pan from Bullock and dumped the crumbs into my trash can.

"Since you mentioned it," Bullock asked. "How far did you get with the building tenants?"

"I'm going to put these back in the closet," I said as I walked away with the broom and dustpan. "I'll be right back."

"So you didn't get anywhere either," he shouted to me as I got further away.

"I got plenty of answers," I said. "But unlike you, I'm waiting to discuss everything in the meeting tomorrow like Captain Leonard said we should."

I opened the door to the janitorial closet and placed both objects where they belong.

"You're a jackass, Brody!" he said.

\* \* \*

After putting the broom and dustpan in the closet, I decided to wash my hands in the restroom. A quick stop to the break room, and I headed back to my desk with a cup of coffee in hand.

"There's a coffee pot in the closet?" Bullock asked.

With cup in both hands, I blew on it to cool the coffee.

"That's not the only thing that came out of the closet today, am I right?" Bullock said.

"Why, did someone else make a mess and need to clean it up?" I asked. "I knew the vacuum was missing, I just didn't know why. Now I do."

"No, you idiot," he said. "I was saying..."

"I know what you were saying, doofus," as I sat down in my chair and started to sip my coffee.

"You know this whole thing got me thinking," he said.

"What thing?" I asked. "The thing where you're an insufferable child most of the day?"

"No, not that," he said. "The case. It's like that episode of *Mice Vice* where Blimpo has to figure out who abducted his partner."

"Who the hell is Blimpo?" I asked.

"Blimpo!" he incredulously said. "From *Mice Vice*. You know, the show that's on that cartoon cable channel. *Mice Vice*. I can't remember his partner's name, though."

"You watch cartoons?"

"Roxie!" he said proudly. "Roxie is his partner's name. Anyway, she gets abducted and Blimpo has to try to find out where she is and who has her and why."

"Well, don't keep me in suspense," I said. "Who had her and why?"

"Oh, it was the Cat Crew," he nonchalantly said. "It's always the Cat Crew. It's what they do."

"Sounds thrilling," I said. "I'm glad you get to relive your favorite old childhood cartoons, again."

"It's not an old show," he proudly said. "It's brand new this year. It's awesome."

\* \* \*

"I think I'm going to head into downtown," I said. "Might walk around a little bit, maybe something will hit me regarding the case. You want to join me?"

"Nah," Bullock said. "I'm going to make some phone calls. I still need to establish a relationship between Lucas Winters and Carson McCall."

I knew he didn't get very far.

"Well, I hope you find out something," I said.

\* \* \*

My plan was to walk up and down Main Street, stop in to the various shops, say hello and just engage in general conversation.

"How you doing?"

"How's business?"

"Enjoying the weather?"

That sort of thing.

I'll drop in an innocent inquiry such as "are there any issues we need to be aware of?" or maybe a more direct "I'm sure you heard of the young man who passed away. Have you seen or heard anything we should be concerned with?"

I wasn't expecting much to come of my stops, other than getting out and meeting some of the local business owners and employees. But you never know when something is going to fall into place that you weren't expecting.

* * *

Two stops remained on my trek: Deb's Donuts and Carruthers Jewelers. I figured I'd swing in to the jewelry shop, talk to Jason Carruthers for a spell and then head in to Deb's for an end-of-shift donut and coffee.

Carruthers has been in business for over 40 years. Jason inherited the business from his parents, who have since passed. In my time with the force, there hasn't been any police calls dispatched to their store. The story of how Jason's father, Anthony, held a would-be robber at gun point still resonates throughout the town. Especially with the old timers holding court in various establishments serving coffee in the morning or those serving beer at night.

As I opened the door, the buzzer sounded letting anyone in the store know that someone was entering. Everyone ended up being just Jason, who was standing off to my right, behind the counter.

"How can I help you, officer?" he asked as he set down his jewelers eyepiece onto the counter next to a tray of rings.

"I'm Brody James," I said.

151

"Ah," he said. "I've read about you."

Fantastic.

He took the tray and returned it into the glass display cabinet and adjusted it perfectly.

"Well, not everything you read is true," I offered as I looked about his store. "I just wanted to stop in, say hello and see if there's anything we can do as a department that would be helpful to you and your business."

"Nothing comes to mind," he said. "Business is good. I can't complain, and even if I did, who would care?"

I glanced over some of the rings he had on display and made my way down the display case, stopping at some of the watches.

"Are you looking for a timepiece?" he asked. "We have the latest from F.P. Journe, the Octa collection, as well as the very popular Classique 1801 tourbillon from Bregeut."

"Not really," I said as I leaned down and gazed into the display case.

The price tag for the two watches: nearly $50,000 for the former and nearly $30,000 for the latter.

"You sell a lot of these?" I asked as I continued perusing the available watches.

"We sell enough," he said.

As if my uniform wasn't a huge red flag, my reaction to the price of the watches must've been the moment he realized I wasn't capable of buying much from his high end merchandise.

I began to browse the rest of the store as one does when they're not really shopping, but more so, seeing what others spend their money on. The whole time I was trying to get to the front door as nonchalantly as possible.

Something, however, caught my eye. I wasn't expecting it. In fact, it never dawned on me until that very moment. Maybe it was in the deep recesses of my mind waiting to move to the forefront for quite some time. Maybe it wasn't. Maybe it just rushed to get there at that moment. But there it was. Staring at me.

Jason knew I had stumbled across something. He could sense that whatever I was looking at, had my attention. He started to gradually move closer to me. He was an expert fisherman. He was letting the bait do the work before reeling me in.

He eventually was a little off to my left. Almost shoulder to shoulder. He began staring at what I was staring at. Neither said a word for quite some time. It's possible it was only a few seconds, but it felt much longer than that.

What caught my eye was a picture. A regular everyday picture that you find in stores all the time. I had seen similar pictures, but this one, at this time, grabbed a hold of me.

A young man, well-dressed in a black suit with an unbuttoned white dress shirt. His left arm was wrapped around a beautiful woman his age, holding her hand. She was was elegant in a red dress. His right arm was holding her right hand, at the wrist and palm, while her hand was on display with fingers together. Everything was beautiful. Particularly the ring.

"We can create something spectacular, no matter the budget," Jason said.

# 17

# Worst Case Scenario

My cell phone rang. I tried as best as I could to open my eyes. Nonetheless, I rolled over and reached for my phone that was on my nightstand.

"Hello?" I asked as I was able to open my eyes enough to see the time on the clock. It was a little after 4 a.m. With my head still pressed comfortably into the pillow, I set the phone atop my ear and balanced it there.

"Can you be here by 8 a.m.?" Captain Leonard asked.

"Yes, sir," I said with eyes closed.

"Good," he said. "Our meeting is getting moved up a little."

Before I could say anything, Captain Leonard hung up on his end.

Bullock's phone calls must've been productive, I thought as I closed my eyes and went back to sleep.

* * *

I walked into the conference room and Bullock was already there eating a donut.

"Good job," I said as I pulled out a chair, sat down and put the notepad and pen I was carrying on the table.

"What do you mean?" he asked.

"I figured you caught a break in the case," I said. "Isn't that why we're here so early?"

The conference room door opened and Captain Leonard entered, followed by Evans and Betsy.

I looked at Bullock. He looked back at me. We shrugged our shoulders in unison.

"I knew you guys would shake something free," Bullock said as he looked at me with a wide grin.

All I could offer was a halfhearted, "Congrats."

Leonard stood at the front of the table with the whiteboard behind him and flanked on each side by the women.

"We got forward movement on this case," Leonard proudly said. "I'm going to let Officer Evans tell us the events of several hours ago and then we'll formulate a plan from there."

Evans had the floor.

* * *

"Betsy and I had a brainstorming session on Monday," Evans said. "Which proved to be very fruitful. I can't thank her enough for all the information she was willing to share."

Evans gave a warm smile towards Betsy, who reciprocated.

"What we established was that Betsy had pretty much covered all possible business hours of surveillance on the Booker Building."

155

"The Booker Building?" Bullock asked.

"Correct," Evans said. "The Booker Building is the property owned by Don Barton and has four tenants, including his office, on the top floor and Good Health is the lone tenant on the first floor."

"There's great history regarding the building," Betsy said. "Did you know an elephant is rumored to be buried on the sidewalk in front of the building? Story is it died when the circus visited about a hundred years ago. But that's another story for another day."

I am all about solving cases. But at that moment, I would've been lying, if I said I didn't want to learn more about the elephant.

"During the lengthy conversation Betsy and I had," Evans said.

"With fantastic wine," Betsy added.

Evans stopped dead in her tracks, with a scared stare toward Chief Leonard.

"We were officially off-duty, sir," Evans apologetically said.

"Go on," he said as he smiled.

"During our conversation," she continued. "We thought that maybe, just maybe, if there was something nefarious happening at the Booker Building, it would be later in the evening."

"After Good Health closed," Betsy added.

"Well, even later than that," Evans said. "We waited until everybody was closed. All the shops up and down Main Street. The last business on the whole block to close was Primo's Pizza at the far end of the street."

"Isn't that your buddy?" Bullock asked me.

"Yeah," I answered. "Brian and I were high school best friends."

"Well, he closes at 10 p.m.," Evans said. "Betsy parked her car on Main Street at about 9 p.m. I strategically parked on Carpenter to give me a straight shot look down the alley."

Evans turned to the whiteboard and started to diagram the downtown area and her vehicle as well as Betsy's car.

"With how we were setup," she said. "We were fairly confident that any of the action would be in within the sight angles we established. Or at least we thought that was a fair assumption."

"To be honest," Betsy said. "I think I was there simply to see if something spilled, for lack of a better term, toward me."

"Like more wine?" I chided her.

She gave me an angry stare. I winked at her. She so wanted to laugh. A small crack at the corner of her mouth appeared. She turned away as not to break from her pretending to be mad.

On the whiteboard, Evans drew arrows coming from the alley, south down Carpenter and turning left and right onto Main Street. Betsy's vantage point would have given her clear eyesight on activity that headed in either direction.

"Not much happened until after midnight," Evans said.

"Nothing ever does, am I right?" Bullock gleefully said.

Eliciting no response, he shrugged is shoulders in defeat and sat there like a sad puppy.

"At about 1 o'clock," Evans continued. "A white van backed into the alleyway. I watched a white male, early 20s, get out and open the rear doors to the van. At this point, I exited my vehicle and began to approach."

Evans drew a small stick figure on the left side of the van.

"Art major?" I asked. Bullock laughed. I laughed. No one else laughed. Tough room today.

"From here," she said ignoring my comment.

She drew arrows toward the building, passed the van.

157

"I could see clearly that the young man was unloading boxes into the van from Good Health" she continued. "I had suspicion, but nothing more than that. So I played it as cool as I could."

Leonard interrupted. "Backing up a little bit, Officer Evans had already called in suspicious activity and dispatch sent out another squad car."

Leonard gestured for Evans to continue.

"Knowing backup was on the way," she said. "I continued forward. When the male suspect exited the building, I identified myself as a police officer and then said, 'a little late for deliveries.' The suspect laughed a little and said, 'yeah, I know. They got me working all hours.' He got a little closer and then took off running down the alley toward the street. I chased after him."

"Meanwhile, I was listening to *Phantom of the Opera*, the Michael Crawford version, and enjoying some nighttime tea while all of this was happening," Betsy said.

"I love *Music of the Night*," Bullock said. "So moving. It just gives me goosebumps thinking about it."

"I know, right?" Betsy said back. "Andrew Lloyd Webber is so good."

"As he exited the alley, I was able to tackle him," Evans said trying to finish her presentation among the snide comments and side stories.

"At which point," she said. "A gun fell out of the waistband on his jeans and landed in the street. I cuffed him and checked him. All he had on him was a small amount of cash, some wrapping papers and loose tobacco, and a couple tokens for the arcade. His name is Phoenix Kester."

"This is where it gets interesting," Betsy said.

"Please tell me he had our 9 millimeter," I said.

"Unfortunately, he was carrying a 45," Evans said. "When

everything was settled and we were about to ship our guy, we finally got a hold of Wesley Nelson. Sort of."

"Sort of?" I asked. "What does that mean?"

"Well, we were able to connect with Mr. Nelson's caretaker," she said. "Apparently, Mr. Nelson is quite old and is in declining health. He's owned Good Health for quite some time, but in the last couple of years he has deferred much of the business decisions to his younger partner."

"Phoenix Kester?" I asked in disbelief.

"Oh, hell, no," Evans said. "Phoenix can barely dress himself. No way someone's giving him the keys to anything. I'm surprised he has keys to the van he was driving."

"Ian Parker," Betsy said. "Ian bought into the business after being the manager for quite some time."

"How old is Wesley Nelson?" Bullock asked.

"He's 83," Evans said.

"And Ian Parker?" he added as he wrote what they said onto his notepad.

"He's just turned 55," she said.

"Pretty nice looking 55-year-old, if you ask me," Betsy added.

"Noted," Bullock said with a chuckle.

"So where does that leave us?" I asked.

"We were eventually able to get a hold of Mr. Parker," Evans said. "He confirmed that Phoenix Kester is employed at Good Health, but he stated several times that he has no idea why Kester would be at the building at that hour and he stressed even further, that he's unaware of any reason why things would be taken from the building at all by Phoenix."

"Do we believe him?" I asked. "Parker that is."

"He seemed sincere," Evans said. "I can't see Kester being the brain trust of any illegal operation, however."

159

"He's a worker bee for sure," Betsy added.

"So are we to assume that Ian Parker is lying to us or that someone else is calling the shots, and Parker is oblivious to what's going on in his own business?" I asked. "Which is more likely?"

"Are you asking what I believe?" Evans asked.

"More like asking aloud and seeing what the room thinks," I said.

"Well, we're about to find out," Captain Leonard said. "I wanted to bring everyone up to date before we start interviewing Kester and Parker. Evans will continue with Kester, since it's her collar. Brody and Bullock, I want you to talk to Ian Parker and see if he reveals more than he's alluded to already."

"Kester is in interrogation room number one," Evans said. "Parker is room number two."

"Betsy, if you'd be so kind," Leonard said. "I'd like you to just watch the Parker interview. It seems like you've had a feeling about this guy, or at least his business, and you can fill some gaps in his story. If there is any."

We all agreed to return to the conference room for a debriefing when we finished with the interviews.

"Will you be providing lunch, sir?" Bullock asked.

* * *

"I don't appreciate being left in this room like some like common criminal," Ian Parker said as I opened the door to the interrogation room. "I came down here of my own free will to answer your questions and you just left me in here."

160

"I'm sorry about the delay," I said as I pulled out a chair.

It let out a loud screech as the metal scraped the floor beneath it.

"Jeepers creepers," Bullock said.

He picked his chair up and moved it back and set it down to not make a sound.

"Is this a comedy routine that you two put on?" Ian angrily asked. "Because I'm not amused."

"We just have a few questions," I said. "It shouldn't take too long. You'll be out of here momentarily."

Bullock opened a folder and slid a couple pictures across the table toward Ian.

"As you're aware," he said as he flipped a few pages in his folder. "An employee of yours was found unloading boxes from your building last night into a van. When he was approached by an officer, he fled and during his apprehension, a weapon fell from his waistband."

"Officers, I have no idea why Phoenix would be carrying a gun," Ian said.

"But would you have an idea as to why Phoenix would be loading boxes from your place of business at 1 o'clock in the morning?" I asked.

"Our business has changed dramatically over the years," he said.

"Yeah, I would say so," Bullock said.

"I'm not sure what that is supposed to mean," Ian tersely said. "My point was, that I have worked there since I was in my early 20s. I worked for Virgil Nelson and then his son Wesley. I've done anything and everything there. And now we've taken it in a different direction."

"That's an understatement," Bullock said.

Looking toward me, Ian asked, "what is he getting at?"

"Mr. Parker," I said. "Why don't we back up a little bit and you explain to us what you folks do at Good Health, and what specifically do you mean about a 'different direction'."

"I've been with this company for a very long time," he said. "Virgil Nelson hired me when I was still in college. Virgil had us wearing white coats, because he thought it made us look more medical."

"Aren't you?" I asked.

"Not really," he said. "Not in the same sense. We are sales people, to be honest. We sell things that medical professionals need and people with health issues need. We don't prescribe anything, nor diagnose anything. And that has changed over the years as well."

"Such as?" Bullock asked.

"Well, for one," he said. "We no longer provide as many supplies to doctors as we used to. There's less and less private practices that need us. They're all getting gobbled up by larger hospitals. We still do referrals, but most of our business is to the end customer, the patients."

"And that has you looking for other revenue streams?" Bullock asked.

"This guy and his insinuations," Ian said while looking at me, but pointing to Bullock.

"Go on," I said.

Ian shifted in his chair so that he only faced me.

"Virgil passed and Wesley inherited the business," Ian said. "Wesley didn't want to have anything to do with it, to be honest. He was already in his 60s. He was in nomine solum."

"I'm sorry, my Latin is a little rusty," I said.

"He was the owner in name only, basically," he said. "For

example, Virgil always signed one to two year leases. In 1984, when the lease was to be renewed, Wesley told me to take care of it and to get the longest lease I could. I was able to get one for 20 years."

"And that ends in two years," Bullock said.

"Correct," Ian affirmed, without actually looking in Bullock's direction.

"And so you'll be out on the street?" Bullock asked.

"Not exactly," Ian said, this time turning and looking at Bullock. "It's one of the changes I decided to make a few years ago. I knew Wesley didn't care, as long as we continued to make money. I bought into the ownership as a sign of good faith. It also allowed me to make some drastic changes. I read the tea leaves as to where this business was going."

"And where's that?" I asked.

"Delivery," he said. "Simply put, our customer base is the old and frail. The sick. They weren't coming in on a whim. And now with technology making it easier for people to order things via the world wide web, I thought we'd move from waiting for people to come to us, to more of a business that went to them. So we stopped being open to the public, per se, and more delivering our products directly to the customer."

"So why keep the space at all?" I asked.

"Storage and rent costs," he said. "I was going to close up entirely, but when I looked around, the costs for storage units or industrial buildings were way more expensive than just staying put and using this space as a quasi storage unit."

"Where does Phoenix Kester fit into all this?" I asked. "And we still haven't determined why he was there at one in the morning. Although, I'm getting somewhat of an idea. I think."

"We've come full circle," Ian said.

"How so?" Bullock asked.

"I'm now Wesley Nelson and Phoenix is now me," he said.

"I don't follow," I said.

"Not literally, but figuratively," he said. "Phoenix is a great kid and a hard worker. He's my right hand man. I needed someone to watch the store, help me put orders together for me to take to customers, keep a supply readily available and do general maintenance and cleaning."

"So now you're nomine solum," I said.

"Not entirely," Ian said. "But as far as the building is concerned, sure, we could say that. It's been very liberating for me at my age. I have much more freedom."

"And maybe so does Phoenix," I added.

"True," he reluctantly said. "But I trust him."

"Do you trust him enough that his taking things from your building in the middle of the night isn't alarming?" Bullock asked.

"The time of day doesn't concern me," he said. "But removing things from the building, well that is definitely peculiar. As long as we can account for everything, and he's not stealing from me, then to be honest, while it may be weird, I'm okay with it. I just have to ask him. He'll tell me."

"Are you going to ask him about the gun?" Bullock asked.

Ian sat stoically.

"The gun isn't registered," I added. "That does send a red flag. As does the materials in the boxes. They are, in fact, medical supplies. So it does appear he was stealing from you."

"You know what other heading they fall under?" Bullock asked.

"Much of the equipment is used in the manufacturing of narcotics," I said. "It appears that Good Health may be supplying

164

equipment for a drug lab."

"Is that the 'different direction' you were speaking about?" Bullock asked.

"Gentlemen," Ian said. "I can assure you I have nothing to do with anything illegal. And with that, I will respectfully say that any additional questions can be directed to my attorney. We are done here without my lawyer."

* * *

At our debriefing, Bullock and I explained to the group what we discovered in our interview with Ian Parker.

"I'm not speaking for Bullock, sir," I said. "But I don't think Ian Parker is directly involved in anything criminal. He may be totally oblivious to what Phoenix Kester was doing within the walls of Good Health, but I don't think there was direct involvement."

"I'm not willing to let him off so easily," Bullock said. "But it does seem like he has one foot out the door and is more than willing to, at least, let Phoenix do whatever he pleases as long as it doesn't impact Ian."

"From what I observed from behind the glass," Betsy said. "I didn't get the feeling he was too aware of what was happening at his own business. Additionally, it appears he's at least two years away from being financially impacted as he has a sweetheart lease agreement that Don Barton can't wait to squeeze for more money."

"We're getting a warrant to check his office, his home and all records pertaining to Good Health," Captain Leonard said. "He could very well be giving himself plausible deniability, but still reaping the rewards of whatever Phoenix Kester is sowing."

"If anyone might be needing some additional cash, maybe it's Don Barton himself," Bullock suggested. "He already told Parker his rent is going up when the current lease expires, maybe he's pressing others as well."

"Which, if you think about it," I added. "Would make a lot more sense than Kester being the mastermind behind this."

"Which kind of goes with what Kester wants us to believe, anyway," Evans said. "When I talked with him today, his story was, he gets to work whenever he wants and was only stocking equipment that was ordered. He kept stressing that he wasn't aware of what the equipment was used for."

"Worst case scenario," Leonard said. "We have a renegade employee using his work as a small drug center. I think we all can agree that we don't think highly enough of our Mr. Kester to think he's the brains behind such an operation."

"Do you ever notice that people never actually use 'worst case' correctly?" Bullock asked. "Worst case we have a major criminal enterprise or thousands are killed."

"Wouldn't millions dying be worse?" I asked.

"Exactly," he said. "That's way worse."

"Are you through?" Leonard asked.

"Worst case, I'd say no," Bullock said.

Leonard let out a prolonged sigh.

"Moving on," Leonard said. "When the warrant is approved, let's check all their records. And let's find out where Kester was taking this equipment."

# 18

# So You Say

Finding a judge in a relatively rural part of the country that would be willing to issue a warrant after a murder, a situation where one suspect lawyered up and the other was caught in possession of an unregistered weapon, was fairly easy.

Although Kester's gun wasn't a 9 millimeter, the fact he had one at all helped our request. Guns scare people. The specifics of guns is an area few want to tread.

After pouring through the records, we had sufficient information to ask both Ian Parker and Phoenix Kester more about their involvement. Phoenix was still in our possession on the gun charge, and since Ian was going to bring a lawyer (something Phoenix couldn't afford), we knew starting with the younger, and less polished, of the two could expedite the process of discovery.

\* \* \*

"Tell us about Niezao Pharmaceuticals?" I asked.

"Not much to tell," Phoenix said as he squirmed in his seat.

Neither Bullock and I moved. We didn't smile. I don't think we even blinked.

Phoenix blinked. Phoenix blinked pretty quickly.

"I mean, it's a Chinese company we order products from them," he said. "Standard stuff. You know we're a medical supply company. So we buy medical supplies. That kind of stuff."

"Like pill pressing machines?" I asked.

"I guess," he said. "Ian tells me what to order and I order it. I don't ask what he's ordering."

"You don't ask what he's ordering, but yet you're the one who orders the equipment?" Bullock asked.

"Well, I mean," Phoenix said as he became restless and started to rub his wrists where the handcuffs were placed. "I know what he's ordering, but I don't know why he's ordering it. Like I don't know what he uses the stuff for."

"You're saying you wouldn't know what a pill press is used for?" Bullock asked.

"I mean, yeah, it's like in the name and stuff," he said. "But not everything you can tell what it is by the name of it."

"How long have you worked for the company?" I asked.

"A couple years," he said. "Maybe two. I don't know. Maybe three. Somewhere between two and three."

"And in that time you haven't learned what the products you sell do or what they're used for?" I asked.

"Yeah, sure," he said. "I mean, I guess I do now. With a lot of stuff. Sure. Not everything. Like the new stuff."

"What would be some examples of the 'new stuff'?" Bullock asked.

"Well, there's not that much new, I guess," he said. "Maybe, well, like the pill press thing. That's fairly new. Maybe like a year or so. Maybe more."

"It seems like several other items have increased in the last year," Bullock said as he looked over a printout of Good Health purchases in the 12 months. "Looks like you guys have increased in glass beakers and stirring rods and rubber gloves. Jeesh. Rubber glove orders are through the roof."

"If you say so," he said.

"You don't think there's been an increase in orders for those items?" I asked.

"I can't remember all the orders," he said.

"But you do the ordering, correct?" I asked. "It seems like when you do something regularly, whenever there's some oddities, it would be apparent."

"Yeah, I guess you're right," he said. "Yeah...maybe if I thought about it more, I'd think we've ordered more."

"And Ian Parker asked you to order these?" Bullock asked.

"I mean I order what he tells me to, so yeah."

"How does he tell you what to order?" I asked. "Does he tell you in person? Does he call you? Does he send an email?"

"Yeah, I think he kind of does all of those things, I think." he said.

"So how would you prove, to us, that what you ordered was on a directive from Ian, and not, let's say, something you wanted to order?" Bullock asked.

"I don't understand what you're asking?" he said.

"Let me be very clear here," I said. "We have a dead body. We have you on a gun charge. We have you taking equipment out the back door of your employer in the middle of the night."

"All of the equipment you had in your possession is used in

169

the production of illegal narcotics," Bullock said.

"Do you see where we going with this Phoenix?" I asked. "It's not going to take long for us to connect the rest of the dots and charge you with a whole litany of things that will find you heading to Jackson."

"Man, you are definitely going to have a full dance card when you get to prison," Bullock said.

"I didn't kill Carson," he vehemently said.

"Then who did?" I asked. "Let's get that off the table and then we can discuss our options with the drug operation."

"I don't know," he said. "I'm telling the truth. I don't know. I'm a little freaked out, you know? That's why I had the gun. Someone killed Carson right where I work. That's why I was there so late, dude. I figured no one would be there. Then when I saw the cop lady, everything went hazy. I thought I was going to die. I really did."

Neither Bullock or I immediately responded to what Phoenix just said. We let it sit there for a moment. Now was the time to shift gears a little bit. It was time to become an ally of Phoenix. At least as far as he was concerned.

"I believe you," I comfortingly said. "I know you're just doing what you were told. All we're trying to figure out is who killed Carson McCall and who is in charge of this little operation."

"Is it Ian Parker?" Bullock asked.

"Nah, man," Phoenix said. "Ian is good people."

"So that leaves us with you, my man," Bullock said. "Unless of course, you want to get out from under this rock. Maybe it's time to save yourself."

"I knew this was going to happen," he frustratingly said. "I knew I never should have said anything."

"You never should have said anything to whom?" I asked.

"Shit!" Phoenix yelled out as he slammed his hands onto the table. "Shit, shit, shit, shit, shit."

"With you so far," Bullock said.

"Relax and just explain to us what you got yourself into," I said.

"We were just talking one day, you know?" he said. "I was out back on a break, smoking a drag. And we started chatting. Nothing too serious. What do you do? Ah, yeah, cool, what do you do? That sort of stuff."

"Who?" I asked. "You and Don Barton?"

"I don't know who that is," he said.

"Who are you talking about?" Bullock asked.

Phoenix hung his head and started crying.

Among his tears, he said, "over time he just kept asking me more and more about my job and what I do there."

He raised his head up, wiped his eyes and let out a huff.

"And then one day, he said he had an idea."

* * *

"Do you think he killed McCall?" Bullock asked.

"He would fit the profile, don't you think?" I said as I pulled off to the side of the road. We strategically positioned ourselves behind a row of trees, allowing us to see the building where our suspect was thought to be, while also giving us cover if he happened to look in our direction.

"You don't think he's the one pulling all the strings of this whole thing, do you?" Bullock asked.

"That's the part that seems unlikely," I said.

"He seemed so chill the last time we talked."

"Does chill mean calm?" I asked. "Because it's the calm ones you always have to be leery of. The spastic ones, they're just riding on emotion at that time. But the calm ones are the devious ones. The plotters and planners. Those are the true masterminds."

Two Monroe police cars pulled up behind us. Three officers got out. We briefly exchanged pleasantries and outlined our plan on the trunk of my car.

Jameson McGuire, a Sargent for Monroe, was a tall man whose physique widened as you looked up from his feet to his shoulders.

The other two were lower on the food chain but looked like capable officers. Brandon DuBois was a little shorter than McGuire, a little thinner but had a bulldog presence to him. I got the impression he wasn't too scared to pursue much larger suspects.

Elle Stanway was the third officer. Much shorter than her partners, hair pulled back tightly with a noticeable tattoo on her right wrist. It read "intrepide."

"I noticed your tattoo," I said. "Is that French?"

"Yes, sir," she said. "It means fearless."

"You play softball?" Bullock asked.

"Used to," she said.

"I thought so," he said. "You give off that softball player aura."

"Is that a good thing?" she asked.

"It is in battle."

Elle nodded her head as if she accepted Bullock's comment as a compliment. When the plan was finalized, we made our way back to our respective vehicles and moved in.

Bullock and I pulled up to the building and parked next to the entrance. We sat for a few seconds just staring at the building.

"At least we know what door to go through this time," Bullock said.

* * *

We let the locals take point on this mission, since it was their jurisdiction.

Jameson McGuire opened the door while Brandon DuBois peered inside. There was a haze from where the sunlight met the darkness of the interior.

"Does it smell like weed?" Bullock asked.

"Do you always ask that on an entry?" McGuire said as he stood just off Bullock's right shoulder.

I followed DuBois as we entered the building. We moved quickly to the left where I assumed our suspect would be sitting.

Bullock and McGuire went to the right. Stanway stepped back outside the door and gave herself cover, in case any suspects might try to escape.

As we approached the last office, I positioned myself so I could sneak a peek around the corner, but unfortunately, I realized our suspect wasn't in his usual spot.

"Police!" I head McGuire shout from the opposite side of the building.

A shot rang out. Several shots followed.

DuBois and I took off as fast we could through the darkened hallway and into the larger area of the facility. We bobbed and weaved through various industrial barrels and pallets full of shrink-wrapped boxes.

"He went out the side door!" Bullock yelled.

I turned, with DuBois in tow, and headed toward the only door I was aware of. As I swung the door open, I shielded myself just in case bullets would have been the first thing I encountered. Thankfully, none were shot, and in particular interest to me, in our direction. When I looked out, Stanway wasn't where she was supposed to be. Looking left, I saw her running around the southeast corner of the building.

"Let's head this way," I said to DuBois as we went right, hoping to box our suspect in.

As we rounded the northwest corner of the building, I could see Bullock wrestling our suspect to the ground as McGuire and Stanway approached.

I jogged over to the mass of people as Bullock handcuffed our suspect, face down in the dust and oil and debris often found at industrial sites.

"Hello Lucas," I said as I knelt down and tapped him on his head.

"Hey Brody," Bullock said as he seemed out of breath.

He took a deep breath, and said, "I'm starving. I think there's a great burger joint around here some where."

"I'm sure there is," I said. "But let's take care of this first."

* * *

We set Lucas down in a somewhat working webbed lawn chair we found tossed to the side of the building. A couple of the polyester straps were a bit warn and the aluminum legs may not have been as stable as you'd prefer, if you were to sit in the chair. Nonetheless, it was better than the three tires that were stacked together. And even if it wasn't the better option, I wasn't sitting in it.

"Hey, Lucas," Bullock said. "You didn't happen to shoot at us with the same 9 millimeter you used to kill Carson McCall, did you? Because that would be super helpful, my friend."

"I didn't kill Carson, asshole," Lucas barked back.

"Did you say you didn't kill Carson's asshole or you didn't kill Carson, comma, asshole?"

"I didn't kill anyone, or anything," he said. "Are you happy with that answer?"

"Not really," Bullock said. "I was really hoping to wrap this up, and then grab a bite to eat, if I'm being honest."

"Sorry to disappoint you."

"Well, I wouldn't worry too much Lucas," I said. "You shot at cops. You ran from cops. You have a nice little drug production setup inside this building. You're going to face charges in two communities. You're looking at some serious time. So you clearly have other worries at the moment."

"Hope you have a good lawyer, mi amigo," Bullock said as he lifted Lucas out of his chair and walked him toward McGuire, who was pulling up in his squad car.

There was no telling how long it was going to be until we could get Lucas back to Stonington. McGuire was none too pleased to be shot at, and was still fuming when he shoved Lucas into the backseat.

"You guys have a lovely day," he said to me and Bullock as he got into his car and drove off.

Bullock and I walked back toward the building as we were going to have to take a ton of photos and log a lot of evidence, all of which was also being processed by Stanway and DuBois for their cases.

"McGuire said there used to be a Burger Chef down here," Bullock said. "It's a Hardee's now. Do you like Hardee's?"

# 19

## It's The Damn Pillows

Bullock and I waited for Captain Leonard to let us know what the verdict was regarding the two departments, the two prosecuting attorneys and anyone else at the decision making level in Stonington and Monroe, to determine the pecking order in regards to Lucas Winters.

In the meantime, we unloaded boxes into the conference room and began to sort folders, documents, pictures and printouts. Every sort of evidence we collected from Good Health and the Monroe warehouse was strewn across the conference room.

"Hey Brody," Bullock said. "Can I talk to you for a second?"

"Sure," I said as I placed a box on the table.

"It's pretty serious," he said.

"I told you before, always go with your gut. If you think it's burning unnecessarily, have it checked out."

"What?" he asked.

That was an odd response from Bullock. He's usually quick on the draw for our verbal exchanges. Not this time. His response was concerning. Like my mother used to say, "it's not what you said, it's how you said it."

How he said it made it seem pretty important. I stopped what I was doing and gave him my full attention.

"You okay?" I asked.

"Yeah, I'm fine," he said. "It's just that over the last few weeks or so, I've had a lot of things on my mind."

"You thinking about the baby?" I asked.

"Yeah, always," he said. "So it's that and just other stuff. It got me thinking, you know."

"I think so."

I didn't actually, but I figured it was the right thing to say.

"I was thinking about where I'm at, where I want to be, all sorts of stuff."

I didn't like where this was headed. I have to make myself busy, I thought. I opened the lid of the box and started pulling folders out and placing them into various piles. I'm not sure they were even the right piles, to be honest.

"You thinking about leaving the job?" I asked.

"No, not anything like that," he said.

I slowed my pile making.

"Going to another department?"

"No, I like working here," he said. "We're like Starsky and Hutch."

"I'm definitely Kenneth Hutchinson," I said. "He was the thinker. And Starsky was too moody for my tastes."

"You think I'm moody?" he asked. "I think you're more moody than I am."

"Are you saying you think you're the Hutch in this situation?"

"Well, wasn't Starsky in the military?" he said. "You were in the military, he was in the military. You're moody, he was moody."

"Yeah, but I'm more blonde than you are."

178

"Graying is not blonde," he said.

It was nice to know that even in what seemed like a serious conversation, we could still joke with each other.

"But seriously, I need to tell you something."

Bullock went over to his coat that he draped over a chair. When he came closer to me, he was holding a small, black bag. He reached in and pulled out a small, felt box.

"Are you kidding me, you jackass!" I said.

"Well, that's rude," he said. "I haven't even told you what's inside it."

He opened the box and there was a beautiful diamond ring inside.

"Follow me," I said.

The two of us walked back toward our desks. I was walking at a pretty steady pace. Bullock would break into on occasional two to three step jog to keep up.

I opened my desk drawer and pulled out a red felt box. The one I got from Carruthers. I turned toward Bullock and showed him the closed box.

"No shit!" he said. "We're both going to propose?"

"I knew it," said Mike Garrett as he walked by our desks. "You two are finally going to make this official?"

"Keep walking, Garrett," Bullock said.

"This isn't cool Bullock," I said as I opened my box and showed the ring I was planning on giving Chloe.

"Why not?" he asked.

"Let me present some scenarios for you," I said. "Who's going first?"

"What does it matter?"

"Oh, it matters," I said. "It matters a lot. If I ask Chloe first, then when you ask Alicia, she's going to think you're only doing it because I asked Chloe. And I'm sure as hell not going to let you get the drop on me."

"The drop?" he asked. "You been watching old gangster movies again?"

"You know what I mean," I said. "I'm not going to propose to Chloe after you ask Alicia, and then Chloe thinks I'm only doing it out of guilt or a sense of obligation."

"Why don't we propose at the same time?" Bullock said as he turned his attention away from me to Garrett who was standing there with a mug in his hand.

"Don't say a freaking word Garrett," Bullock said.

Garrett just turned, walked away sipping his coffee.

"Then we have to hear how it wasn't their special moment," I said.

"But it would be," he said. "It would be their individual, special moment. But together. Sort of."

"Huh?" I said. "What the hell does that even mean?"

"We won't do it together," he said. "Like at the same spot. But we could each do it at the same time, but somewhere different so it's together but separate, and then they'll be super excited for themselves. Then when they talk about it, they'll be like doubly excited."

"Yeah," I slowly said. "That clears that up."

"It'll be fine," Bullock said. "Trust me."

"Trust you is the last thing I'll do," I said.

"For a second there," Bullock said. "I thought you were mad because the ring I got Alicia is way nicer than what you got Chloe."

"You're a dick," I said.

Now I have to worry about not only the when, but also which ring is better. This future moment of mine is already ruined.

\* \* \*

I wasn't sure when I was even going to pop the question. I actually thought that the gesture of buying the ring bought me some time, in my own head, even though Chloe had no idea. It seemed logical to me. I must've been in deep thought sitting at the conference room table.

Bullock took a bite of an apple.

"What are you thinking?" he asked breaking my trance.

"You couldn't have asked that before chewing?" I asked.

"I could've," he said. "But I didn't. "

I stood up and looked over numerous pictures that were affixed to the dry erase board. The photos were collected from Good Health, the van used by Phoenix Kester, and Lucas Winter's operation in Monroe.

I turned and scanned the information spread out across the table. I grabbed a random pile and thumbed through various pieces of paper. I realized it was going to be a daunting task. Bullock and I poured through every document we could find and matched every item that was received by Good Health, and every item they sold. We compiled a list of every item that was still was in their possession. With the exception of the lone shipment received from Niezao, everything matched. Ian Parker was very diligent in keeping meticulous records.

Everything that was received at Good Health could be accounted for. There wasn't anything we could find that would indict Ian Parker of criminal activity.

"We got bupkis on Parker," Bullock dejectedly said.

"I still don't trust Phoenix Kester," I said. "It may not involve Ian Parker, but it does involve Good Health somehow. I'm sure of it."

We needed something concrete to connect Good Health with the Monroe warehouse. It was going to take us through the night.

"I think we both know there's a strong connection between the two, right?" I asked not expecting an answer.

"There's got to be," Bullock said as he was leaning back in his chair staring at the ceiling. "We've been through a lot of papers. I've never looked at so many numbers before in my life."

"No?"

"I don't think so," he said. "What do you think the largest number is that you've personally seen?"

"Do you mean the largest amount of numbers or actually the largest number?" I asked.

"I don't honestly know," he said. "My brain is fried."

"Good," I said. "Because I wouldn't know the answer to either question."

I turned over an invoice and stared at it a little more thoroughly. Good Health received six pillows from a company called Almohada Secreta. There was something about it that kept drawing my attention.

"What do we know about this Almohada Secreta?" I asked Bullock.

"I have no idea," Bullock said as he slowly lowered his chair back and started looking over notes he had written.

"What's it for?" he asked.

"Pillows," I said. "Six pillows."

Bullock thumbed through several pages.

"Good Health sold them to a Dr. Schneider," Bullock said. "Looks like he's a sleep therapist. That's not a guy I'd need right now. I could fall asleep on this table and be fine."

"Good to know," I said. "I don't know what it is, but something is off about this."

Bullock flipped through a couple pages in his notebook.

"I should've written these down alphabetically," he said. "I don't see anything like that. Maybe I'm not spelling it correctly. How do you spell it?"

"Just like it sounds," I said. "Sound it out."

"That's certainly more helpful than just spelling it for me," he said.

Bullock stopped shuffling.

"Hey, it looks like it's a company from Mexico," he said.

"We don't have record of them receiving anything from Mexico," I said. "Not one direct shipment from Mexico. Where did they get these pillows from?"

Bullock rose from his chair and walked over to the table. He started looking over more notes he had written down.

"Well, shit," he said.

"What?" I asked as I got up quickly and walked over to Bullock.

Looking over Bullock's shoulder, "Son of a bitch."

I walked over to a stack of papers, thumbed through a few pages, and stopped on a specific page.

"It's the damn pillows," I said.

# 20

# I'm A Buckwheat Pillow Smuggler

After the dust had settled, and Monroe and Stonington had filed all of their charges, Lucas Winters was shipped off to prison, awaiting his numerous court appearances.

His stay on the public dime allowed us to head down there and have a chat with our young criminal mastermind.

* * *

"You put together quite the operation, my friend," I said to Lucas as the guard set him down in a chair across from me at the table.

The guard secured his handcuffs to the table and said, "knock if you need me."

"Will do," I said.

"I think he was talking to me," Lucas said.

"Who were you talking to?" I yelled toward the guard as he was leaving the room.

"Whomever knocks, I guess," he said pulling the door shut.

"You enjoying the view?" Lucas said to Bullock, who had his back to the both of us and was staring out the small window that looked out to the yard. Dozens of inmates were lifting weights, playing basketball, smoking some cigarettes, or just generally relaxing.

"Just checking out your friends," Bullock said.

"You're facing some serious time, Lucas," I said.

"Time is all I have, now," he said back.

Lucas grinned. I surmised that this was to give us the impression he was in charge of this particular interaction.

"Well, hopefully you're making yourself comfortable, because you'll probably be here for awhile," I said.

"Although," Bullock said as he turned from the window and approached the table. "I bet you're first few nights weren't what most would consider comfortable. I noticed you were walking a little different when you walked in here."

"Bullshit," Lucas said. "You were looking out the window the whole time. You didn't see shit."

"But you're not denying the walk was different," Bullock said.

"Screw you dude," Lucas countered.

"Was that the pickup line?"

"Alright, let's keep this civil," I interjected. "Listen, Lucas, we have two choices here. We really do. We can either proceed with you taking the hit for all of this, throw the book at you, and Bullock and I can go about our merry way."

"Or?" Lucas asked.

"Well," I said. "Let's be honest. Neither my partner nor I think you put this together. If you work with us, and point us in the right direction, we can help alleviate a little of your problem, and a lot of the problem our town is facing with your operation."

"You think me ratting out someone else is going to solve

Stonington's drug problem?" Lucas asked. "You assholes are dumber than you look."

"Says the guy chained to a table," Bullock said.

"I don't like him," Lucas said.

"That's irrelevant," I said. "He probably doesn't like you, either. But the fact of the matter is, you are facing a whole bunch of charges that pretty much leaves you in here for a very long time."

"The fact of the matter is, Officer James," he said as he straightened up from the slouch he was sitting in. "The bigger charges aren't coming from you guys, so unless we're talking about those, I can handle the time you guys throw on top of the pile."

"I wouldn't be so confident," I said. "Let's take this one step at a time, and maybe we can all come to an agreement that serves all of our interests."

"I got nothing to say," he said maintaining his position that we were not the department that had him worried.

"Well, then let me have a go at it," I said. "I'll tell you what we know, and if you feel compelled to clarify anything just speak up."

"Does this technique work?"

"It does for those that want to hear their options," I said.

I opened a folder I had set before me. I flipped a page.

"I just want to preface this with the fact that Bullock and I know you're running a drug lab," I said. "The questions we have, are you capable of killing someone? Probably need to be in your line of work. But really, let's be honest. Are you capable of running this whole thing? That just seems way outside your specific skill set."

"You guys drove all the way down here to tell me that I'm too stupid to run something?" he asked. "Doesn't matter. I'm not involved with what you think I'm involved in. I mean, I just let some people store some stuff at an empty warehouse."

"But then you went ahead and shot at cops," Bullock added.

"I didn't know who they were," Lucas said.

"That seems to be a common answer these days," I said. "So you're saying you were just renting space. Is that right?"

"Yes, sir," he said as he crossed his arms in an act of defiance.

"And you, I'm assuming, know who these people are who are renting your space," I said. "Names, phone numbers, that sort of thing."

"I didn't ask their name," he said.

"I'm assuming they paid cash for this rental space?" Bullock asked.

"They seemed like good people," Lucas answered. "I had the space, they had the need. I just let them use it."

"Well, my friend," I said. "It seems like we have a whole slate of new charges to add to the pile. We got conspiracy on the drug charges, conspiracy on receiving stolen property."

"Don't forget money laundering," Bullock added.

"Absolutely," I said. "I mean we can't account for any of these other people, so I mean, I guess it would be conspiracy. But since we don't know about anyone else involved on this end, I guess it all falls on you."

Lucas took a deep, defeated breath. He still didn't relent and offer any information, but he was a man without an island.

"Let me add some information that might help you in your decision," I said.

"What decision?" he asked.

"Come on, Lucas," Bullock said. "We all know where this is heading. If you want us to dance, then play some music. But I prefer we just skip to the end."

"I bet you say that to your wife all the time," Lucas said.

"That's a good one," Bullock said.

"I bet she never said that, though."

"You might want to stop while you're ahead," I said.

I presented a couple pieces of paper and spun them around so Lucas could read both clearly.

"What's this?" he asked as he looked them over.

"It's an invoice for Almohada Secreta," I said.

"Never heard of them."

"Well, allow me to elaborate," I said. "Good Health receives about a half dozen pillows from them every month or so."

"If you say so."

"The problem is, Almohada is a Mexican company," I said. "But we don't have record of them shipping directly from their factory in Cuauhtemoc, Mexico to Good Health."

"Cuauhtemoc is the apple capitol of Mexico," Bullock added. "Not pertinent to the case, but something I found interesting."

"This is riveting so far," Lucas said.

"We're getting there, trust me," I said. "Turns out, Almohada sends them to an office in El Paso."

Lucas adjusted himself in his chair. He swallowed and took a deep breath.

"The puzzle is coming together, isn't it?" I said. "In all the documents we looked at, we missed it, to be honest. But upon further analysis, there it was. On a shipping label. The pillows were being sent from El Paso to this address: 29378 Edward, Monroe, Michigan."

Lucas was losing color in his face. His posture stiffened.

"That's the address of the warehouse," I said. "You get steady shipments from Almohada, as well as regular shipments from

Niezao, it turns out."

"You got me," Lucas said. "I sell pillows."

"Well, sort of," I said. "You see what we were trying to figure out was how could you get pillows passed through customs?" Bullock asked. "Buckwheat."

"The guy from Little Rascals?" Lucas sarcastically asked.

"No, dipshit," Bullock said. "Buckwheat pillows. You see buckwheat has fagopyrin."

"Fago what?" Lucas asked.

"Fagopyrin," Bullock continued. "It's a flavanoid. It has a strong odor. So strong that it can mask the smell of certain narcotics. Which allows a product, such as buckwheat pillows filled with drugs, to pass through easily undetected."

"Even easier when you have people willing to assist in the delivery at the border," I said.

"So, I'm a buckwheat pillow smuggler?"

"Not so fast, my friend," I said. "This is where it gets interesting."

"I certainly hope so," Lucas said.

"The pillows come to you as buckwheat pillows," I said. "But there's no record of these buckwheat pillows going out. And Good Health hasn't received any buckwheat pillows."

"Wow, that is interesting," Lucas said. "Can you guys say buckwheat pillows more?"

"Well, I can say polyester fiberfill, if that helps," I said. "Turns out, you get regular shipments of polyester fiberfill. Ironically, Good Health receives six polyester fiberfill pillows each month from Almohada. Who, it turns out, doesn't produce such a pillow."

Lucas leaned forward, raised his eyebrows in feigned astonishment and said, "well, don't keep my in suspense. Finish your story."

"Here's our working theory," Bullock said as he stopped and put both hands on the table directly off to the right of Lucas. He leaned close.

"See if this is interesting enough for you," he said softly in Lucas's ear. "You extract the buckwheat, sort out the methamphetamine, fill the pillows with a cheaper alternative fill and send them off to Good Health to sell."

"Seems like a nice little operation," I said. "Until Carson McCall and Phoenix Kester decided to call an audible. We figure they worked for you."

"Is that so?"

"Most of the products were coming directly to you," Bullock said. "From what we're thinking, Carson was the delivery man from you to Good Health. Phoenix would receive the pillows and enter them into the store's inventory. But maybe the two of them got a little greedy. And they ordered directly from Niezao. Were they going to set up their own shop?"

"Is that why you killed Carson?" I asked.

"I told you, I didn't kill anyone," he said.

"Maybe, maybe not," Bullock said. "Nonetheless, the operation had taken a turn. And like you said during our first meeting, there's no way you could make it out to Stonington. So someone else had to kill Carson. Someone who was very involved, and would be just as mad."

"Let me add a few more colors to the painting for you," I said. "What's odd is you said you were sort of shipped off from your stepdad to manage a warehouse in the middle of nowhere. And magically, this warehouse quickly becomes a drug manufacturing center."

I paused and stared at Lucas. Nothing. Colder than ice.

"So our initial thought is simple," Bullock continued. "Don Barton sent you down there to establish this side business. How am I doing so far?"

"Not very well, if I'm being honest," Lucas said.

"Which part?" I asked. "Because we know the timeline fits."

"Is there more to your theory?" he asked.

"Sure," Bullock said. "Maybe you're right and you didn't kill Carson McCall. Maybe Don Barton did?"

\* \* \*

Bullock and I met with Evans and Captain Leonard's in the conference room.

"I think we're starting to get a good handle on the operation," I said. "We just have to connect the last few pieces, and get to the nitty gritty on who pulled the trigger that killed Carson McCall."

"All the evidence says the drugs are coming inside pillows through Mexico into El Paso," Bullock said. "From there, they ship them to Lucas Winters in Monroe. He removes the interior, separates the drugs, fills the pillows with polyester and sends them to Good Health."

"It won't take for the three-letter agencies to take over this investigation," Captain Leonard said. "We need to make sure we have everything on lock down before they get involved. And it goes without saying, we need to close out the murder of Carson McCall. First things first. Where do the pillows go from Good Health?"

"They sell them to a doctor who specializes in sleep therapy," I said.

"What do we know about the doctor, other than the specifics of the practice?" Evans said.

"From everything we could put together," Bullock said. "The doctor is using the pillows for their intended use. We think he's just a guy who buys, what he believes, are legitimate products from Good Health. He's not a suspect. And from what we can put together, Good Health, as a company, is innocent."

"However, Phoenix Kester may have used his position, un-beknownst to ownership, to help the operation," I said. "Ian Parker is no longer involved in the day-to-day operations. That left a door wide open for Kester. We believe Carson McCall was the delivery man, if you will, to and from Monroe."

"It looks like McCall and Kester tried to venture out on their own by eliminating Winters in the supply chain," Bullock said. "And that's probably why McCall was killed. Maybe kept Kester around for the access to the ordering system? It's much easier to replace a driver."

"Libby, I want you to go back and press Kester," Leonard said. "See if he breaks now that we can add more layers to this operation. I'm probably stating the obvious. We're all in agreement someone is pulling the strings, and I don't think I'm out of turn by saying this seems like Don Barton would be the obvious person of interest, would it not?"

"I asked Lucas Winters point blank if Don shot McCall," I said. "He remained silent. I think Barton is pulling the strings. He owns the two buildings. He conveniently sent his stepson down to watch a vacant building, which we now know is the headquarters, if you will, for this whole operation."

"The question I keep coming back to is where's the money?," Leonard said. "We find the money, we find out who all is involved. If it's under a mattress, then we know it's these three

192

geniuses, who somehow put this together themselves."

"But if we think someone else is in charge," I said. "Then it's highly likely they moved the money somewhere else."

"And what better guy to do that, then the dude who has his fingerprints all over everything, in some way," Bullock said.

"Evans, see if Kester will crack," Leonard said. "You two, find the money trail."

"Captain," I said. "I have an idea I'd like run by you. Preferably in private."

Captain Leonard looked at Bullock and Evans, who both were surprised by my request.

"Come with me to my office then," he said. "There was something I wanted to ask you as well."

* * *

"What's on your mind Brody?" he asked as he walked around his desk, hung his coat on the rack and sat down in his chair.

"It really isn't as big of a deal as I may have alluded to," I said as I pulled out one of the two chairs in front of his desk. "Do you mind if I sit?"

"Help yourself," he said. "What are you thinking?"

"I didn't want to put you in a bind," I said. "But I was thinking, particularly when you said 'follow the money'. We know product is coming to Winters in Monroe. We know the product is coming directly from El Paso, indirectly from Mexico. The equipment is sent directly from China. What I'm thinking is, what if I go down to El Paso and get a firsthand view of the location that is receiving the products from Almohada. We might be onto something much larger."

"Are you just going to waltz into the building and see if they tell you everything?" Leonard said.

"I just feel like if I get a better sense of what we're dealing with down there, it can help us here," I said. "What if this is much larger than anything we're aware of? Maybe this is just the tip of the iceberg. Maybe, it's the whole iceberg."

"What are you asking, specifically?" he asked.

"I'd like permission to go down to El Paso and check it out in person," I said.

"I don't have the budget to send you down there, Brody," he said. "Is this going to be a regular thing with you? Running all over carnation to nab the bad guy on every case that comes your way?"

"No, sir," I said. "Unless, of course, you think there might be some nefarious activity in Bermuda. Then I'm your man."

The comment got a chuckle. Neither of us spoke for several seconds. I was hoping he was rethinking his position. I had one last card to play.

"What if I took a couple of vacation days?" I asked.

"Wasn't that your tactic last time?" he asked.

"It worked, didn't it?"

He moved the mouse to his computer. He tapped a few keys. He stared at his computer. He let out a sigh. He brought his hand to his chin and rubbed his jowls.

My father used to use a similar tactic when I was younger. I would ask him something, and he would often look like he was pondering my question, but in the end, he was just stalling until I got bored standing there and then I'd walk away. I was hoping this was not the case.

"What about a week from Tuesday and Wednesday?" he asked

finally breaking the tension. "I can cover those two days."

He was not stalling.

"I appreciate that, sir," I said.

He turned his attention back to me and gave me a serious stare.

"On several conditions," he said. "Number one. You're down there as a civilian on a fact-finding mission. Absolutely no way do you involve yourself with anything beyond what you observe."

"Got it," I said.

"Number two," he continued. "Two days. That's it. Whatever you find out in two days is good enough. Don't call me and ask for me to extend your vacation."

"Yes, sir," I said. "Is that it?"

"One more thing," he said. "Just you. No one else is going with you."

"No problem," I said. "Bullock is going to stay here and man the fort, if you will."

"I wasn't talking about Bullock," he said. "I know Bullock is staying here. I'm talking about Chloe. You don't get to take her on every covert mission you dream up."

I had no alternative other than to laugh a little.

"Understood," I said as I stood to leave his office.

"And while we're on the subject," he said. "When are you going to do the right thing and move this relationship from girlfriend to something respectable?"

"Don't get me started, sir," I said.

"Well that sounds like a story for another day," he said.

I shook his hand and headed toward the door.

"Hey, before you leave," he said. "I forgot to ask you my question. Do you play poker? I have a semi-regular game at my place and we're down a couple guys this weekend."

"Sure," I said.

That was the first time Captain Leonard had ever asked me to do something social before. At that moment, I thought that I was moving from employee to friend. He wanted to ask me this in person and that could mean only one thing: he wasn't asking anyone else in the department. I was in a special place in his eyes.

"Do me a favor," he said.

"Yes, sir," I proudly said.

I no longer looked at him as the boss. I looked at him as a friend. As he clearly looked at me.

"Ask Bullock if he wants to join us, too," he said as everything inside of me deflated. "We need another guy."

"Does he play poker?" I asked.

"Do you?" he asked. That was a good point. I actually don't play much poker and he still asked me.

"Thanks for the invite, Captain," I said with still a sense of pride.

Bullock or no Bullock, Captain Leonard could've asked anyone else and he chose me.

"You're welcome," he said. "And if what I'm thinking about Bullock is true, I'm hoping he's the type of guy who won't admit he doesn't play that often. That will just put a few more dollars in my pocket."

Yeah. Imagine someone not admitting they don't play poker very often. Bullock is so dumb.

# 21

## We're Not Going To Subway

I knocked on the door and waited a few seconds.

"Knock again," Bullock said.

"Why?" I asked.

"Maybe they didn't hear you?"

"Or maybe they're on their way and we just be patient and wait for them to get to the door."

We waited a few more seconds.

Bullock stepped around me and knocked on the door.

Again we waited.

"Do you want to pound on the door, now?" I asked. "Maybe you could kick it in."

I barely got the last word out, when the door opened and Grace Leonard, the captain's wife, stood there in a floral house dress with an apron.

"Sorry, gentlemen," she said. "I was just putting in some chicken wings in the oven. I hope you're hungry."

"Yes, ma'am," I said.

"Well, come on in," she said. "Please take off your shoes and don't mind the dog. He can be a little much with strangers."

I love dogs. In fact, I have a saying that always remains true: I always trust a dog that doesn't like a person, but I never trust a person who doesn't like a dog.

I was anxious to meet the Leonard's little ball of joy. As I turned the corner I was greeted by Murphy. A 140-pound German shepherd that nearly knocked me to the ground.

"Murphy, down boy," Grace said. "He loves people. Don't let his size fool you, he's a big ball of mush."

"I had several dogs growing up myself, Mrs. Leonard," Bullock said as he knelt down and scrubbed Murphy's fur vigorously.

"Please call me Grace," she said. "What kinds of dogs did you have?"

"We had two chocolate labs," Bullock said. "Chewy and Rocky. We didn't have them at the same time, though."

"I had a small shepherd," I said. "We named him Tigger. We thought he was going to be pretty big. But he never really grew. My mom called him a combination of a German shepherd and a hamster."

"A Germster," Bullock said with a laugh.

"We also have a few cats walking about," Grace said. "They'll let you know when they've decided you can pet them. They'll just appear in your lap."

"Noted," I said.

"Well, let me show you guys to Alex and his friends," Grace said.

* * *

Captain Leonard was sitting out in enclosed deck at the back of his house. He had two other men with, both about the same age, all in their early to mid 60s. When we approached the table, I could tell that the other two were either former or current law enforcement. We have a look.

"Charlie and Frank," Grace said to the two guys. "This is Brody and...I'm sorry. I apologize."

She placed her hand on Bullock's shoulder.

"I don't know your first name," she said to Bullock.

"People just call me Bullock," he said. "Even my mom."

"Well, Brody and Bullock, I guess," she said. "I'll leave you gentlemen alone until I bring out some more food."

Bullock held aloft a six-pack of beer.

"Where should I set these, sir?" he asked Captain Leonard.

"Probably back in your car," Leonard said. "My friend Charlie here is a recovering alcoholic."

Bullock's faced turned ashen. He looked like he was going to throw up all over the table.

"I'm," he stammered. "I'm very sorry."

"He's just bullshitting you kid," Charlie said as he stood up and grabbed a bottle out of Bullock's stash.

"Brody, Bullock, this is Charlie," Leonard said. "And that handsome devil over there is Frank. Charlie is the captain up in Flushing, and Frank retired a little more than a year ago after serving the great folks of Mason for 30 years."

Bullock and I shook each man's hand and then I moved to the chair in the corner.

"You a gunfighter son?" Frank asked me.

"Not really," I said with some confusion.

"Well, you're sitting in the gunfighter seat," he said. "That's why I asked."

I looked over at Bullock. He had a face that said so much. Most of it was "I told you so."

"You guys familiar with Texas Hold 'Em?" Charlie asked.

"Yes, sir," Bullock said confidently.

I remembered back to the conversation I had earlier with Captain Leonard how Bullock would be in this exact spot: saying with great confidence he was a fine card player, when in reality, he probably wasn't very good.

Right when I was about to respond to Charlie's question, I realized that it was I, who wasn't very good at cards, or at least having not played them very often and now it was the moment of truth.

"I'm not too bad," I said.

"He's bluffing," Frank said. "You can always tell. It's the quiet unassuming guys who you have to look out for. Poker players and criminals are all the same."

* * *

We had been playing for more than hour and the talk was the standard ribbing and joking between men. Bullock was actually doing quite well. I was not. I actually lost a hand when I had a full house. Frank had a four-of-a-kind.

"Kind of a tough night for you, am I right?" Charlie asked me.

"I don't play cards very often," I said in defeat.

"That's okay," he said. "I hear you solved a murder case a little while back."

"He even got an award for it," Bullock said.

"Is that so?" Frank said.

"Yeah," I said with embarrassment. "It was no big deal. I made a lot of mistakes. We didn't even really solve all of it, if I'm being honest."

"Don't worry about it, kid," Charlie said. "Let me tell you a story."

Charlie set his cards down. The game was officially paused.

* * *

"So I'm a detective out near Birch Run, right?" he said. "Sure as shit we get a call that the local apple orchard has been robbed."

"Someone stole some apples from an orchard?" Bullock asks.

"Not some apples," Charlie said. "They stole the whole freaking orchard."

"How the hell do you steal an apple orchard?" Leonard asked.

"That's just it," Charlie said. "We don't know. We never solved the damn case. One night, all the apples disappeared."

"Were there tire tracks?" Frank asked.

"There's tire tracks all over that damn orchard," Charlie indignantly said. "Truck tracks, wagon tracks, Bobcats and mowers. We had tracks upon tracks. Do you know what we didn't have?"

We all sat silently waiting for the answer.

"Cameras or witnesses," Charlie said.

"How is it possible take to take all the apples off all the trees and escape with no one seeing or hearing?" Frank asked.

"That's just it," Charlie. "That had to take several hours. In the middle of the night. Not one damn witness."

"You think it was an inside job?" Leonard asked.

201

"Hell yeah," Charlie said. "Twenty years later and I still think they cleared their own orchard out, sold all the apples, filed an insurance claim and doubled their money. But here's the rub. At no time over the last two decades did they ever buy anything for the business, or themselves, that would've stuck out. Nothing. We have no idea where the money went. We have no idea who would've bought an orchard worth of apples either. But every time I eat applesauce, I wonder."

"You eat a lot of apple sauce, do you?" Frank said. "Is it because your gums are getting soft?"

"Kiss my ass, Frank," Charlie said.

"That's nothing," Frank said. "I got a story for you guys."

\* \* \*

"You know those guys that dress up like kings and queens and stuff?" Frank asked.

"For Halloween?" Charlie asked.

"No, more like festivals," Frank answered.

"When I was in Virginia, they did a lot of Civil War reenactments," I said. "Do you mean like that?"

"It's more like dragons and shit," he said. "They walk around and say stuff like, 'pardon me, my fair lady' and 'welcome to ye royal castle'. Stuff like that."

"You mean a Renaissance Festival?" Bullock said.

Frank pointed at Bullock in victory.

"Renaissance Festival!" he loudly proclaimed. "So check this out. It's the early 80s and Ingham County decides to put on one of these things, right? It starts off small. We help police the event, and it's a few kids and families and stuff and they're all having a grand time. A few years later, it grows. Like, there's a thousand people coming to this thing. And for the most part, it's a cash haul. And we were like, 'you guys might want to have better security and oversight of the cash'.

I mean, anyone, at any time, could stuff wads of cash in their pockets and no one would be the wiser. I'm figuring they're getting ripped off left and right. Because no one is really watching. And we didn't have the technology that we have now. There was no fax machines. We didn't have pagers or mobile phones. None of that. So I'm assuming this place is ripe for a theft. Well, guess what? "

"Someone robbed them," Leonard said in a matter-of-fact sort of way.

"You could say that," Frank said. "By this time, the festival had jousts and all sorts of, if I might admit, pretty cool shit. When I first went, I thought they were a bunch of dorks. But by the fourth or fifth year, I'm into it. Seriously."

"We believe you," Charlie said.

"Anyway," Frank said. "One day, these four guys come riding into the festival on these huge horses. I mean they're decked out. They looked like knights right out of Arthur's Court. Their horses too. Everyone is clapping and cheering. These dudes were legit riders. They're riding around, whooping and hollering. The crowd is going crazy.

They get off their horses with their swords and they go over to the entrance where they had, I don't know, four or fives bushels. When you entered the festival, you paid, I think, five or 10 bucks. You just threw into the bushel. That's how they collected the money.

Well, these knights walk over to the bushels, push over a

couple of the workers and grab as much money they could. One dude, held his stack of money high above his head in victory. The crowd is going crazy. This is the best show the festival had ever put on.

These dudes hop on their horses, ride around kicking up dirt and high tail it out into the parking lot."

Frank stopped. He looked at each of us waiting for us to realize what had happened.

"Exactly," he triumphantly said.

"Exactly, what?" Leonard asked.

"They robbed the damn festival," Frank said. "Not only right in front of everyone. But while everyone was cheering them on."

"That's awesome," Bullock said. "I mean, they're thieves, but that's an awesome story."

"We're all just standing around and cheering them on," Frank said. "The ballsiest robbery I ever heard of."

He leaned back in his chair as if he had just told the greatest story ever.

"What about you, Alex?" Charlie said to Captain Leonard. "You have anything that matches?"

"Not really," he said.

"What about your old man?" Charlie asked.

Turning to Bullock and I, Charlie said, "did you guys know that your boss is a third generation cop?"

Neither Bullock and I did.

"Yeah, I'm sure there's a story in there somewhere," Frank said.

"The only thing I could think happened when I was a kid," Leonard said.

\* \* \*

"As you know," Leonard said. "My mom and dad divorced."

I know I didn't know that. I'm pretty sure Bullock didn't either, based on how he was looking at me.

"My mom moved up to Bad Axe, in the thumb of Michigan," Leonard said. "My dad was working in Madison Heights at the time. So I would come down on the weekends and visit. My mom dropped me off one Friday afternoon. I can't remember why, but it was much earlier in the day than usual. I was just hanging around the department. Goofing off, getting into things I probably shouldn't have. It was a different time.

Anyway, my dad and I are going to his apartment. As we enter the apartment complex, there's some dude standing by a car. I didn't think anything of it. But my dad was the best cop I ever knew. He knew that guy was up to something. So we turned around. As we're heading back toward the guy, three other men come sprinting behind one of the apartment buildings. Paper is flying all over the place."

"Paper?" Charlie asked. "Like money? Or just regular paper?"

"I'm thinking it was money," Leonard said. "I'm pretty sure my eyes got wide because as we got closer, I see these guys are carrying guns."

"Armed robbery?" Charlie asked.

"Don't forget," Leonard said. "I'm about 10 or 11 at this time. I'm sitting in the front seat of my dad's unmarked car. These dudes all get into their car and they take off. My dad reaches over with his right arm and presses into me so I lean back into my seat. He says, 'Buckle up, son'."

"Holy shit," Frank said. "Your dad took you on a chase?"

205

I looked over at Bullock. He was already looking at me with the same expression I probably had. We always thought Captain Leonard was a stud, back in the day. Now we know that Captain Leonard's dad was a total bad ass.

Captain Leonard continued.

"We're flying through this neighborhood," he said. "These dudes are probably looking back at some dude and his kid following them wondering what the hell was going on. We followed them for, probably, 10 minutes or so until backup arrived and boxed them in."

"That's freaking hilarious," Charlie said.

"Here's the funniest part," Leonard said. "They made off with $38. That's it. They robbed a gas station on the other side of the apartment complex. I mean, if you think about it, they put some thought into it. They were expecting a big score, which I get. They weren't expecting me and my dad, which I also get. Talk about a bad day going worse. Armed robbery for $38. That's got to sting a little bit."

* * *

At the end of the night, I walked out of the Leonard's home with $50 less than when I walked in. Which wasn't good, because I only brought $50 with me.

Bullock fared much better than I did, but he still had a chunk taken out of his initial amount.

"All I have left is five dollars," he said. "How about you, Brody?"

"Flat broke," I said.

"You lost all $50?" he said.

"You lost almost the same amount."

"No, I didn't," he said back. "I still have five dollars. I could buy a foot-long from Subway. What are you getting? Napkins?"

"We're not going to Subway," I said. "First off, they're closed."

I opened the driver's side door of my car, but before I could get in, Bullock peered over the roof of the car and said, "And second off, you don't have any money."

"Okay, we have to back up a second," I said. "First off, there's no such thing as second off. And..."

I sat down on my seat and buckled my belt.

"Second off," Bullock said as he did likewise on his side. "You know you want to say it."

"No, I don't," I said as I turned the ignition. "It's stupid."

"But it works, doesn't it?"

"And secondly," I said stressing the last syllable. "I want to go home and get some sleep. I'm getting up early to go to church with Chloe."

I turned on the headlights and backed out of the driveway.

"Church?" Bullock asked. "I didn't know you went to church."

"I've been going lately with Chloe," I said.

"You like it?" he asked.

"I don't hate it," I said. "I have a lot of questions."

"Such as?"

"Dude, we don't have time for all the questions I have," I said as navigated our way out of the neighborhood.

"Give me one," he said. "What's the most pressing thing that's got you thinking?"

"Okay," I relented. "If you were God, and you had this whole thing planned from the beginning. Why wouldn't you skip all the hassle and all the stupid people and just build what you're going to end up with in the end?"

"That's a good question," he said.

"And?" I asked.

"And what?"

"What do you think?"

"About what?"

"What do you mean about what?" I asked. "What do you think about what I said? The question. Why did God do all this if he knew the end?"

"I don't know," he said. "Maybe he just wanted to be sure that the people who end up with him actually love him."

Both of us spent the next few minutes considering the enormity of Bullock's comment. At least, I did. I didn't take Bullock for being overly religious, but I think most of us, if we're honest, are hoping there's something beyond this world.

"You know," he said, breaking the silence. "Losing Kendan was probably the most difficult thing I've ever been through. I know it was the worst thing ever for Alicia. I know it's not true for everyone, but that moment, no matter how tragic it was, brought us closer together. Me and Alicia."

There wasn't anything I could offer in that moment.

"Maybe that's your answer," he said. "Maybe, God realizes that when times are good, it's easy being in relationships. But when the chips are down...like you tonight in poker...that's when you find the real value in your connection with other people. Maybe that's why there's pain on earth. To find out who truly loves him."

# 22

# I'll Be Damned

"Did you know El Paso International Airport was where the first hijacked plane in the US landed?" the guy sitting next to me asked. He hadn't said a word the entire trip from Detroit Metro until this moment when the plane landed in Texas. And that's the tidbit of information he used as an icebreaker, seconds before we never saw each other again.

"I did not know that," I said.

That was it. He didn't elaborate or change the subject. I never spoke another word to this man. Whatever time I have on the planet, the only exchange between me and him will be about a hijacked plane.

We landed in El Paso a little before 8 a.m., Mountain Standard Time. Meaning my individual clock was still thinking it was two hours later in the day. Exiting the terminal, the early morning was already beaming, and it took me several seconds for my eyes to adjust.

With eyesight intact, I was able to see the general area where my rental car was located. People are funny in the small moments of life. Looking over numerous options of the same

Ford Taurus, I literally thought to myself that I hoped I was given a blue car. I was not. Mine was gold. I was sincerely disappointed. Life is hard sometimes.

Once I buckled into my gold Taurus, my plan was simple. Drive north on the Patriot Freeway, past Fort Bliss and just east of the Franklin Mountains.

As I approached the El Paso office of Almohada, I realized it was a part of a collection of buildings, which due to their proximity of each other, gave off the feel of a strip mall, but none of the buildings were actually connected. Each building was separated by the narrowest of gaps. You could barely fit a fist between them, but nonetheless, separate buildings they were despite appearing as one at quick glance.

The lot was at the corner of Dyer and Hercules. I was able to initially drive by the front of Almohada, turn right onto Hercules, and then turn right again into a parking lot that gave me a view of the backside of the building. Nothing stood out other than the fact there wasn't a loading dock to speak of, meaning any and all shipments received were small in nature and possibly delivered through regular mail or courier.

As I returned to Dyer, I noticed across the street was a FoodMart, that had a large parking lot that I could use to sit and view Almohada without people being suspicious. The market was fairly busy, even for a weekday afternoon. Traffic came and went throughout much of the day.

I found a parking spot that gave me a straight view to Almohada. To the right was the Bueno Suerte pool hall, which according to their window displays, had hundreds of slot machines. To the left was a small taco truck, Super Almuerzo, which blocked my view of the building to the left of Almohada.

For the time being, I sat positioned among a flurry of activity in the supermarket lot. I sat and watched. Nothing happened. For a very long time. I took a respite and went inside to the supermarket, used the men's room, bought a soda pop and a small bag of chips and returned to my stakeout in the now early afternoon heat of southwest Texas.

I rolled down the window of my car and let the morning heat consume me. I reached for the bag of chips when my phone rang.

"Hello?" I said as I opened the bag.

"How's El Paso?" Bullock asked. "Have you had any authentic food yet?"

"I'm about to have a bag of chips."

"You can have chips anywhere," he said with great disdain.

"I can have Mexican food anywhere," I said.

"Not authentic Tex-Mex, my friend."

"Did you actually call me just to ask if I have eaten any local food?" I asked.

"Yep," he said. "See you when you get back."

And that was it. He hung up. I shook my head and returned my attention to my chips, which were delicious by the way. Took a sip of my soda and then returned my attention to across the street.

More nothing happened. A lot more. As the minutes crept into a couple of hours, and the soda pop took it's toll, another men's room trip was in order. I figured enough time had lapsed that the market was a good option, but if I went across to Bueno Suerte, I could get a closer look of Almohada as I crossed the street.

As I approached the pool hall, I could see above their one story building to the second level of Almohada. It looked like any other two story business on every street of commerce in America.

211

I went inside the pool hall and looked around a bit. For an early afternoon on a Tuesday, the place was hopping. Lights were flashing, horns and sirens were filling the air, and smoke engulfed you upon entry.

I was wearing cargo shorts and a button up shirt. It's pretty common style for men my age. But not in southwest Texas apparently. I should've worn jeans, a huge belt buckle, a long-sleeve buttoned-up shirt and a cowboy hat. And that was just the women.

My camera bag was probably a dead giveaway that I wasn't a local. Nonetheless, I wandered around the place for awhile and sat at the bar. I ordered an Estrella Jalisco and sat and watched the crowd.

No one paid me any attention, other than an occasional, quick glance at my outfit. I walked back toward the entrance and sat at the bar tabletop that gave me a front row seat to Dyer Avenue.

While I enjoyed my beer, I watched dozens of people come and go from Super Almuerzo. I figured they probably had a good sense of what great local food was, and who was I to argue with local opinion. Drinking on a fairly empty stomach probably wasn't the best idea I had, as well.

I finished the beer, no sense in wasting it, and headed back out to the street and ordered two tacos de cerdo with guacamole.

While waiting for my order, I decided to take a peak at Almohada. Nothing to write home about. I guess I was hoping for a large, neon sign that flashed "drug manufacturing center".

I sat down at a small table, set my camera bag on the chair next to me and looked about at the activity, occasionally zeroing in on Almohada.

"Your tacos, senor," a young man said as he set my food in front of me.

"Thank you," I said as he disappeared as fast as he arrived.

I took a bite of taco and continued to look about at the other buildings in the makeshift mini plaza. Something caught my eye next door to Almohada. I slowly stood up and focused my eyes on the listing of the tenants. There were a small handful of businesses listed on the glass door. But there was one that I zeroed in on. I approached slowly, not losing my lock on the words until they were crystal clear.

"Well, I'll be damned," I said aloud.

I pulled out my phone, flipped it open and dialed, all the while never taking my eyes off the listing outside the double-door entry to a run of the mill building that you find in every town. Even Stonington. But with much less Spanish.

"Captain," I said into the phone. "Well, Almohada didn't produce much of anything, so far. But what is interesting, is what's next door."

I explained to the Captain what I saw, that I was going to cancel my hotel for the night and book an earlier flight home.

I pulled out my camera and snapped a few photos.

I returned to the table and took another bite of taco. I wiped my mouth with a napkin and tossed the remnants in the nearest trash can. I dodged a few cars crossing the street, heard a few honks of car horns and received a friendly one-finger wave from an agitated driver.

It wasn't a long stay in El Paso. But it was potentially a very rewarding one.

# 23

# You Definitely Look Like A Peter Pan Guy

I was still a little jet lagged from my two flights in a 12-hour span. Not sure how pilots do that everyday as it drained a lot of energy from me. When I got to the station, I bee-lined straight to the coffee pot. I poured a cup of straight, black coffee and gave it a short, cursory blow to cool it. Close enough. Down the hatch it went.

The second cup I poured, I paid closer attention to how I actually like my coffee. Two cream, two sugars. I gave it a little stir and headed toward my desk.

"So, how was Texas?" Bullock asked.

Blowing on my coffee, I answered, "It was hot."

"Hot!" he said while raising his arm in the air. "Like your mom, am I right?"

Bullock slowly lowered his arm in embarrassment. He was pondering something. It must've been deep.

"Are you okay?" I asked.

"Did your mom pass away?" he asked with deep concern.

I was totally baffled. I had no idea where he was going with this.

"I don't mean recently," he said. "I mean, did she pass away? Like awhile ago? If so, I feel horrible for that joke."

"Nah," I said. "My mom lives in Arizona with my dad."

"Oh thank God," he said with deep relief.

"You want to see a picture of her to see if you still think she's hot?"

"Dude," he said. "That's not cool."

"But saying my mom is hot is cool?" I asked.

"Hot is cool?" Bullock said while laughing. "Anyway, mom jokes are fair game. It's not about your mom specifically, but your mom in a more of a general sense. You know, like, much wider than an individual person."

"Speaking of wider," I said. "How's your mom doing?"

\* \* \*

I stood at the podium at the front of the conference room. I was surrounded by pieces of evidence we had collected in trying to solve the Carson McCall murder. That investigation lead us to discover something much larger than we had anticipated. It was about to increase even further.

Evans, Bullock and Captain Leonard were present. Betsy was invited, but she said she would be late.

"As you know," I opened. "Yesterday, I was in El Paso. My goal was to check out the activity at the Almohada branch there."

I passed pieces of paper to each of them and slid one to where I assumed Betsy would sit when she arrived.

"What the hell is this?" Bullock asked.

Captain Leonard was squinting at the paper and then it turned it on it's side.

"Well," I said. "I got a new camera and each photo is saved on a little disc. But I couldn't figure out how to get it from the disc to the computer."

"Did you photo copy your camera?" Evans asked.

"Well, I loaded the photo into the screen on the camera and then photocopied that," I said.

The three of them stared at me for a few moments.

"Never mind the photo," I said. "What the photo is supposed to tell you is there's a law firm that sits right next door to Almohada in El Paso."

Bullock tried to make out the photo more clearly to no avail.

"What's name of the firm?" he asked.

"Well, the name is Salazar, Soto and Gonzalez," I said. "But that's not really the important part. It's what's underneath their name."

"And what's that?" Evans asked. "Because I sure as hell can't figure it out."

"They're part of a larger collection of attorneys," I said.

I walked toward the board and wrote down the name.

"Wait, why do I know that?" Bullock asked.

"You know Trade Logistics Group?" Evans followed.

I started to smile because I knew it was coming together for Bullock. I was just going to give it the time he needed.

"Holy shit," he said.

There it is.

"What?" Evans said with great excitement. "What is it?"

Bullock stood up and walked toward the board.

"That's the group that Constance Capel belongs to," he said.

"Exactly!" I said as if he answered the final question on a

216

game show.

"How the heck do you know that?" Evans asked.

"It's on her door," I said. "Underneath her firm's name, it says the same thing. They're part of the same organization."

"After Brody called me to tell me of his find," Captain Leonard said. "I made a few calls and was able to get the lowdown on Trade Logistics Group. From the information I was provided, by two very valuable resources, it's a small firm with four offices. Obviously, the one here in town, and equally obvious is the location down in El Paso."

"During my initial contact with each of the tenants after the murder of Carson McCall," I said. "Sera, the receptionist for Constance Capel mentioned they had four offices. The other being in Miami and one across the bridge from Detroit in Windsor. What I didn't understand at the time, but I do now, is the 'we' wasn't referring to Constance Capel specifically, but this Logistics Group."

"My sources were able to tell me that there's only one to three attorneys at each office," Leonard said. "All told, they only handle a small amount of clients and none of the shipments imported, or exported, are very large."

"Small enough to stay underneath the radar?" Bullock asked.

"What's weird is," Leonard said. "They're almost too small. Each shipment they receive, apparently, is too small to be of significance at all."

"What do you mean?" Evans asked.

"Neither of my contacts said that any shipment coming in would be large enough to be profitable for a large smuggling operation," he said. "What's funny is, they both said it's too small-time for the cartels to even bother with and it's not enough for the DEA to get involved, either."

"So, it's large enough to be profitable for someone here, and perfectly small enough to go unnoticed," I said.

"The crux of the group appears to be clients who need a small amount of materials shipped from one vendor," Leonard said. "For example, they have a few interior decorators who will need a chair, or a vase, or something. This group helps the process of securing the product and getting it through customs."

"And if they facilitate a small amount of narcotics traffic simultaneously," I said. "Who's to know?"

"Not be the bearer of bad news," Leonard said. "But their role in all of this is moot. We can't go after the attorneys, as any communication between them and any of their clients is going to be protected. It's going to be nearly impossible for us to crack that egg."

"What do you suggest is our focal point from here?" I asked.

"If we can find a money trail," Leonard said. "We can find the brain trust."

"I think I can help with that," Betsy said as she entered the room.

"You heard all that in the hallway?" Bullock asked.

"No," she said. "I was standing there listening for a few minutes. Do you think I have the ears of a rabbit or something?"

Betsy sat down at the table, opened her briefcase and pulled out several pieces of paper, binder clipped together, and started passing them out to everyone like a card dealer at a casino.

"What are these?" Bullock asked.

"I'll explain," she said.

"Well, they appear to be pretty clear photos of people," Evans said as she thumbed her way through the stack of papers she received. "How did you ever master the technology to take photos and then transfer them so effortlessly producing such quality images for us?"

"I'm sorry, I don't understand," Betsy said. "It's not that hard."

Betsy was confused, I wasn't amused, but everyone else in the room had a hearty chuckle. How nice for them.

"Inside joke," Leonard said. "Please ignore them and continue."

"Well, I spent the last few days thinking about how we got here, to this point," Betsy said. "I mean from the young man in the park to Carson McCall, everyone and everything in between, to this moment."

"You spent the weekend at the arcade?" I asked.

I said the words. They flowed off my lips so easily. But as I was staring at the pictures Betsy took of the arcade, I realized the importance of what I was seeing.

"Son of a bitch," I said.

"You got it," Betsy gleefully added, as she knew she and I were on the same page.

"If this is, in fact, how they are moving the money," Leonard said. "How do we connect it to the case?"

"Let me go back," Betsy said. "I literally spent hours staring at the evidence photos and pouring through every detail I could. I had a nagging thought. We know Tom Downing and Carson McCall are connected, right?"

Everybody in the room nodded in agreement.

"But why?" she asked. "Why do we know they're connected? It's kind of obvious. We do. We just do. Pieces came together that connected them. But it gnawed at me. I couldn't shake this question. How are they connected?"

"One was a dealer," I said. "The other was a customer. Pretty simple."

"That's just it," she said. "We know one was a dealer. And we know one was a customer. But does that complete the story on these two?"

"Are you saying there's more?" Evans asked.

"Maybe, maybe not," Betsy conceded. "I'm not sure who Tom Downing was, as a complete human being, to be honest. That being said, I looked over the report you and Brody wrote concerning his death. It was all run-of-the-mill information."

"Thanks, I guess," I said. Not sure if run-of-the-mill is a compliment or a criticism.

"I did the same thing with McCall's death," she continued. "Again, nothing that I would say set off bells and whistles."

Betsy took out additional papers from her briefcase and distributed them across the table to each of us.

"On the left column," she said. "Are things found at the scene of Downing's overdose. What he was wearing. What was found on him."

I, like I'm assuming everyone else did, gave a look over the list. Nothing alarming. Until the bottom of the list. There it was in black and white. Normally, it would not have caused me any concern. But now I have context. My heart started to race. I knew it was going to say the same thing on the list of items found at the scene of Carson McCall's death. I glanced to the right side of the page. The same words appeared.

"Holy hell," Bullock said.

"Right!" Betsy excitedly said.

We all now had the connection that was needed. Sort of.

"They both had tokens from The Funhouse on them," Leonard said. "All we can do is make assumptions. But we do need more, as this is circumstantial. Also, are we saying Tom Downing was also dealing?"

"And are they dealing out of The Funhouse?" I asked.

"I don't think so, on the latter," Betsy said. "As for the former, Captain, I'm not sure what Tom Downing was doing to be honest. All I know is the two of them had enough of a connection, in my eyes, to The Funhouse, that I thought I would keep an eye on it for a few days.

Here's how I spent the last few days. On Friday, I went over there and actually went inside. An old lady in the arcade would stand out. So I approached the counter, told them I had never been inside before and I had my grandsons coming to visit this weekend."

"You have grandsons?" I asked.

"For the story, yes," she said.

That's a peculiar answer to a pretty common question. At least for people of Betsy's age. I think.

"The employees were very nice," she continued. "They showed me around and let me know what all was available to the boys. I wasn't able to stay too long, as that would've been weird. What I learned, however, is an old woman creeping about is only weird because young people assume that's what old people do, especially when it involves new technology such as video games."

"Video games have been around for decades," Bullock said.

"Newer video games," she said stressing the first word. "The next day I returned. Busy Saturday. I let the boys run wild. Spent a hell of lot of money, mind you."

"So you do have grandsons," I said.

"Stop interrupting," she fired back. "With the boys running amok, I was able to sit at their small, I don't know what call it, lunchroom, maybe. They have a few tables and chairs and you can buy junk food and such. It's not really a room, as there

221

aren't any walls or doors separating you. Whatever. I sat at one of the tables and drank a Diet Coke and watched. And watched. And watched."

"So you're saying you did some watching," Bullock said.

Betsy glared at Bullock.

"Brody is right about you," she said.

Bullock looked at me with sad, puppy eyes. I shrugged my shoulders as a sign to him that I had no idea what she was talking about. Betsy and I will discuss boundaries later.

She continued.

"Over the several hours we were there," she said. "A couple young men came in and went straight to the token machine. They didn't come in together. They came in a couple hours apart. But anyway, both of them probably put several hundred dollars into the token machine."

Despite the shooting and us arresting people, one thing was evident.

"Business must go on," I said. "Despite us putting a clamp on any new deliveries, there's probably still product out there."

"And these guys had to follow procedure," Bullock said.

"Especially if they believe someone was killed for not sticking to the rules," Evans added.

"What made it more obvious what they were doing, again, in my eyes," Betsy said. "Is both guys, almost to a T, did the exact same thing with the tokens. They just walked around and passed them out to kids playing video games. I don't think there's that many generous people walking around Stonington. Especially teenagers."

"Yeah, they're the worst," Bullock said.

"Do we know owns The Funhouse?" Leonard asked.

"Faron Martin," Betsy said.

"And what do we know about him?" Leonard asked.

"Not a lot there to raise our antennae," Betsy said. "I kept a close eye on The Funhouse all weekend. I couldn't say definitively, as I wasn't inside, but it seemed to me, at least, that Sunday they had a few more of these foot soldiers come in. They all have that look. You know what I mean?"

We consider that profiling in law enforcement, but none of us were going to correct her.

"We also happen to have the benefit of the calendar," Betsy said.

None of the rest of us knew what that meant.

"What was Monday?" she asked.

"I'm assuming Monday isn't the answer you're looking for?" Bullock said.

"More specifically," she said. "What date?"

"June 30th," Leonard said.

"Correct," she said. "June 30th. Now the rest of this story just happened to fall into place. The final day of the fiscal quarter, which in itself isn't definitive, but what happened after, was a roll of the dice."

"And what was that?" I asked.

"I waited all day yesterday and nothing happened," she said. "I was hoping something was going to happen today. I would have waited until tomorrow and since Friday is July 4th, I would have been willing to wait until next week. Even though I wasn't guaranteed it would happen at all."

The rest of the room was anxious to hear where this was going.

"This morning," she continued. "Faron Martin exited The Funhouse with a briefcase. Faron Martin isn't a briefcase kind of guy. Wherever he was going, he wanted to look professional. Horrible shirt and tie combo, wrinkled pants. The works."

223

"Where did he go?" I asked.

"Hold that thought," she said as she pulled out another piece of paper. This time she only had one copy. She held it high and showed it to each of us for greater impact. It was a picture of two guys near a car.

"The guy all dolled up is Faron," she said. "The other guy is one of those soldiers who came in and dumped some serious amount of cash into his token machine. I watched him pass out tokens like they were fliers to strip clubs in Vegas."

She paused and looked right at Bullock.

"Not a word from you," she pointedly said.

Looking at Bullock's wide grin, he was about to pounce on the strip club comment, before she halted his progress.

"At that point," she continued. "I knew that Faron was not only well aware of the scheme, he was quite possibly behind it. Now the key would be where he was going."

She paused. She gave a wry smile. She wanted to build drama.

"He went straight to the Booker Building," she said breaking the tension in the room.

"To meet with Don Barton," I confidently said.

"That wasn't my first guess," she said bursting my bubble. "Remember the date."

"He met with Drake & Brahms," Captain Leonard said.

"Bingo!" she exclaimed. "He was meeting with his accountants since the quarter just ended. I can imagine you'd want to have pretty concrete paperwork with a cash business such as an arcade."

"And if I'm their accountant," Evans said. "I wouldn't want everything at the end of the year. I'd want it as often as I could to cover my own ass."

Everyone looked at Bullock. He had a smile. He even had a

comment in his little head. He kept it to himself.

"What happened to the other guy?" I asked.

"Last I saw him, he was leaned up against the back of Faron's Saturn smoking a cigarette," she said.

"Are you sure that while you were following Faron, they weren't also following you?" I asked.

"Well, not until you just brought it up," she said.

"Brody and Bullock," Leonard said. "I want you to head over there and see what you can find out. In the meantime, I'm going to go see if we can get a whole slew of warrants for both the accountant and The Funhouse."

\* \* \*

Bullock and I headed up the stairs of the Booker Building. We turned right at the top of the stairs and headed for the second door.

"We're going to play it cool, and see what they offer up while we wait for Captain Leonard to let us know if he got the warrant," I said.

"I know," Bullock said. "I was there when he told us the plan."

"Just want to make sure we're on the same page," I said.

"We're always on the same page."

"Are we?" I asked as I opened the door to the office.

"I thought so," I heard Bullock mumble as I entered the office.

\* \* \*

Delilah Rendon was sitting behind the welcome counter.

"May I help you officers?" she asked as we approached.

"Yeah, I hope so," I said. "Are either Alexander or Jim here? We're working on a case and, I'm kind of embarrassed to admit this, but we have some technical aspects to it that is beyond our knowledge. I was hoping they could help guide us to a more definitive answer."

"Let me check with the boys," she said as she got up. "Wait right there and I'll be back in a jiffy."

Off she went down the hallway.

"Which do you like better?" Bullock asked. "Jif or Skippy?"

"What?" I asked with as much confusion as I've ever had with one of his questions.

"Jif or Skippy?" he said. "She said she'll be back in a jiffy, which I thought was funny because it combines Jif and Skippy. Which then made me think of peanut butter and how I'm a Jif guy. I was wondering which one you prefer."

"To be honest," I said. "I loved Velvet growing up."

"Velvet?" he asked.

"It was a pretty popular Detroit brand back in the day," I said.

"I figured you were going to say Peter Pan," he said. "You definitely look like a Peter Pan guy."

"What the hell does that mean?" I asked as Delilah returned.

"The boys will see you now," she said followed by a wave.

\* \* \*

With her left hand, Delilah opened the office door and stood off to the side as we entered. Alexander was seated behind his desk,

Jim was standing off to the left just a few feet behind Alexander's shoulder.

"Gentlemen," I said to Jim and Alexander. "I appreciate you making time for us."

"No problem, officers," Alexander said. "Do we need our attorneys?"

The question was followed with two very uncomfortable laughs from the two of them.

"Why?" Bullock jokingly asked. "Do you need attorneys?"

"I hope not," Jim said. He wasn't joking at all.

"Well, let's hope not," I said as I pulled out a chair. "Do you mind if we sit?"

I thought by offering to sit, it might ease some of the tension in the room. It's less formal than standing. At least when dealing with police officers. I wanted both of them to feel more comfortable.

"Sure thing," Alexander said. "Delilah, thank you."

"Would you officers like anything to drink?" she asked.

"I'll take a water if you don't mind," Bullock said.

"Nothing for me, thank you," I added.

Delilah made her way out of the office. She left the door ajar. I figured she was going to be as within earshot as she could. She seemed like a dedicated and loyal employee. I turned back to the two accountants and sat down. Bullock followed suit.

"I appreciate you helping us," I said.

"Well, I'm not sure what we can help with," Alexander said as he moved his chair forward slightly and placed his arms atop his desk and clasped his hands. Jim remained where he stood, almost statuesque.

"We are working on a case that has us baffled a little bit," I said. "We can't divulge too much information, as you can assume, but

227

this case is more, I don't know, technical in regards to business and accounting, if you will."

"Sounds intriguing enough," Alexander said.

"What we need you to do is pretend, for a second, you're trying to help a client of yours hide illegally gained money," I said.

"And from that," Bullock added. "How would you cover your bases. Legally."

Jim Abrahms looked a lot less comfortable. He didn't exactly exude confidence when we walked in, but whatever comfort level he had at the beginning, was much lower. Alexander was the better of the two at playing poker. Either that, or he had nothing to worry about and was demonstrating that belief accurately.

"What do you got?" Alexander said.

"Okay," I said. "How do you make sure a business, any business really, that deals in cash, is doing everything on the up-and-up? At least on your end."

"Receipts," Alexander pointedly said. "Listen, we have numerous clients that are cash based. Hair salons, restaurants, even smaller operations."

Alexander turned to Jim.

"What is Johnny?" Alexander asked. "19, 20-years old? Maybe."

"I think he's 20," Jim answered.

"Kid is 20 and running a lawn care company," Alexander said turning back toward us. "All that kid deals in is cash. We tell him to have receipts for everything. We meet with him every couple of weeks and make sure everything is good as far as the IRS. You'll be surprised who those bastards will go after. Can't be bothered to investigate a Congressman, but you bet your ass they'll hunt down a 20-year-old mowing lawns who can't account for $30."

"That's good," I said.

Delilah returned carrying a bottle of water.

"I don't mean to interrupt, gentlemen," she said as she handed Bullock the water.

"Southpaw?" Bullock asked Delilah.

"I'm sorry?" she asked, not understanding his question.

"You handed me the water with your left hand," he said. "I assume you are a southpaw. A lefty."

"Oh, yes," she said, still not quite sure what he was talking about.

"Southpaw, it's a baseball term," he said. "I played baseball."

"That's nice," she said as she went on her way.

As she left, she once again positioned the door strategically to allow her to eavesdrop if she so desired.

"Let me give you a different scenario though," I said continuing the conversation we were in prior to Delilah's water delivery. "Using that same kid, for example. Let's say Johnny has a side gig, maybe collecting money from another business."

Neither Jim nor Alexander reacted.

"Johnny's dealing weed to some of his clients," Bullock bluntly said, apparently thinking I was being too subtle in my scenario.

"What is the likelihood that you would know that?" I asked, building off of Bullock's directness.

"Would we know what?" Alexander asked. "Would we know he was dealing marijuana? As long as, in this case, Johnny, and I'm not comfortable using a good kid's name this way. As long as Johnny can account for every dollar spent and received, let's just say, for his primary business, and we can verify this through proper documentation, then we have no alternative to believe our clients are conducting business honestly."

"Have you ever had clients that you think might be less than honorable in their reports to you?" I asked.

"We have some clients that make it difficult to track their expenditures, sure," Jim said. "But all of our clients are able to provide the necessary documents."

"I got a scenario for you," Bullock said. "Let's just pretend you do know a client is engaged in an illegal activity."

"We wouldn't have them as a client," Alexander abruptly said.

"But let's pretend you, or another accountant, if you will, did," Bullock continued. "And the client had income that couldn't be accounted for. What would you recommend they do?"

"Strictly hypothetical?" Alexander asked.

Bullock and I nodded in the affirmative.

"We would probably recommend they take those funds and invest them," he continued. "Preferably in an offshore account. Hypothetically, of course."

"Have you ever heard stories of people around here that did stuff like that?" I asked.

There was a knock on the office door. The knock was louder than the other two times Delilah had knocked. If a knock could be angrier, this was it.

Bullock and I turned around. There was Delilah. But behind Delilah was Evans and few other members of the Stonington PD. Evans held up a piece of paper. It was the warrant we were waiting for.

I turned back to our dual accountants.

"Such as an arcade?" I asked.

* * *

We took everything that was pertaining to The Funhouse from the offices of Alexander Drake and Jim Abrahms, CPA.

In the conference room back at the station, we separated boxes by year. Any disks that were retrieved we placed at a work station with a computer. Evans was assigned the task of analyzing each disk to see what information could be found that was pertinent to our investigation.

"I never should have told anyone I minored in computer technology," Evans said as she started sorting the disks. She was really demonstrative in her sorting, as if she wanted us to fully realize her annoyance.

It didn't matter to the rest of us, we had our own mundane tasks we had to handle.

"I didn't go to college at all," I said. "Maybe Captain Leonard thinks I'm too stupid to work a computer."

"A computer technology degree is a little more advanced than putting a disk into a drive and reading the contents," she continued. "Any of you idiots could do this. Well, maybe not Bullock."

"Doesn't hurt my feelings," Bullock said as he dropped a pair of boxes onto the table. "All I know is I don't have to sit there staring at a computer all day."

"What's the difference between looking at a computer and looking at a ledger?" she asked.

"I don't know," he said. "I'm not doing your thing, so I'm not concerned about how it is similar or different from what I'll be doing."

\* \* \*

Bullock, at his desk, and me at mine, were both nose-deep into ledgers produced by Drake & Brahms for their client The Funhouse.

Captain Leonard came out of his office and without stopping his gait, said to the two of us, "let's go."

Like puppies following their mother, Bullock and I trailed him, not knowing where we we're going or why.

We walked into the conference room, where we could barely see the top of Evans' head from behind a computer terminal.

"What did you find?" Leonard asked Evans.

"Well, it wasn't very hard," she said. "Everything they've brought in is accounted for and well-documented. The arcade can show every nickle and dime received with invoices and receipts. Not sure the involvement of Drake & Brahms, at least as far as the paper trail is concerned. The accountants appear to be operating honestly. At least as far as a paper trail, we wouldn't have anything on them."

She stood up from her chair and walked toward a printer that was rigged up on the table next to the computer.

"But," she continued as a document was being printed. "They invested some of the money into an offshore account."

She pulled the paper from the printer and handed it to Leonard.

"Who's they?" I asked.

"The Funhouse," Leonard said not looking up from the paper he was given. "It looks like we have a couple more dominoes to knock down. I'm going to call Judge Long and let him know we need another warrant. He should have the one requested for The Funhouse prepared. We'll add this guy to the list. In the meantime, I need you and Bullock to go have a chat with him."

Leonard handed me the paper. I glanced it over and handed it to Bullock.

"Let's go for door number three," I said.

# 24

# Your Aunt Is Slutty

Bullock and I headed up the stairs of the Booker Building. We turned right at the top of the stairs and headed for the third door.

"Showtime," Bullock said as he opened the door and walked into the office of Colton Moore.

"Still no receptionist," I said as the two of us bypassed the lobby area and went straight to his office.

Before we reached the door, Moore, who was eating a bagel, looked up at us. Both Bullock and I flashed our badges. The look on Moore's face signaled to us he understood the magnitude of our visit.

"Colton Moore?" I rhetorically asked.

"Yes," Colton said, still holding half the bagel.

He answered with great fear in his voice. His face conveyed the same emotion.

"We'd like to ask you a few questions regarding your business dealings with The Funhouse," I said.

"Damn it," he angrily said.

He tossed the half bagel onto his desk, missing the napkin that held the other half. It slowly rolled about his desk until finally stopping cream cheese side down.

"I knew those assholes were up to something," he said.

"Why don't you go ahead and explain that," I said.

"I'm trying to get my book started, you know?" he said. "We're all small firms here in this building. We try to scratch each other's back when we can. I figured I could trust those people."

"What people?" Bullock asked.

"Next door," he said.

"Can you elaborate?" I asked.

"They said they had a client who wanted to protect assets as part of a future custody settlement," he said.

"Are you speaking of Faron Martin?" I asked.

"Yeah," he said. "Apparently, he took over the arcade from his stepfather. Faron has been running the business for a few years. I guess it's all sort of weird or something."

"How so?" I asked.

"Okay, let me explain it to you how it was explained to me," he said. "So there's Faron? Right? Well, Faron assumes the arcade from his mother's husband - Faron's stepfather. So Faron's stepfather, this is is second marriage as well, right?"

"As difficult as you made that, I'm surprisingly with you so far," Bullock said.

"Okay, then," Moore said as he took a napkin and wiped a little cream cheese from the side of his mouth. "Faron is running the business, his stepfather gets sick. The family thinks if they take some profit and move it to an offshore account - for Faron and his sister - that if something happens to the old man, his kids from his first marriage don't have a claim. That's what I was told."

It appears that at every turn, we've got a local business involved, unknowingly, in the distribution of drugs in Stonington. Whomever put this whole thing together had everything planned out.

"Let me ask you a question," I said. "To your knowledge, did the information you receive from Drake & Brahms seem legitimate?"

"What do you mean?" he asked.

"Did you have any reason to believe they were trying to skirt tax law or do anything else that seemed illegal to you?"

"Dude," he said. "I don't know what all this is about. Jim and Alex are just regular guys. We're all just trying to survive and help each other out. She asked me to help a client of theirs and I did. When I talked to them, they said all the information was accounted for and everything I received said the same thing."

"Who's she?" I asked. "You said she."

"Delilah," he said.

"Delilah Rendon is the person who referred Faron Martin to you?" I asked.

"Yeah, that's how we help each other," he said. "I was outside in the alley, smoking a cigarette and we got to talking. She said she had a client who might need my help. We talk a lot of shop out there. Sometimes I think it's weird, most of the time it's just fun chatter."

"It's weird between you and Delilah?" Bullock asked.

"Me, Delilah, Lydia and Sera," he said. "Me and three chicks. A lot of times they go off into some pretty raunchy territory. I didn't know women talked like that in their little groups. I always thought one day it'd get me in trouble. I just didn't think this would be the way."

"How did you think it was going to get you in trouble? Bullock asked.

"Let's just say my girlfriend isn't too keen on me being chummy with three women," he said. "I mean, come on. Get real. One could be my mother and another could be my slutty aunt."

"Your aunt is slutty?" Bullock asked.

"What the hell dude," he said with disgust. "I don't even have an aunt. But if you got a penis and you walk next door, Lydia is all over you. Delilah, on the other hand, is like the building mom. She's knows everyone's business and is always looking out for everyone. She's a sweetheart. She really is."

"What about Sera?" I asked.

"That's the one my girlfriend hates the most," he said.

"Why's that?" Bullock asked.

"Look at her," he said with a laugh. "You're not throwing her out of bed for eating crackers, if you know what I mean? Carmen, my girlfriend, says she's a fiery one. Not sure what that means, but Carmen says she can tell by just looking at her. Women always say they want equal rights, you know what I'm saying?"

"Not at all," I said.

"What I'm saying is," he said before pausing as if was about to unleash the wisdom of Aristotle. "That women say they wanted to be treated like men. You know who treats women the worst? Other women. It's true. There's not a sisterhood. There's absolutely a brotherhood. For sure. Bros before hos, you know what I mean? But there sure as hell ain't no sisterhood. Get one of them mad and it's a cat fight to the end. Even when there isn't an issue. That's how Carmen is with Sera, who I barely know. But Carmen is convinced she doesn't like her."

"That's a great story," I said. "However, all that being said, we have to get down to the nitty gritty. You're going to have to provide us with any and all documents regarding your dealings with The Funhouse."

"I hate to be a noodge, officers," he said. "But I have to protect myself. I can't lose clients because they found out I willingly betrayed a client's trust. I'm going to need a warrant. "

I reached into my jacket and pulled out a warrant.

"Like this one?" I said as I handed it to him.

Grabbing the paper, he unfolded it and looked it over.

"Yeah, like this one," he said.

\* \* \*

Bullock followed me to the car, as I set a few folders from Colton Moore onto the backseat.

"Do you think this leads back to Don Barton?" he asked.

"I have no idea," I admitted. "I was hoping so, but the further we get down this rabbit hole, the less likely it is, it seems."

"I was thinking the same thing," he said. "Only because no one has mentioned him in any of the interviews we've had recently. Official or unofficial."

"Who else would be able to pull all these strings, though?" I asked.

"I don't know, but we're getting close. I can feel it."

"I sure as hell hope so."

\* \* \*

"Man, I hope this doesn't take very long," Bullock said.

"Why's that?" I asked.

"I'm hungry," he said.

"You're always hungry. How is now any different than any other moment of the day?"

"Because now I'm super hungry," he said. "I'm hungry like the wolf."

Neither of us spoke for a few as we drove directly to The Funhouse. All I know, was I was instantly humming the classic Duran Duran song that Bullock, knowingly or unknowingly, put into my head. That was until he started belting out the chorus. For the next several minutes we both just sang like we didn't have a care in the world.

\* \* \*

We pulled into the gravel parking lot where only a few cars were parked. In fact, automobiles were outnumbered by bicycles by about four-to-one.

As I got out of the car, I looked across the street to an otherwise nondescript white van. Inside, I knew sat Evans, and two other members of the Stonington PD. The warrant to wiretap The Funhouse had been approved.

On the sidewalk, next to the van, were two city employees hanging signs on the lampposts. In two weeks was the annual Squash Bash, a downtown festival to celebrate the areas largest agricultural crop. Unbeknownst to the employees, and pretty much everyone else on the street at the time or the area as a whole, we were about to break wide open a drug dealing operation in its infancy. They were more focused ahead to the great social gathering of the summer.

I followed Bullock to the front door, but before entering the building, I took a look up into the sunlight beaming down. I took a deep breath. Sometimes being a police officer can be very rewarding, and not very satisfying, simultaneously. I felt that, at that moment.

Bullock opened the door and waved me inside.

"Age before beauty," he said.

Not an original line.

As we entered, reinforcements arrived in two other cars to help us execute our warrant.

* * *

In the Navy, I was a Master-at-Arms. Basically, we were called sea sheriffs. Most of my time as an MA was on shore, particularly when I was stationed at the base in Norfolk. I recalled an evening where I was to patrol Sewells Point, specifically many of the buildings in the oil recovery area.

It's a tedious and boring process going from door to door, checking the handle to see if it's locked or not. When your evening's excitement is an unlocked door, you know most of the time in your career can be drab.

One particular evening, I found my unlocked door. It was like manna from Heaven. I may actually have a story to tell my loved ones when they asked me how I was enjoying my military service, I thought to myself.

Well, it was indeed a story. Apparently the door in question was well-known to the more seasoned MAs. This particular section of the building had long been forgotten, and lost its usefulness. I was about to find out who, or what, had use for this closet-sized room.

I opened the door, turned on my flashlight and was greeted by the movement and sound of thousands of cockroaches scattering every which way the could. Including toward me. My feet were surrounded by the tiny offspring of the devil himself.

I'm sure I gave a pretty feminine squeal. I slammed the door and vigorously brushed every inch of my body to be free from my attackers.

That night came to mind as soon as I stepped foot inside The Funhouse. Without the squeal.

The room was full of preteens and teens, as well as a handful whose teen years weren't that long ago. Except one guy who was clearly trying to relive his teen years, although they were during the 80s.

When I say none of them were excited to see two members of the local police force, that is an understatement. Even the innocent looked guilty. A few were calculating the probability of them being able to make it to the front door. Some had an instant need to use the restroom. Some froze. There was a few of them that I recognized. A handful, based on their experience with law enforcement, knew enough to mind their own business and don't bring attention to yourself.

We were there for only one person. I turned to the young man standing behind a counter full of cheap toys that were given out as prizes.

"You, in the Nirvana shirt," I said to the pimpled-face, scrawny teenager in the band tour shirt, and pants that sat way too low exposing his drawers for the world to see. "Where's Faron Martin?"

All he could muster in his panicked state was to point to a door at the far end of the room.

"Thanks," I said as Bullock and I continued on our way through the heart of the arcade.

Teenagers pressed themselves as closely to their various video games as they could.

"You think this is what Moses felt when the sea parted?" Bullock asked.

That was funny. I had to suppress a laugh. It didn't seem right to laugh as kids looked at you petrified.

"I got high score on that once," Bullock said to me as we passed Galaga. "Did you ever play video games?"

"I was okay," I said. "I played Joust a lot, and Ms. Pac Man, of course."

"Joust?" he asked. "Never heard of it."

"You flew on a duck or some large bird, I think," I said. "And you had a giant sword or something and had to joust opponents."

"Little hazy on the details," Bullock said.

"Regardless, it was super fun," I said. "I also liked Dig Dug, now that I think of it. And Rampage."

"Are you just making these up?"

"They're actual games," I said.

"Sounds like you played some pretty lame games."

"What did you play?" I asked. "Other than Galaga."

"I was pretty legit at Mortal Kombat," he answered.

"That sounds about right," I said.

"What does that mean?" he incredulously asked.

The door to Faron Martin's office opened as we approached. Someone must've notified him of our arrival.

"Officers," he said with a slight crack in his voice. "Can I help you?"

I reached into my pocket and pulled out the warrant.

# 25

# Not My Concern

I leaned back in my chair and attempted to stretch out my neck. I turned my head in every possible direction hoping that I could get a soothing crack, to no avail. I sunk my head and took both hands and rubbed my eyes, moving towards my ears and down my cheek bone. I had been staring at spreadsheets and reports and receipts and anything and everything that had either a Western Arabic number or an English letter on it.

I was in charge of all the files we grabbed from The Funhouse. Bullock was analyzing the information from Drake & Abrahms.

I glanced over to see how Bullock was faring with his task.

His head was leaned back in his chair. Only he wasn't trying to stretch. He had a long string of taffy from his mouth all the way up to his right hand, which was high above his face. He let go and let the taffy fall into his mouth.

"Busy?" I asked.

"Not really," he mumbled as he started chewing. "I pretty much went through everything already. There was only a few folders. You're the one who picked to review all those boxes."

The truth of the matter is, everything I found of value was

already in the folders provided by the accountants. No new information was unearthed. Everything was accounted for. Sure, the arcade had a serious uptick in revenue in the last year, but all of that could legitimately be attributed to the business being transferred into younger management. At least that's the argument I'd make if I was a defense attorney.

Captain Leonard and Evans entered the conference room. Evans was beaming. She looked like she was about to explode from excitement. Leonard seemed unfazed by what was about to happen. Either he had no idea, or he was a much cooler cookie. No wonder I lost money to this man playing poker.

Evans set a tape recorder down on the table.

"As you can tell, Evans is quite excited to share something with the two of you," Leonard said.

Evans sat down. She looked at me and then turned to Bullock. Back to me.

"Are we getting this telepathically?" I asked.

"I wanted to make sure I had your attention," she said.

She reached over and pressed play. She hit the stop button almost as quickly.

"That was riveting," Bullock said.

"I have to set it up first," she said. "The first voice you'll hear is Faron Martin. The call he made is a little after you guys left the arcade. The second voice was unknown to us until we ran the number. Listen."

She pressed play a second time.

"The cops were just here," Faron said with distress in his voice. "This shit is getting serious."

"You need to calm down," a female voice said. I knew that voice, but I couldn't place it. "Where are you calling from?"

"The arcade," he said.

"You're such an idiot," she said. "You call me from the arcade and you call my cell phone. Hang up and we'll meet in person. You should've called the office."

"Why?" he asked. "What difference does it make?"

"Because the office line would be protected by attorney client privilege, you moron," she said.

I placed the voice.

"I know who that is," I blurted out.

"Shh," Evans said before hitting the stop button again.

"But it's Sera from Capel's office," I said.

"I know," Evans said. "But you missed it. Listen to what she said."

She hit rewind and then pressed play again.

"She's going to be pissed you called my cell," Sera continued. "I'll get with you later."

Evans stopped the recording.

"Is she talking about Constance Capel?" I asked.

"It has to be, right?" Bullock said.

"We don't know officially," Leonard said.

"What we do know," Evans said. "Is that we were able to trace the call and identify who he called."

"It's the receptionist, Sera," I emphatically said.

"Shh," Evans responded.

"Why does she keep telling me to shh?" I asked Bullock.

"Shh, I'm paying attention," he said.

Jackass.

"When we traced the number it came back as a personal cell phone for Sera Gonzalez," Evans said.

"It's a huge break that it's her personal cell number," Leonard said. "If the law firm provided that phone to her, anything we had collected would have been thrown out. But her personal

246

phone is not covered by privilege, since she herself, is not an attorney."

"So we're not going to be impeded by using that conversation?" I asked.

"I'm proceeding that we're okay to use it," Leonard said. " They could argue otherwise, but I like our chances. We need to find out who the female referenced by Sera Gonzalez is."

"It has to be Constance Capel," I said. "Correct? And if so, is she running everything? Because if so, we're kind of screwed."

"I thought you liked Don Barton for this?" Bullock asked.

"Him too," I said. "He could be hiding behind Constance Capel."

"Well, if the attorney is involved," Leonard added. "This case just got a lot harder. We know we're not going to get anywhere with Capel. We're probably not going to get much further with Gonzalez. We got to see if Martin will crack somehow. Go find him and see where it leads."

\* \* \*

"Man, we haven't been on a stakeout together for quite some time," Bullock said.

"Nope," I answered.

"So," he said. "How's it going?"

I looked over at him. He had a weird grin on his face.

"Good," I said wondering what his deal is this time.

I knew he wanted to say something. He was like a puppy dog waiting for their owner to arrive. I was surprised I couldn't see his tail wagging.

"Are you okay?" I asked.

"Yep," he giddily said.

"That's nice," I answered knowing I was going to have to eventually say what he wanted me to say. I let him wait a little longer.

"How are you?" I asked allowing him to release all his energy.

"I think this weekend is the weekend," he said. "If you know what I mean."

"Nope," I said.

I had a feeling. The bastard was going to beat me to the punch, I just knew it. Questions filled my head. When was the weekend it was going to be the weekend in my case? Did I have to make it a weekday now? Did it have to wait until fall? Is he doing it in the day time or night? Will I have to pick a different time of day? Is he making it formal? Casual? Inside? Outside? Son of a bitch I had a lot overwhelming me.

"I'm going to ask Alicia to marry me," he said.

"Yeah, I figured that's what you meant," I answered.

I didn't mean to sound disappointed in my friend's exciting moment.

"I'm sorry, Bullock," I continued. "I didn't mean to ruin your moment. I'm happy for you. And Alicia. I bet you're pretty excited."

"It's going to be the greatest day of my life," he said confirming what I had thought for a very long time. Alicia was the most important thing to him. Nothing else mattered.

"She's my everything," he added.

Sometimes, you got to just love this guy.

"Marrying one friend is awesome," he continued. "But beating another friend to the punch, makes it even better."

What a dick. I hate this guy.

* * *

"What time do they close?" Bullock asked.

"8 p.m.," I said.

We had been sitting in the car for four hours and in the last two hours not a single soul entered the arcade. We had less than 10 minutes remaining until Faron Martin was closing his business.

Bullock and I figured he already had phone calls with his sister and her attorney. Who is now probably his attorney. The door was closing and it was closing fast. We needed a break.

* * *

"How long does it take to close an arcade?" Bullock asked.

"How the hell would I know," I said. "I've never worked at an arcade."

"Have you been to an arcade?" he asked.

"Yes, I have been to an arcade," I said, annoyed that the question suggested I was some old, decrepit geezer. "They had them in my time."

"It was probably hard to put the two bits in the machine, though," he said.

"Did I ever tell you that no one likes you?" I asked.

"People like me," he said. "I happen to love me, but I understand, that that level of appreciation is pretty rare. But most people like me. I'm like candy."

"I'm going to regret this, but how are you like candy?" I asked.

"You know it's bad for you," he said. "Like it's so good in your mouth, and you know you enjoyed it. You shouldn't have. You vowed you'd cut back. But you'll want some more. You'll want some more soon."

"If you ever say so 'good in your mouth' again, I'll knock the shit out of you."

"So good," he said. "So, so good."

"Don't," I said, raising my hand to him like a parent to a child when the parent has had enough.

"In your mouth," he continued.

That was the longest night of my life.

* * *

At nearly 9:00 p.m., Faron Martin opened the front door of The Funhouse and exited the building. He turned to check the lock on the door and walked over to the mailbox on the wall and took a peak inside.

"Who gets their mail at the end of the day?" Bullock asked.

I wasn't sure if that was an actual question or rhetorical. I treated it as rhetorical.

Faron got inside his rust-filled Taurus.

"I bet he hasn't washed that car in years," Bullock said. "If he washes it, all the rust will fall off and he won't have a car at all."

Faron started the car and turned on the lights.

"Hell yes," I said.

"We caught out break," Bullock said as he sprung to life.

Faron backed out of his spot near the front of the building and prepared to exit the lot. Before he did, he checked traffic to his left and his right. He then looked across the street right at us.

"Do you think he sees us?" Bullock asked.

"I'm sure he sees us," I said. "The question is does he knows it's us us or just some regular people."

Faron turned on his signal to turn left.

"He knows it's us," I said. "He's going to try to be a textbook driver. Except he's forgetting one thing."

I turned on our car. Faron turned left onto the road and passed by us as our front lights lit up the interior nearly blinding him. We turned right and didn't make the pursuit last very long. We hit the flashers and he immediately pulled over.

* * *

I approached the vehicle on the left. As I reached the trunk, I touched his vehicle to mark my presence there in case something went sideways with this stop. Many police officers use this tactic to prove that they pulled over this specific vehicle.

Bullock strategically positioned himself near the rear, right door. He also was prepared in case it became eventful. If he had to shoot his weapon, I wasn't in his line of fire.

Despite being a summer night, Faron had his windows up. He rolled down the driver's side window slightly.

"Can I help you officers?" he asked as he tried to peer through the small crack in the window.

"Do you know why I pulled you over?" I asked.

"No, sir," he said.

"Your right tail light is out," I said.

I took a step back to check out the rear seat. I smiled.

"License and registration," I said. "Sir, have you been

drinking this evening?"

"Huh?" he said as he fidgeted in his wallet to retrieve the documents I requested.

"Have you been drinking sir?" I reiterated.

"No," he emphatically said. "I've only been in the car for a few minutes. I was working. I just closed."

"Where do you work, sir?" I asked.

"Are you kidding me?" he incredulously asked. "You know where I work. You know who I am. And you've been watching me all day. This is unbelievable."

He turned to see where Bullock was. He looked around as if he was hoping someone would be there to help him out.

"Are you looking for someone, sir?" I asked.

"This is bullshit," he said. "I'm hoping there's witnesses."

He was getting more and more agitated.

"Sir, I see a few empty cans in your back seat," I said. "I'm going to have to ask you step out of the vehicle."

"Are you freaking kidding me?" he asked. "This is entrapment."

He swung opened his door and stepped out of the vehicle.

"Partner, this gentleman wasn't wearing a seat belt," I said as I looked across the roof of the car to Bullock. "Please make note of that."

"You guys are assholes," he said.

"I'm going to ask you to step to the back of the vehicle," I said. "My partner here will be conducting the rest of the search of your vehicle."

Faron Martin got pale. Very pale. Panic was setting in. His look was a clear indication there was something in the car he didn't want us to find.

"Bullock," I said as I kept my eyes focused on Faron. "Look

very carefully."

While Bullock searched the vehicle I wrote down Faron's information into my notepad. Faron was fidgety and kept trying to turn around to see what Bullock was doing.

"Is there something in the vehicle you need, sir?" I asked.

He didn't answer. His breathing increased in pace. He was swallowing more frequently.

"I'm almost done here," I said. "But I am going to have to give you a breath analyzer."

"Whatever," he said. "You know I wasn't drinking."

Clunk. The sound was unmistakable. I turned to see if what I knew that sound to be was confirmed. It was. I smiled at Faron Martin. He did not smile back.

"Sir?" I asked. "Is that weapon registered?"

\* \* \*

Downtown Stonington at night during the summer, is what is right about small-town life.

People were milling about, the restaurants were full and smiles were had everywhere.

Well except for the back seat of our patrol car.

Faron Martin had an unregistered Colt 1991 hmm Luger in the glove compartment of his car. That gun was tagged and sat in the trunk of our car. Our hope was that ballistics would match the weapon to the murder of Carson McCall.

Looking in the rear view mirror, it was quite clear that Faron was making some serious life decisions. The realization that he was looking at a life sentence was sinking in. His head hung low for most of the trip. When he did lift his head to look out the windows, we could see tears streaming down his face. He could see other residents of Stonington enjoying their evening, but when they noticed us, they tried to catch a glimpse of the backseat passenger of our car. Faron would quickly drop his again.

I never liked talking to people I've arrested while I'm transporting them. I always felt my best questions were asked during the interrogation process. I felt like, for some reason, most people who are arrested are still bargaining with themselves, thinking there's a way out of this while we're en route. But once processed and sitting in an otherwise barren interrogation room, reality sinks in and there's less hope and more willingness to listen intently to their options. Most times.

Bullock was more of an small-talk chit-chatter.

"A Colt, huh?" he asked. "I got a Sig Sauer P226. Which is weird, you know?"

Faron wasn't as interested in conversing.

"The reason it's weird is," Bullock continued. "Is my partner here was in the Navy. He told me he used to have a P226 specifically made for the Navy SEALs. Isn't that right, partner?"

I simply nodded in the affirmative.

"Not sure how he got it?" Bullock said as he turned to look at Faron in the backseat. "He never told me. So I think it's weird. You know what I'm saying. It's like doubly weird."

Faron never looked up. I never looked away from the road.

"Doubly weird," Bullock said. "Weird because we - my partner and I - both have used the same gun. Not at the same time, mind you. But what's weirder, at least to me, is he won't tell me how he got his hands on his P226, and you, my friend, aren't telling me how a Colt ended up in your glove box. Don't you find that weird?"

Faron's head remained hung low.

We stopped at a red light in the heart of downtown. Passersby tried as best they could to sneak a peek at Faron, without looking too obvious. Everybody is interested in gazing upon others when they're at their lowest. A morbid curiosity that gets the best of us.

I looked in the mirror again. Faron had his head turned to his left. I looked out my side window and a little behind me. Sitting in the passenger seat of a minivan was a small child in their car seat staring at Faron. The child was too young to understand what was going on. But Faron kept his eyes fixed on the child. To be inside Faron's mind would be quite interesting at this moment.

The light turned green and we continued on our way.

* * *

After being processed, Faron was placed in one of our interrogation rooms. Bullock and I were more than ready to ask him several questions. But we sat in the adjoining room, behind the one-way glass and watched him for several minutes. We didn't speak to each other as I assumed Bullock was doing what I was doing: formulating the best and most concise questioning we could muster. We had to get this right. By observing him for a few minutes, we caught a glimpse into this mental state and that gave us a pathway we could stroll down to our destination.

"What are you thinking?" I finally asked Bullock. "Direct or indirect?"

"I'm thinking go right for the jugular," he said.

I agreed.

"Let's go," I said.

* * *

"Well jeepers creepers," I said as Bullock and I entered the room. "You are facing some serious time, my friend."

Bullock sat down first, as I slid a manila folder to Faron.

"Here," I said to him as he just stared at the closed folder.

"Let me open that, since your hands are otherwise restrained."

I turned the first page. Then the second. I paused a few seconds, then turned another. I repeated the process several more times.

"You're never getting out is the point," I said. "Luckily, there's no death penalty in the state of Michigan. Otherwise, you'd be lit up like a Christmas tree on the people's dime."

I moved to the other side of the table, pulled out a chair, and sat down. I stared at Faron for a few seconds. He was emotionless. I think every possible feeling he could have had during the last several hours had escaped him. He was mentally and physically taxed. I reached across the table, closed the envelope and slid it back towards me.

"Listen," I said. "You know there's no way you're escaping this. We have so much incriminating information on you, it's just a matter of how much time are you willing to do."

I leaned back in my chair. I turned to Bullock. That was his cue.

"Did you kill Carson McCall?" my partner asked.

Faron looked at Bullock and looked at me and pursed his lips.

"Let me be straight with you," Bullock continued. "Your attorney is on their way. Not sure if you two have ever met. But when that door opens, any deal we may have for you is long gone. Do you understand?"

Faron looked at the two of us. He was mulling his options over. He was going to crack any moment.

The door to the interrogation room opened. It was Captain Leonard.

"Parking lot," he said. "Don't act surprised."

"I think it takes five minutes to get from the parking lot to this room," I said as I was letting the captain know how much time I thought I needed.

Leonard shut the door. If he had a stall tactic, I needed him to use it. I knew who was going to open the door next, I just needed the time to get my answers from Faron Martin.

"We only have a few minutes remaining on the clock," I said. "It's time to call your play. If that door opens before you decide, we are charging you with everything. I mean, if we have to settle for you being the mastermind behind this whole thing, we will. We already have Lucas and Phoenix and we'll just end it all with you."

I stood up and grabbed the folder as if to leave.

"When we get the ballistics report and it matches our murder weapon, you'll spend the rest of your life in prison," I said as my last ditch Hail Mary throw. "At least with your build, you won't be lonely."

"Okay," he said, finally breaking his silence.

Whatever strategy Leonard implemented to halt the forward progress of our approaching attorney was sufficient. By the time the door opened, we had everything we needed.

The door swung open.

"I'm the attorney for this man," she said as she brushed by me. "Don't say another word, Faron."

"Too late, Constance," I said. "We already made our deal."

Constance had a surprising reaction. She shrugged her shoulders and looked at Faron.

"You're not as smart as your sister Sera," she said. "I'm sure your public defender can help you now."

"You're not going to be his attorney?" I asked. "That's kind of cold, don't you think?"

"Not my concern," she said as she made her way out of the room.

\* \* \*

"Her brother?" I said to Bullock as we walked back to our desks. "Brother and sister. Two different last names."

"Could be their heritage," Bullock said. "Or it could be maybe a divorce in their family."

"What do you mean?" I asked.

"Well, some kids might keep a different parent's name in a divorce."

"Not the divorce part," I said as I stopped as the drinking fountain. "I meant about their heritage. You said something about it being their heritage."

"In Hispanic cultures, the passing on of surnames is different than white culture," he said. "When a child is born, they technically get both their father's surname and their mother's.

So, I would assume that their parent's names were Martin and Gonzalez. Not sure which is which, of course."

"Of course," I said as I quickly stood up after getting a few sips of water. "Well, that's annoying."

"You think Hispanic culture is annoying?" he asked.

"No, that's not annoying," I said in agitation. "When you stand up quickly and you get dizzy."

"It is?" he asked while bending over and standing up quickly. "Is this a major issue in your life?"

He did the same thing again. Then a third time.

"I don't feel any different," he said.

"Never mind," I said as I continued toward my desk.

"I mean, if it is, maybe we could talk to Captain about it," he said.

"Never mind," I said as I had moved from agitation to border-line anger.

"Maybe you need a cat scan," he said, pressing on.

"I don't need a freaking cat scan, you ass," I said as I plopped myself down into my chair.

"Sorry for caring," he answered as he continued toward his desk.

"Are you going to finish your story about names?" I asked as I turned around to face him.

"I'm just saying that I bet one parent was Martin and one was Gonzalez," he said as he stood behind his chair, pulled it out and sat down. "I had a buddy that I played college baseball with at Saginaw Valley, and he went by Garcia, but Garcia Cruz was actually his technical last name."

"Technical?" I asked.

"Technical, official, actual," he said. "Whatever the term is. Doesn't matter, he wanted to be known as David Garcia. Said it was simpler. Maybe that's what Sera and Faron did and they just picked differently. One took the mom's and one took the dad's."

"Or maybe they didn't want anyone to know they're related," I said.

"That could be it, too," he said.

# 26

## I Don't Trust You At All

Bullock and I headed up the stairs of the Booker Building. We turned right at the top of the stairs and headed for the first door.

Coming out of the office of Don Barton was Lydia Wright.

"We're going to have to start charging you two officers rent?" she said.

She wasn't as flirtatious as before.

"And here I thought you liked when we visited," I said.

Ignoring me entirely, she set her gaze upon Bullock.

"I wouldn't mind you visiting more often," she said. "I wouldn't mind that at all."

There she is. What's the saying about a leopard and spots? She may not be a leopard, but she sure as hell is a cougar.

I opened the door to the office of Constance Capel and turned to Bullock.

"Let's go lover boy," I said.

"Utter a word of this to Alicia and I'll kill you," he said.

\* \* \*

There wasn't anyone in the lobby area of Constance Capel's office. Bullock and I approached the desk where Sera Gonzalez is normally working this time of day. Bullock reached over and gave several taps on a small, silver desktop bell.

"Hello?" he called out in a soft voice.

"You okay?" I asked.

"Yep," he said as if he does such a thing all the time. Which he probably does.

Appearing from the hallway was Constance.

"Officers," she said. "What do I owe the pleasure?"

She was calm as if she didn't have a care in the world. It was as if our recent meeting at the police station never happened.

"We're looking for Sera Gonzalez," I said.

"I'm sure you are," she said. "She's not here."

"Do you know where we can find her?" Bullock asked.

"I do not," she said with a smarmy look to her.

"If you say so," I said. "I'm sure we'll be back. And for what it's worth, counselor, I'm not convinced you aren't involved in all of this."

"You won't be back," she said. "We're just a small firm that helps small companies import products from all over the world. I was asked by Sera to help out a friend who was trying to buy some pillows from Mexico. I was able to do that. I did my job within the boundaries of the law. What she and her brother may, or may not, have done beside what they told me they needed. Well, that's a discussion for another day."

"One I think we'll have," I said.

"Have a great day, gentlemen," she said as she turned and walked away toward her office.

\* \* \*

Bullock and I left Capel's office and turned right.

Lydia was leaned up against the door to Don Barton's office. She looked like she was attempting to be a pinup girl from the middle of last century.

"You fellas going to go door-to-door today?" she asked.

Neither Bullock and I responded as we stopped at the door to Drake & Brahms.

"Just remember," she said as she started into her office. "My door will always be unlocked for either of you."

The door closed behind her.

"She's all yours," I said to Bullock as I opened the door to the accountants.

\* \* \*

Jim Abrahms was standing behind the front desk. He looked frantic.

"I'm assuming she's not here," I said.

He looked up at my partner and me.

"We were asked to help out some friends," he said. "That's all."

He continued diligently tossing papers across the desk.

"We got every freaking agency investigating us now," he said. "The damn IRS. The state. We'll be lucky to get a client ever again."

"At least you're not going to jail," Bullock said.

263

Jim looked up at us. Bullock's words were little consolation. They were ruined. And they actually were just doing their jobs. And they, unfortunately, did it well.

\* \* \*

We knew the answer, but out of curiosity, we decided to check any way.

As we assumed, the office of Colton Moore was devoid of any semblance of his business.

"Where do you think he went off to?" Bullock asked with his face pressed against the glass.

"I have some idea," I said. "I bet it has a beach."

We started back down the hall.

"Weird isn't?" he asked. "All these people just trying to get by. And one person saw an opening and took everyone down with them."

"It's why I don't like to trust people," I said. "You're not disappointed if you don't trust anyone."

"Ah, come on," he said. "You trust some people. You trust Chloe. You trust me."

"I don't trust you," I said. "I don't trust you at all."

"Sure you do," he said. "I'm the one who will be there when you get your cat scan."

# 27

## That Seems Plausible

After several days of waiting, one of our two fleeing suspects was apprehended at the Blue Water Bridge that connects Port Huron, Michigan to Sarnia, Ontario.

Bullock and I stood outside of the precinct as she was being brought back to Stonington.

The patrol car pulled up, the officers got out and opened the rear door and extracted our suspect.

We followed the trio into the station and waited patiently for the Border Patrol to finish their paperwork to transfer her to us.

Once everything was finalized, we escorted our suspect to the interrogation room.

\* \* \*

I sat down. I looked up the single light dangling from the ceiling. I stretched out my neck and turned hoping to get a relieving crack or two. Again, to no avail. I took a deep breath.

I looked across the table at the lady staring at me.

"Let me tell you what we've been able to put together, so far," I said.

I opened the folder in front of me.

"This all started with cigarettes," I said. "You and a few other people would meet in the alleyway for smoking breaks."

"Cigarettes will kill you," Bullock said. "Of course, so will a 9 millimeter handgun."

I nodded in agreement.

"One day, you and your friends are out, enjoying a smoke and you see a couple guys who are engaged in a small-time drug deal," I said. "Marijuana."

I turned a page in the folder.

"One of you," I said. "You, according to everyone else involved, gets an idea. Why think small, correct?"

I looked up. Her expression didn't change.

"Would you like to add anything?" I asked.

She just continued to stare.

"Well, anyway," I continued. "While we waited for you to be apprehended, we did some followup discussions with Phoenix Kester and Lucas Winters, since they're both still incarcerated."

"Which you'll be soon," Bullock interjected.

"Here's what the others had to say," I said.

* * *

Jackson State Prison is no joke. It screams bleak. The facility, which served as the world's largest walled prison until the early 80s, is the final stop on eastbound O'Leary Street. It's literally

266

the end of the road for many of its residents.

Our presence there was not greeted with warmth and love. Other than Lucas Winters, we didn't know anyone who was assigned there. But they hated us just the same. At least based on the looks and comments we received. Although, a couple did make some offers to Bullock. So he was slightly more popular than I was.

The guards there weren't much friendlier. I think in their line of work, showing any sense of humanity was also showing weakness. So cold and distant was the common emotion.

Lucas Winters was sitting among a long row of prisoners whose only connection to the outside world was the thick piece of glass separating them from any visitor and the phone each had access to.

"We've made some more arrests," I said into the receiver.

"Good for you," he returned.

"I just want to close this all out," I said.

"I don't give a shit," he said as he started to hang up.

"Hey, hey, hey," I said as I tapped the window. "We might be able to drop some time."

"Say what you got to say," he said.

"We arrested Faron and we're waiting for two others to be returned back to Stonington," I said.

"Who?" he asked.

His question wasn't out of true curiosity. He knew who. It was more of me showing my cards and letting him know if I was speaking honestly.

"Sera," I said.

He waited patiently.

"And Delilah," I added.

"What do you want to know?" he asked.

267

"Tell me how it got away from you?" I asked.

"Simple," he said. "I was dealing a small amount of grass. I would sell to Phoenix and Carson and some other kids in the back alley. Carson said he became friends with some people in the building who were looking for weed. So I had him sell to them. Then one day, Carson says these people want to talk with me."

"About what exactly?" I asked.

"They said this chick had an idea to grow the business," he said. "Said they read some magazine article about Mexico. I met with Sera one night and she said she was able to make some connections in El Paso. She said those connections could hook us up with a supplier in Mexico. But we needed a product we could use to get across the border. I was like, shit, I don't know anything about Mexico and shit like that."

"Is that how Phoenix got involved?" I asked.

\* \* \*

Bullock and I waited at one of three circular tables with four metal chairs at each table.

"Why don't you slide a little more to the right," Bullock said. "You're making me uncomfortable."

I slid my chair a little further away. It made a hideous sound that echoed through the common area.

"You could pick it up, you know," he said.

"You could shut up," I said.

County jail is a lot nicer than a state facility. It's brighter. It has more hope. Everyone there knows there's an end to their time.

Phoenix Kester was ushered into the room by a correctional officer.

"Mr. Kester," I said. "Have a seat, please."

"I don't have to talk to you," he said as he sat down.

"I think you'll want to," Bullock said. "We've made several arrests, waiting for a couple to be returned back to Stonington. We thought maybe we could help you, if you helped us."

"What do you mean?" he asked. "I get out in a couple of months."

"True," I said. "But we talked to Lucas and we could, legitimately, add more charges."

"You guys are joking, right?" he asked.

"Yes," Bullock said. "We're joking. We took time out of our day, drove all the way over here to make a joke."

The three of us just sat there for a few moments.

"We're not joking, jackass," Bullock said.

"Here's what we know," I added. "Lucas was talking to you one day about the idea of expanding his business. He told you he was looking for products that came from Mexico. That's where you came in."

"I said I didn't know of any products from Mexico," Phoenix said. "I wanted to help him out. He's my friend."

"So what specifically did you do?" Bullock asked.

"I knew we ordered this polyester fiberfill pillow, but they weren't from Mexico," he said. "I told him about them. Told him where we ordered them from. That was it."

"For awhile, right?" I asked.

"Yeah," he said. "Next thing I know, Lucas is asking if we could order a different kind. I told him that Ian Parker only orders certain products. The only pillows we order are the fiberfill ones. He asked me how hard it would be to change the inside. So I checked. I told him it wouldn't be too hard."

"Who discovered the pillows from Almohada?" Bullock asked.

"I did," he said. "I told Lucas about the different types they had. Then he said he had a great idea."

\* \* \*

"I did some research based on what Phoenix said they sold," Lucas said. "What if we ordered these buckwheat pillows? They have an scent and I figured if we ordered in small batches, we might be able to pass it through at the border."

"You figured that out?" Bullock asked.

"Well, Sera suggested it first," he said. "But I did the followup. So Sera told her contacts in El Paso and they told their people in Mexico."

"At Almohada?" I asked.

"Nah," he said. "I think someone else just paid some employees there to stuff our product in. I don't think Almohada, the company, had any idea. But, you never know."

"What do you mean? Bullock asked.

"Shit," he said. "If you pay enough money, people are willing to do a lot of illegal shit. Everyone has a price."

"So you get these pillows across the border," I said.

"Yeah," he said. "Sera had an office down in Texas. She said they're part of some larger lawyer thing."

"And the lawyers helped you knowing it was drugs?" I asked.

"I don't think so," he said. "I think all along the process people were just doing what they thought was their job. I'm pretty sure most had some idea. But as long as they never asked, we never said anything. Everyone was happy."

"Well, not Tom Downing," I said.

For the first time in our exchanges, I saw remorse from Lucas Winters.

"No, not Tom," he said. "My idea was we could exchange the buckwheat out and put in this fiber stuff and keep the product moving so we could account for it all."

"So you need somewhere to process all this, correct?" I asked. "Is that when you involve Don?"

"Don?" he asked. "He doesn't know shit. He hates me."

He paused for a few seconds.

"Now he really hates me," he said with a hearty laugh. "I knew he didn't like me and I asked him if he minded if I crashed down at the warehouse in Monroe. It's a dump and he has plans to demolish it and build something else or sell it. But he's got other things going. To get me out of his life, he agreed. He has no idea what we were doing."

"So now you got your nice little setup," Bullock said. "And you send the pillows and the drugs up to Stonington."

"Carson would come down and get everything," he said. "He'd give the pillows to Phoenix, and the two of them would set up our street guys."

\* \* \*

"Carson would bring the pillows to me," Phoenix said. "I knew Ian wasn't scrutinizing things. So I figured I could enter the pillows into the system and continue to sell them to Dayal, like usual."

"Dayal?" I asked.

"Dr. Wilbur Dayal," he said. "He's the sleep doctor who orders them."

"What about the drugs?" Bullock asked.

"Carson would take care of that," he said.

"Let's get to the crux of the matter," I said. "How did we get to Carson getting shot?"

"I guess it doesn't matter now," he said. "Carson thought we could cut the product even further. Mix it with some other stuff, double our supply. He said everyone already had their cut, so the rest would be profit. He needed me to order the equipment. I knew it was a bad idea."

"But you did it anyway," I said. "Why?"

"I don't know," he said. "I honestly don't know."

"So who shot Carson?" Bullock asked.

"I just freaked out," he said.

"What do you mean?" I asked. "Were you there."

"I was standing right next to him when they shot him," he said.

"They?" Bullock asked. "Who's they?"

"Sera said we owed them," he said. "She said we stole from them and we better pay up or else. Then she shot him."

"Sera killed Carson?" I asked.

\* \* \*

"Those two dumb asses screwed everything up," Lucas said. "Carson got greedy and Phoenix is an idiot."

"So you killed him?" I asked.

"You're not pinning that on me," he said. "Listen, I've screwed up enough times that I don't have a license. I can't drive. I couldn't get to Stonington."

"You, the drug dealer don't want to break a driving law?" Bullock asked.

"Can I shoot you straight?" he asked.

"You haven't so far," I said.

"I don't like to drive," he admitted. "To be honest. I thought it was cool that I had this set up and everyone came to me. Like Scarface."

"I don't think that's how Scarface operated," I said.

"Whatever," he said. "It's who I pictured."

"So who killed Carson?" Bullock asked.

"Hell, if I know," he said. "Sera was pissed. Faron was pissed, but I can't see him doing anything like that."

"But you could see Sera doing something like that?" I asked.

"Nothing she does surprises me," he said.

"When did Faron get involved?" Bullock asked.

* * *

I walked into the county jail, Bullock in tow, and signed in.

"Back again?" the desk clerk asked.

"Different inmate," I said.

She buzzed us in and we headed back to the cell area. We sat in the common area at a metal table that served as card table, lunch table and anything else that could pass the time until the residents have court or are released.

Faron came strolling out in his orange jumpsuit. He didn't

273

look comfortable at all being locked up.

"You okay?" I asked.

"Peachy," he said.

"How did you get involved in all of this?" I asked. "Listen, the house of cards you all built is falling apart. Might as well tell us what you know. We're going to find out eventually."

"Simple," he said. "Sera came into the arcade one day. She said I could make some easy money."

"How?" Bullock asked.

"She said she had some people that needed to get rid of some cash that they didn't want to report," he said. "I knew it was dirty. But I didn't know where it came from."

"A bunch of raggedy teenagers come walking in with hundreds of dollars and you didn't know where it came from?" I asked.

He knew we knew he knew.

"So how did you hide it?" I continued.

"Concessions," he said. "No one knows how much soft drink goes into a cup. Or how much popcorn we sell. A lot of stuff like that, that's hard to account for. We just made it seem like we sold a lot and bought a heck of a lot more than we did. And it worked. Sera talked to mom, who talked with her bosses and they said cash businesses should make sure everything is accounted for."

"Wait a second," I said. "Delilah Rendon is your mother?"

"No sense in hiding it now," he said. "She took her new husband's name when she remarried."

"So your mom's new husband is the man who gave you the arcade?" I asked.

"Now you know," he said. "He was a client of her bosses."

"Do you think the accountants knew what was actually going on?" Bullock asked.

"Not based on when I met with them," he said. "They

asked questions. I answered them. Anytime they needed to see paperwork, I made sure they had it. As far as they were concerned, we were just doing better since I took over."

* * *

"I told you," Alexander Drake said as he was packing boxes. "We had no freaking idea. We were just doing our job. And this is the thanks we get."

Jim and Alexander had most of their office packed up into small boxes. At least the portions that weren't covered in yellow police tape. Two IRS agents stood off to our side listening intently into our conversation.

"Delilah asked if we could help Faron like we helped Armand," Alexander said. "So we did. Why wouldn't we?"

"Now we're under investigation," Jim said. "Colton is nowhere to be found. A fugitive at large. I can't believe it. And pretty much everyone in town thinks we're criminals. My daughter was asked what's it like to be a drug kingpin's daughter. I'm a damn accountant!"

"So the only one who actually has access to the funds in the offshore accounts is Colton?" I asked.

"Pretty smart," Alexander said as he looked at the IRS agents. "Everyone else is ruined and he's down in the Caribbean spending all the money, I bet."

* * *

275

"So now we're back to you," I said. "Where's your daughter, Delilah?"

"I don't know," she said. "I haven't seen her."

"Why don't you explain to us how you fit into all of this," Bullock said.

"It's pretty simple, really," she said. "My son explained that he was able to make a lot more money with the arcade since Armand gave it to him. So I knew Alexander and Jim could help him. Make sure everything was done properly."

"Are you saying you didn't do anything wrong?" I asked.

"I don't know what you're talking about," she said.

"So when everyone says you were present at some of the early alley meetings where everything was discussed," I said. "That wasn't true?"

"They must've been mistaken," she said.

"At every stop, with everyone we've talked to," I said. "Your name has come up. But it's all just a coincidence?"

"It has to be," she said.

"That's weird," I said. "Because Phoenix Kester said you were present when Carson McCall was shot. He said you were there with Sera."

"Listen," she said in a very serious tone. "Are you parents? Well I am. And I protect my children."

"What are you saying Mrs. Rendon?" Bullock asked.

She paused and a tear appeared in right eye. She wiped the tear. That must've been hard to force out.

"My daughter is with Colton," she said. "She's never coming back. It breaks my heart."

Neither Bullock nor I said a word. We wanted her to continue to speak. She looked up at us. Another tear came trickling down her face.

"Sera killed Carson McCall," she said before bursting into tears. "She put this all together. And one night, we were in the alley on a break and those two dimwits showed up and she lost her cool saying all these things that I was absolutely shocked to hear. I couldn't believe my beautiful daughter was caught up in all this. And she lured my son in as well. "

She paused and looked at us. We remained awestruck at what we were hearing.

"She killed Carson," she continued. "I told her to get rid of the gun. I guess she gave it to Faron. I don't know. I don't know why she would do that. I can't believe he would be so stupid to keep it. I know for sure she would've told him to get rid of it. Throw it in a lake or something."

"That seems awfully specific of what you think she would've told him," I said breaking my silence.

"I'm just saying," she said. "That would seem like something she'd say."

"Gotcha," I said.

"I knew she and Colton were involved," she said. "I'm sure as soon as everything fell apart, the two of them took off. Never to return."

"That seems plausible," I said.

"Yeah, I could see her never returning," Bullock said. "Especially if you're accused of murder."

"Which, by the way," I said. "Why were you going to Canada?"

"Armand and I were going to go on vacation," she said. "I heard Sudbury is nice this time of year."

"You had a lot of belongings for a vacation," I said.

"Well, Armand has a summer home up there," she said. "So I wasn't sure if we were going to stay awhile."

"I just have two more questions for you," I said. "Why would

Phoenix Kester say you killed Carson McCall?"

"What?" she said with surprise in her voice. "Why would he say that?"

"I don't know," I said. "Do you know, partner?"

Bullock shook his head side-to-side.

"I do not," he said.

"I have one last question for you, Delilah," I said. "So in talking to Faron, he mentioned that Sera was right-handed. Which means if she was holding the gun, her three fingers not on the trigger would've left prints on the left side of the gun handle."

Her eyes widened. She knew where I was headed.

"But you're left-handed," I continued. "And my question for you is, guess which side of the gun we found fingerprints?"

"Are you going to say the right side?" Bullock sarcastically asked.

"I am," I answered. "And when we match the prints to what we collected today, I'm pretty sure we answered the question of who killed Carson McCall."

"That little bitch had all these ideas and then when those two punks started to cheat us, she didn't want to fix it," Delilah said. "I told her we needed to send a message. The message was sent."

"Loud and clear," I said as I stood up and read her her rights for the charge of Murder in the First Degree.

# 28

## A Politician, His Chief Of Staff, And A Pimp

I sat on my deck as the sun was setting on a midsummer night. Chloe was closing Brown's, and I had an early morning in court to testify on the murder case against Delilah Rendon. I thought I would take a few moments and just enjoy some peace and quiet and an iced cold beer.

"Quite the case," Betsy said from the adjoining deck.

"Yeah," I said. "All because you had intuition."

"Glad I could help," she said followed by a long drag on her cigarette.

I took a sip of my beer, she took another puff of her lung dart.

"What's next for you?" I asked her.

"Not sure," she said. "Might read a book. Might write a book."

"Really?" I asked. "You write? I never knew that."

"I'm pretty sure I mentioned it before," she said followed by a laugh cough mixture.

"If you were going to write again, what would you write about?" I asked.

"I have to admit something, Brody James," she said. "This

case, despite me playing a very small role. It got my juices flowing. It made me realize, I missed the action."

"Is that so?" I asked. "You thinking about getting back into the game?"

She didn't immediately answer. I didn't want to press. I took another sip. She took another puff.

"Not in so many words," she said.

"What do you mean?" I asked as I heard her chair move.

I turned to look in her direction. She was standing up at the railing facing me. She broke our thing. We always sat, never facing each other, and just talked. She wasn't following protocol. At least what I thought was protocol. I figured this had to be pretty serious for her to go against the rules.

"Are you okay?" I asked.

She didn't answer. She just stared. I got out of my chair and took the one step to the edge of my balcony.

"Seriously, Betsy," I said. "Are you alright over there?"

"Brody," she said. "I have had the craziest thought all day."

"What is it?" I asked.

"I've never really told you about the case," she said.

"The case?" I asked with some confusion. "Which case? The Booker Building case?"

"No, not that case you idiot," she said. "You know that case. You closed that case. The case case."

I felt bad that I didn't know immediately what she was talking about. So I sat in my bewilderment. She couldn't stand it anymore.

"The case that forced me to the sidelines," she said. "The one that put an end to my career and sent me packing to Podunkville living next to the world's most clueless cop. Sometimes."

I think she was talking about me.

"Oh, that case," I said when it all clicked in my head. "Do you want to talk about it?"

"I want more than that, Brody," she said. "I want to do what you just did. I want to close this case. And you're going to help me?"

"Me?" I asked. "Why me?"

"I need access to police information," she said. "And you can provide that. And there's no statute of limitations on murder cases."

"Murder?" I asked. "Who got murdered?"

"It's a long story," she said. "But involves a politician, his Chief of Staff, and a pimp."

"Sounds seedy," I said. "What kind of politician was he?"

"He was a state Senator," she said. "But he's in Congress now."

"He's still alive?" I asked.

"Yeah," she incredulously said. "Why wouldn't he be alive?"

"To be honest," I said. "I wasn't sure who was killed. And I figured it was awhile ago and, you're, I mean, he was, probably. Well, anyway, I just figured it was some time ago."

"Are you saying I'm old?" she said. "You little shit. I'm not old."

"How old are you, if I may ask?"

"No, you may not," she said. "But the fact of the matter is, *he* is getting older. He's in his 70s. He's been in Congress for quite a few years. He may not be around much longer. And if there's going to be justice, I need to do something soon. Or I'll miss my chance forever."

"So the Congressman killed someone?" I asked.

"I don't know," she said.

"The Chief of Staff?" I asked. "Is he still alive?"

281

"Yes, he's still alive."

"Or the pimp," I said. "Is he alive?"

"How the hell would I know that?" she asked.

"You knew about the Congressman and the staffer," I said. "I figured you knew about the pimp."

"Do you know how many members of Congress there are in Michigan?" she asked. "Sixteen. It's not that hard to keep track of. And he's had the same Chief of Staff forever. Again, not hard to find out about."

She looked at me as if I was supposed to know the rest of her point.

"How many pimps are there?" she asked.

"Here? In Stonington?"

"No, in the state of Michigan," she answered.

"A lot," I said. "I bet a lot."

"Yeah," she said. "A lot. And that's a group that's a little harder to find information on. Especially after 20 years."

"20 years," I said. "You are old."

"Are you going to help me or not?" she asked.

"Let me see if I get this straight," I said. "There's a Congress-man, who used to be a state Senator. How does the Chief of Staff fit into this?"

"Not sure," she said.

"The pimp?" I asked pressing on.

"Again, not sure."

"Well," I said. "I'm not sure what any of this means. But, sure, if you need my help, just tell me what I can do."

"Thanks, Brody," she said. "I appreciate it."

# 29

# I Can Explain

Statute of limitations. Each crime has an established time limit where legal action can be taken.

About five weeks ago, Bullock had asked Alicia to marry him. She said yes. Why? No one knows. But she did. They have since set the date for next summer. With only a month to go before the summer closes and the school year begins, and the fact that nothing memorable happens in August, I figured this would be the perfect time for me to finally propose to Chloe. In my mind, the statute of limitations expired from the time Bullock asked Alicia and I could then ask Chloe.

I started the planning process. At first, I thought we would go out to dinner. It had to be somewhat classy, but not too classy. She'd see through that right away. It had to be a little more casual, but not too casual, as I didn't want her to remember how her fries were on the night she was proposed to. But I couldn't find a happy medium.

Once I decided that no restaurant offered the perfect backdrop, I remembered that the one thing Chloe values more than flash is time. I decided to really commit to this. I decided to make a basket and have a picnic dinner.

The setting would be downtown on the shore of Tompkins Lake. I would time it so that we were there just as the sun started to set. Only the hardened boater tried to navigate the loading area when it was dark, as the only light provided in the area was by the moon itself.

The menu was thoughtfully put together. I selected a Brie de Meaux. Dubbed the "Queen of Cheeses". I chose it specifically because of that moniker, as I wanted Chloe to know she would be forever my queen. I complemented it with a spicy, Spanish blue cheese knowing that Chloe has an affinity for bold flavors.

I chose a cracker with Rosemary, raisin and pecan, as well as a simple sea salt cracker. I packed some smoked salmon, a few slices of choice roast beef, a vegetable risotto, some mixed nuts and some grapes.

The perfect wine to finish off the menu was a Pinot Noir.

I packed everything in a nice basket and headed out of my apartment to pick Chloe up from her house.

* * *

As usual, Chloe was splendid in a purple, smocked strapless dress. I told her we were having dinner, but didn't provide much more in details.

"Am I overdressed or under-dressed?" she asked as I gave her a light kiss and opened the passenger door.

"Did you ever think you might be perfectly dressed?" I asked.

"That was not an option I considered when I was getting ready," she confessed.

284

"You look perfect," I said as I felt her eyes looking over what I was wearing, while also mentally comparing my outfit to hers and what eatery would be suitable for each.

She wasn't sold. I could see a question brewing.

"Are you overdressed or under-dressed?" she asked while looking me up and down still.

For the record, I was wearing cotton khaki pants with a button-up Hawaiian-style shirt. Nothing gaudy. It was soft-toned with light pink and blue fauna of the island state. I had a pair of light brown top-sider boat shoes on. The salesman told me the color was cream. I couldn't picture myself telling other people the color was cream. So I just say light brown.

Without even trying, I thought our outfits complemented each other very well.

"We're going to the same place?" she asked as she sat down in her seat.

I thought we looked great.

"I'm just messing with you, James," she said. "You'll never pick up on the fact that you're an easy mark, will you?"

She pulled me by the shirt toward her and gave me a much more passionate kiss than the peck of a greeting I gave her.

\* \* \*

I spread out a blanket, set the basket into the corner and sat down. I gave a couple taps of my hand on the blanket for Chloe to sit next to me.

We watched the sun dip below the horizon. We could hear the gentle rumbling of a small fishing boat make it's way to shore.

It was far enough away to not be disturbing. It was like a white noise that actually made the moment even more soothing.

Chloe nestled herself into my arms and we were two lovers who were just there in the moment. I could feel her heart rate slow.

I could hear rhythmic slapping of rubber on pavement. I turned to my right, looking over Chloe and saw a runner on the walking path coming toward us before veering off slightly following the path. Chloe wasn't disturbed. For a second, I wondered if she had fallen asleep.

"This is nice," she said. "Usually when you hold me this long your hands start to, let's just say, move about to more preferred spots on my body."

"Is that an offer?" I excitedly asked.

"No," she said. "We're not doing it in the park."

"So you're suggesting, what?" I asked. "You want to go back to the car?"

She lightly smacked my chest.

"You're into the kinky stuff, I see," I said.

I could literally feel her shaking her head against my chest. While my mind veered slightly to me thinking about Chloe and I getting intimate on the grass in front of fishermen and runners and anyone else in the vicinity, I was, in fact, getting hungry.

"Do you want to eat?" I softly asked trying to steer her into making it seem like she had a choice when in reality I was saying I wanted to eat, but in question form.

\* \* \*

After our meal, we laid on the blanket, her in my arms with her left arm draped across my chest. We just stared up into the stars. I am sure she wasn't sincere as it wasn't really an offer, but the idea of us making out was becoming more and more prevalent in my mind. But it was battling a gnawing thought I couldn't shake.

"I probably shouldn't have packed roast beef," I said, as I finally gave up the thought of rolling in the grass. "That was pretty stupid."

"It's fine," she said.

How stupid could I be? The woman spends almost everyday with roast beef. Why would she want more roast beef? I more than likely ruined the most important night of her life. Unless she says no. If she says no, the roast beef will be a funny side note to the night she crushed a man's dreams.

"I liked the cheese," she said.

"Really?" I asked. "Which one?"

"Both of them," she said. "They were good. And the crackers. They were good too."

"So you're saying they were good," I said. "But not great."

"They were great," she said. "Not the grapes though."

"You didn't like the grapes?"

"I liked the grapes just fine," she said as she rose up from our cuddle and looked me in the eye with a very determined look. "Have you ever had a great grape?"

"Yeah," I said. "I have. In fact, grapes are either great or horrible. No in between. When they're crisp, I could eat an entire bowl. When they're soggy, yuck. That's so gross."

"I didn't realize you put so much thought into grapes," she said. "I've never seen you eat many grapes."

"It's because of all the work that goes into them," I said.

My words were as true as any sentence has ever been uttered. She saw differently.

"All the work?" she said with a tone that she was considering the entirety of our relationship at that moment. "You rinse them. You pull them off the vine. You eat them."

"I know," I said. "But you're not going to eat the whole bushel at once?"

"Bushel?"

"Bushel," I said. "Bunch. Group. All the grapes. The point is, you're not eating all of them. So you got to put the little tree thing back into your fridge. Pain in the ass, really."

"How would you solve the problem?" she asked.

I felt she was really interested in my solution. We're growing as a couple.

"If they just came in a bowl," I confidently said.

"A bowl?"

"Yeah," I said. "A bowl. In the fridge. If they were already in a bowl, you could open the door, grab a handful and go about your day."

"I'll keep that in mind," she said.

Oh. She was keeping that in mind. I don't know if she was admitting she was considering a life with me or if she was pondering coming over with grapes in a bowl every once in awhile and setting them in my fridge. I would prefer the former, but wouldn't hate the latter.

"Green," I said. "If you're going to go through all that work, you should make sure they're the green ones. Purple is good, but the green is way better."

"Noted," she said.

"I feel like I'm going to fall asleep," I said. "Do you want to take a stroll and get the blood flowing?"

"Sure," she said as she got up from the blanket.

The moonlight bounced off her face and she was mesmerizing to look at. A silhouette of her was stimulating as it felt mysterious. I always felt that the idea of mystery as sexually alluring has been replaced by in-your-face nudity. Very little is left to the imagination, and that's a shame.

I grabbed her hand and lead her toward the shoreline. We walked hand-in-hand. She stopped and slid off her shoes and handed them to me. I held her shoes in my left hand and her in my right. She waltzed as the water splashed her feet before retreating back into the depths of itself.

We walked a little while until we reached a pier that stretched itself out into the lake. A lone fisherman was setting himself for a night's catch. We passed by him, but he didn't pay us any mind as he was diligently setting everything he had in its proper place. Buckets, nets, tackle, beer, rods. The works.

We reached the end of the pier and stared out at the still water. A ripple formed where the moonlight and water met. Something came up, but just momentarily. Enough to disturb the water.

I let go of Chloe's hand and bent over to place her shoes on the wooden planks that make up the pier. I got down on one knee and retrieved a small, red case from my pocket.

She turned toward me and immediately put both hands to her mouth. She began to cry.

"I haven't asked yet," I said as I could feel a lump in my throat. My mouth dried but my eyes filled with water.

"Will you marry me?" I asked the most beautiful woman in the world.

* * *

After saying yes, we embraced for a long time. We may have even twirled. After a few minutes, we turned to walk back to the shore.

"Congrats," the fisherman said without turning his attention from the four rods he had balanced against the rail of the pier.

"Thanks," Chloe gleefully said.

"Good luck tonight," I said to him.

"You too," he said before chuckling aloud.

I hope he's right, I said to myself.

"Would you like to walk some more?" I asked.

"Sure," she said as she held her left hand out in front of her allowing the moonlight to hit her engagement ring.

"Passing on left," a cyclist said as he whizzed past.

I may have jumped a little. Chloe didn't react at all. I'm not sure if she's harder to scare than me or was focused on her hand. Fortunately, she didn't even give a reaction to me being somewhat startled.

"What are you thinking as far as a date?" she asked after several minutes of just walking in silence.

"I don't know," I said.

To be honest, I hadn't given that part much thought.

"Are there any months we need to avoid?" I asked.

She gave the question some thought.

"Well," she answered. "We probably need to find out when Alicia and Bullock are getting married. I'm thinking at least a month before or after would work for us."

"What if we pick ours first," I suggested.

"We can be patient," she said. "They've been through a lot. Let them pick a date without worrying about ours. You can be a good friend and wait."

"I am a good friend," I said. "I just want to have ours first."

"I'm sure you do," she said. "But no matter what happens, I will always remember this night. You made me the happiest girl on earth. Nothing will change that."

Ahead of us, about 50 yards or so, I saw a figure dragging something large across the beach. It appeared they were pulling it from the water. I couldn't make out what it was, but my initial thought was it was a man dragging a woman.

I paused to focus my sight. Chloe looked at me and seeing my gaze, turned to look down the path.

The man knelt over the woman and began giving chest compression.

"Oh shit," I said aloud before sprinting toward the two people.

As I got closer, I asked, "what happened?"

Like a baseball player, I actually slid toward both of them.

"I don't know," the man said as he looked up at me.

He knew I knew who he was.

"I was just walking the path," he said as I reached for a pulse on the woman.

I began to perform CPR on her as best I could. Chloe approached the three of us.

"Call 911," I barked at Chloe.

She just stared at the man.

"Chloe," I said getting her attention. "Call 911."

Other people started to gather as the man and I furiously tried to save our victim.

* * *

I sat with my feet in the sand where the water could just barely scrape my shoes. I had both arms on my knees and my held hung low. Chloe was rubbing my back as a way to comfort me.

The other man was pacing back and forth. I wasn't sure if he was distraught at the drowning death of the woman, or the fact that he had to explain the specifics of their encounter and he was worried more about his future.

I could see the flashing of blue and red lights from behind me. They struck the water in front of me. Any other situation, it would have been a mesmerizing and impressive display. Almost patriotic. Not today.

"Brody," I heard Evans call out to me. "What happened?"

Evans had two members of EMS with her as they ran directly toward the woman.

"Don't bother," I said. "She didn't make it."

They continued about their job, disregarding my words. A third member came down with a stretcher, and the three of them placed the woman atop and covered her from her toes past her head.

It's never a good sign when sheets are placed over someone's head.

The man came toward the stretcher.

"You're David Bell, correct?" Evans asked him.

"Yes," he quietly said.

Evans looked at me and Chloe. Professionalism is always the standard. But sometimes we can't contain our animalistic and protective nature from coming out.

"Well," Evans said. "Can you explain how *you* came to be found with our deceased woman?"

David took a long breath. He looked at me and Chloe. He looked at Evans.

"I can explain," he said.

# About the Author

Karl Kling, at his core, is a story teller. A former small-town award-winning newspaper reporter and editor, Karl loves to tell tales that will make people think, as well as make people laugh. Over the years, be it during his time spent working in politics or as a college baseball coach, Karl never lost his passion for writing.

Karl lives in Howell, Michigan with his beautiful wife. They are proud parents to three sons, who are the inspirations for the name Three Dorks Publishing.

**You can connect with me on:**

🐦 https://x.com/KARLKLING3

# Also by Karl Kling

**The Boys Are Back In Town**
Brody James returns to his hometown of Stonington. With his new partner, Bullock, he tries to prove that two recent deaths are more related than just being former classmates of his.

"A fantastically twisted murder mystery" - GoodReads review

"This book gives hard boiled noir vibes and the characters jump right off the pages into your head. The author has the kind of writing style I like - a touch of humor and plenty of quirky descriptors. The plot itself is a fast and fun ride with a satisfying conclusion." - NetGalley review

"It's funny, the characters are well developed, it kept me guessing." - Amazon review

www.ingramcontent.com/pod-product-compliance
Lightning Source LLC
Chambersburg PA
CBHW051413170626
46809CB00006B/2148